The Goodness Algorithm

The Goodness Algorithm

Evolutionary Dystopia

R. de Wolf

R. de Wolf www.rdewolf.com

A catalogue record for this book is available from the National Library of New Zealand.

ISBN: 9780473619015
EPub: 9780473633196

Cover design: Regina de Wolf-Ngarimu
Editor: Ieme de Wolf
Logo Credit https://www.vecteezy.com/free-vector/ornament
Ornament Vectors by Vecteezy

First Printing, 2022

Printed in Australia

R. de Wolf
PO Box 438, Gisborne 4040
New Zealand
https://rdewolf.com

I salute the many people who envision creating a shift
'for a better world' without violence.

In 2022 the peace and lives of the Ukrainian people were
shattered by aggression and war.

Kia kaha - have strength
The madness will come to an end.

CONTENTS

CONTENTS

The Unknown

Throughout my life, I have spent lots of time with many young people. What do they worry about? - the future.

I was born in Generation X. My childhood was relatively carefree. There was no 'checking in' via text, Messenger, or Instagram to my parents on where I was or what I was doing. They couldn't track every move I made by monitoring the whereabouts of my mobile phone, and from their point of view, they didn't have to worry about who was stalking me on Facebook or what I was watching on YouTube. The bully conducted any bullying at school in person, but when you went home, you were safe. When I took off on my OE, I wrote a postcard or the occasional letter, maybe a phone call when I could afford it. I travelled Europe during a time of peace and before mass tourism, not realising how lucky I was.

Now, I look at our army of children trying to save the planet from oceans of plastic, global warming, toxic pollution and political promises that don't materialise – and I feel for them. The responsibilities placed on young shoulders to fix everything grown-ups have cocked up for years can be overwhelming. However, the generations of babies who become eco-warriors early will be better custodians of the planet than we are. Once we die, the generations that follow may be able to shake our outdated ideas, methodologies and the human traits of selfishness and greed. Perhaps the dark side of our DNA evolved in nature for survival and to control the human population.

When I wrote this book, I wanted to provoke thought. One of my observations of how humans function is that we see a problem, come up with an idea for an often one-dimensional or self-serving solution and sell it to everyone else. The best salesperson wins. I don't remember who said 'ideas are like children – you love your own best', but it's often true. Well-rounded thinking is not our forte. So, you end up with a carbon-driven world, global warming, and nuclear energy with no way to dispose of the waste. Still, we will switch to electric vehicles without any thought of how to dispose of all those batteries or generate electricity in large enough quantities to supply the transportation world. I am not anti-electric because we need to do something - just questioning whether it should be the only solution touted in copy and paste policies.

There is also a fine line between efficiency, safety and control. Scientific advancement in genetic decoding has presented a double-edged sword to the human race. So many medical solutions are waiting to be discovered by researchers, and opportunities arise for exploitation. Artificial Intelligence is another field that offers opportunity and risk – the Terminator movies programmed me to be cautious.

Through most of my books, I have included some commentary on leadership – rangatiratanga in Maori. 'Why?' you might ask. I see a lot of political manoeuvring, poll watching and spin every day, but in times of crisis, many leaders seem incapable of – well, leading. Or, the most dominant bully rises to the top by inciting fear. How do we, versus how should we, choose our leaders – food for thought dear reader.

Dive into The Goodness Algorithm, and I hope you will enjoy a story woven with threads of challenges we face.

The door shut. Panic stroked a shiver up her spine, and fear began to pound her ribcage. One of his hands covered her mouth while the other reached inside her garments to caress her skin.

"Why didn't you tell your parents?" the girl screamed inside her head. *"I'm only nine, but I know this is wrong. Why can't anyone hear me in this room?"* she despaired.

He pushed her against the desk, inhaling her fear like intoxicating perfume. Nobody would know he sampled a little of the expensive merchandise. The air was musty, the desk unyielding, warm breath behind, arm-trapped body as her fingers struck cold metal.

Scissors flew into her palm, and she stabbed his right hand with every ounce of strength her tiny frame possessed. As he howled in pain, she yanked her weapon out and plunged it in again – adrenalin staking the hand to the desk before she dashed for the exit. The door was locked. Pounding on unyielding metal, she screamed for help, but nobody could hear her.

The man cursed and activated the extraction protocol. Although he longed to punish the brat, this girl was too valuable and could cost him his life, so he let her scream and claw the door while he attended to his mauled hand.

Within minutes a team deactivated the lock. They administered a mist of drugs to silence the girl instantly, assisted their boss into uniform, and departed.

Goggle-eyed students craned necks to see what was happening before the windows frosted and the virtual substitute tutor demanded their attention.

1

Good Hope

It is incredible how quickly life can transform. Julia Stryker-Petrel woke up inhabiting the perfect life. Great job, a loving family, everything she ever dreamed of having. Then a ripple disturbed the pond's surface, the world tilting in a short time span. Life, as everyone knew it, was undergoing a quiet metamorphosis. The natural world has an uncanny ability to rebalance, and mortals should never doubt nature's power or overestimate their own individual importance.

Julia sat at her desk, carefully transferring the results from the lab experiments for the day into the central information repository. She frowned as she concentrated on the task, sanity checking the results with a practised eye. As the Chief Geneticist in the city of Good Hope, the integrity of data was her responsibility. While Julia selected her scientific staff with the utmost care, they were human and prone to making the occasional error. The magnitude of making an error in their field of work could have enormous repercussions, so she took precautions to avoid unnecessary deaths.

Inevitably, her lab hours increased. Her diligence in the quest for perfection of data and programming produced a brilliant student. The quality of her ground-breaking work made Julia the most sought-after scientist in her field. Julia was a passionate, dedicated perfectionist and these traits contributed to a meteoric rise professionally. What intrigued her about genetics wasn't how much you knew but how much there was to learn. Her field of science continued to challenge and fascinate her. Satisfied everything was in order, she exhaled a sigh of relief. Julia initiated the security protocols, eager to head home to her family.

The year is 2144. One of the benefits of Julia's hard work is she and her partner Alex, an engineer in the military, were approved to have a child. They both possess sound genes, minds and bodies and provide a stable home - a nurturing environment. Julia's aptitude as a scientist makes her an attractive candidate for reproduction.

Obtaining reproduction approval is a complicated process. People are frequently denied a permit or sometimes cannot produce an embryo or child of the required standard. The responsibility of having a child no longer lies with potential parents. The Quality Control Bureau (QCB) terminates any child who fails their tests before reaching maturity. A heart-breaking eventuality for parents, so critical genetic screening must be perfect.

Julia's research provided many refinements to the flawed process inherited, and she is proud of her team's achievements. Terminations late in the life of a child are rare these days. Based on current knowledge, the QCB acknowledged that social, and environmental influences rather than undetected genetic propensities are now the primary cause of behavioural issues. Julia realises some other brilliant scientist could come into her domain and instigate ideas from new research. Maybe they will frown upon her primitive or flawed methodology. Unless she becomes classified AIA (Alpha Indispensable Asset) as most of the Council is. Then she could choose to enhance herself genetically or clone her body and raise herself to continue her work. The option isn't often available for scientists, but if she remains at the top of her field in genetics, a possibility.

Many productive citizens are permitted to clone, especially if they aren't approved to reproduce. The process maintains or improves the skill level of available workers without creating upsurges or downturns in population growth. Parental permits are granted to replace those who die, are in accidents or who leave the planet.

Julia checked her appearance in the mirror. Brown eyes and regular features stared back at her. She pushed a stray lock of dark hair from her chignon behind her ear, grabbed her satchel and headed for the magnetic pod home.

Everyone lives in proximity to where they work—one of the transformational changes to drive efficiency and save resources introduced in the 2060s. The excesses indulged in the 19th-21st century, and the damage caused to the planet as industry flourished and the population ballooned are taught extensively in the education system.

Resources were consumed, like locusts stripping plants in a field. Julia was astounded nobody did anything about it for so long. She interrogated her tutor thoroughly as a child. Her scientific brain struggled to comprehend the irresponsibility and sheer stupidity involved.

When the planet was on the brink of toxic pollution (9-10 billion people was the tipping point), there were shortages of everything. Wars were fought between nations over resources, often nuclear, and the inevitability of self-destruction was imminent. Then, and only then, were changes made. They were sweeping and brutal reforms. Business leaders formed a powerful global Council. The Council developed a new vision for the future, culled the population and no longer gave aid to people or countries who couldn't support themselves.

Organisations didn't send medicine to combat disease outbreaks, and the Council prioritised protecting resources, food production, and restoring the environment. Whole areas were de-populated to provide the planet with a chance to regenerate. It was a dark period of history but the beginning of RPC (Responsible Population Control). Sex without contraception, IVF, and surrogate programs were all outlawed. The surviving leaders introduced strict parental permits and sterilisation. Over time, the Council further reduced the population. They passed laws to ensure the GHN (Global Human Numbers) would never exceed 1 billion people again. The numbers decreased further as people lived longer, worked until they were much older, and fewer children were born. Genetic selection and science played a significant role in building a more empathetic and sympathetic population to environmental realities.

In the late 2040s, a Professor of Humanity wrote a thesis on the Dunedin Study and questioned why monkeys could ostracise antisocial trouble-makers by puberty and humans couldn't. Instead, humans chose to build costly prisons, allow violent crime to flourish and expend valuable resources on the negative impact of a minority percentage.

A group of scientists was assigned to identify the five per cent of the population likely to become criminals and develop antisocial or violent tendencies. The Council wanted the scientists to find ways to influence the behaviour of the minority positively.

In 2049 the Global Council introduced the Goodness Algorithm. Puberty meant every human would submit to a series of tests to measure their predilection of becoming a good person who could contribute meaningfully to society. If a child failed the test, they would be euthanised - humanely, of course. The Goodness Algorithm was a closely guarded secret to prevent any cheating of the system.

The five per cent were often brilliant and displayed extraordinary levels of creativity. Even the early study had shown that if a primary carer nurtured the five per cent and focused them, they could make remarkable leaps that the 95 per cent couldn't. In short, the minority was an essential component of evolution.

Julia studied the data, ran analytics on the longer-term results of the genetic screening, and applied the algorithm. Her instincts were beginning to detect an emerging pattern. It was exciting research that made her leap out of bed early, itching to be in the lab. She kept the details to herself until she had objective evidence rather than a gut instinct.

The pod hissed into place in the apartment building disembarkation area. The concierge scanned Julia's face, and she tubed to her apartment. Ilya Stryker-Petrel leapt off the couch when the doors moved, bounding over to hug his mother. His robot dog Dash - personal pets had been outlawed since the 2040s - yapped happily at his heels, wagging his tail in excitement.

"Mama, Mama, come see what I've made," squealed Ilya, inciting Dash to further yapping and running around in circles. Julia hugged Ilya to her for a moment. He was growing up so fast. Picking him up from his incubator, and bringing him home for the first time, felt like yesterday. She tousled his sandy hair. He had his father's colouring, but his face was all hers, and no mistaking the gleam of pride in his eyes. It was like looking in the mirror when she made a discovery. Alex planted a kiss on her cheek, shrugged his shoulders and held out his hands for her to follow Ilya. What greeted her was a large glass cube full of blooming flowers sitting in the middle of their apartment.

"How beautiful. Did you make this?" Julia raised eyebrows at Ilya.

"Yes, I did," he said, clapping his hands. "My tutor allowed me to have the seeds for these flowers as part of our botanical studies. The building manager gave me the glass cube out of the recycling pile, and all I did was duplicate the perfect conditions in an accelerated growth environment, so I could grow them before you got home. Then I reversed the process. They will live for a long time. Do you like them?" he asked shyly. Breath held, eyes wide, hoping he'd pleased his mother.

"Of course I do! This is the best present I have ever had. I feel really special," she said, putting a hand on his shoulder and feeling teary. Ilya beamed at the praise. An inner radiance lit his face, and he glowed with love. Sometimes Julia couldn't believe they had created this wonderful, clever child who was kind and good beyond belief. They were so lucky. She looked at Alex, whose eyes were glistening. His love for Ilya was naked and raw on his face. They exchanged the look they often did when overwhelmed by their feelings for their son.

"Now you have done it, Ilya. I have to come up with something extra special for your mother. You are showing me up," lamented Alex squeezing his head in his hands. They dissolved in giggles before Julia and Alex turned on Ilya, tickling him until he called 'yield'. Tears streamed down his face from laughter.

"Well, I have organised dinner for tonight," said Alex with a bow and a flourish of his hands.

Julia kissed his cheek, "love your work," she told him and went to change while the boys set the table.

Nobody cooked for themselves anymore. During the wars and before the cull, food and drink were in such short supply almost everyone subsisted on rations. In a few years, obesity became obsolete. New cases of diabetes were rare, and with no insulin available, the disease disappeared with its sufferers. As the new world vision and order evolved, each city centrally managed food as a settlement. Food providers pay careful attention to nutritional intake to manage the health of citizens. Everyone produced food sustainably while the planet recovered from its toxic state, so meat, fish and seafood were grown primarily from stem cell production. Alternative food sources like farmed insects became staple foods, and genetically modified vegetable production boosted plant-based food in the human diet.

Alex unpacked their dinner, which was perfectly balanced with the nutrient intake they needed. Dieticians meticulously controlled the portions for each person's age, height, and weight. He set out the entree of sashimi and seaweed, put the chicken, vegetables, fibre and seed cakes in the warmer, poured some water and a glass of wine for himself and Julia. They both lacked the addiction gene and had healthy bodies, so they were permitted to have small amounts of alcohol. A bottle of wine or four-pack of beer a week was included as part of their food allowance, as were two desserts and treats, as long as they all stayed within their optimal weight guidelines. For Julia, the extra kilojoules helped maintain a healthy weight, as she worked so hard her brain burned energy. Alex and Ilya participated in physical activity to offset the extra nutrition and because they enjoyed it. If they gained weight or developed any adverse physical effects, the food privileges would be suspended or revoked. In their disciplined household, it was never an issue.

A laboratory synthesised the wine and beer. They tasted real with almost no alcohol because viticulture and brewing weren't viable or priority industries. Social engineers acknowledged alcohol abuse's social and physical damage was just as harmful as other substance abuse. As the Council restructured priorities, once-powerful industries like tobacco, alcohol, advertising, social media, arms and fossil fuels descended to the bottom of the list. They didn't contribute to the survival of the human race.

It was the end of the week, and they would spend the day together tomorrow. Ilya chattered about his studies, what he learned and what he wanted to do on their day off.

Julia shrugged out of work clothes and threw them in the outbound chute. The central laundry department would sterilise them before returning the garments to the laundry niche, neatly pressed and folded. Individual dwellings no longer used water for chores, such as laundry or dishwashing, as it was too inefficient. Even shower water was purified and recycled because clean water was a valuable resource.

She ran her hands through her hair, removed the pins, and gently massaged her scalp before brushing it. Julia's closet opened, and she selected a loose powder-blue jumpsuit. Her body was craving comfort and slouching around after a long day at the office. Before she dressed, she washed her face, pinched her cheeks for colour, and examined herself critically.

Eurasian features were regular but ordinary, Julia thought. An oval face framed almond light-brown eyes, high cheekbones and a generous mouth. Julia observed dry skin and tired smudges under her eyes, not the attractive, intelligent woman other people saw. She applied lip gloss, a birthday gift and removed pearl earrings, replacing them with dangly geometric shapes. The change of clothes and refresh made her look and feel younger. Happy with the result, Julia was ready to spend time with her boys.

"You look pretty, Mama," said Ilya.

"Ilya, you need to stop stealing my lines. Julia, you do look particularly gorgeous this evening. I would like you to move in with me. Wait, we already did that. I know; let's have a baby together?" Ilya was in stitches again at Alex's silliness. "Wait, we did that too. How about having dinner with me?" said Alex getting down on one knee.

"What's in it for me?" asked Julia silkily, hands-on-hips and nose in the air. Her teasing made Ilya snort as his father remained stunned and speechless on the floor.

"I offer you this body, everything I have, dinner, and I will throw in that child for free," said Alex, pointing at Ilya.

"In that case, I accept," said Julia laughing and holding out her hand to be kissed. That set the mood for dinner, so Ilya treated them to his latest terrible jokes. The family made fun of each other, pulled faces and unwound from the week. They treasured time together, just the three of them and responsibility gave way to enjoying family life.

Julia and Alex were aware of the privilege they had earned. Ilya added a dimension to their lives, and they couldn't imagine being without him. The partnership was good between Julia and Alex from the start, but Julia wondered if it would have lasted without Ilya. She liked to think it would have. Many of their friends and acquaintances experienced multiple relationships during their adult lives. Partnerships begin and end when one partner no longer wants to live with the other. It is a more fluid arrangement than in previous centuries when marriage was the fashion.

The ownership of fewer possessions simplified matters. You were only ever a custodian of land or an apartment. People shared, and nothing much of value belonged to any one person. Settlements sterilised clothes, jewellery, repurposed items or recycled, as somebody else often wanted what you no longer needed. If you required or desired new dishes, you traded your old set and got one someone else exchanged. Or you waited for a warehouse release of the many items stockpiled after the cull.

If your relationship ended, you went back into the pool to be rematched by the Partnership Department (PD). Unlike the randomness of 'dating', the scientific art of pairing was a complex study of all facets of the matched people. The methodology yielded a high percentage of successful results. Failed pairings were due to incorrect data, often subconsciously loaded by one of the applicants. Most matched pairs formed partnerships for several years once they graduated from the developmental relationship stage.

Couples still met traditionally, at work or when they were studying. They did, however, check their genetic makeup and personality dispositions with the PD before moving in together. Lifetime pairing wasn't the ultimate goal for the PD.

The PD measured its success on the partnership's happiness, which led to increased productivity and social harmony. Julia's best friend Diana was on her third pairing. Each one lasted for about five years, and then it was over. Diana would find somebody new and fall in love all over again. However, a lack of stability did mean Diana wasn't a candidate for reproducing, as a stable environment with two parents was the optimal condition for child-rearing.

The lack of a child meant Diana doted on Ilya. She and her current partner would take the boy on outings when his parents were busy with work. As Diana managed the farming settlement areas south of the city, Ilya visited farms, saw animals, tasted tree-grown fruit and enjoyed the countryside. Ilya loved being outside, and his parents took him hiking and cycling when they could.

The Council chose locations for new settlements in the cleanest environments left on earth. Remote parts of Chile, Canada, Norway, New Zealand, Australia, Borneo, Papua New Guinea, etc. Africa, Europe, America, most of Asia and the Middle East were still largely uninhabitable. The unavailability of land wasn't critical, as most of the remaining population had moved to sustainable, communal village life or efficient, low impact, small cities.

Environmental Scientists abandoned the majority of South America to allow the regeneration of the Amazon rainforest to improve the air quality. They hoped to reverse the slashing and burning that created farmland. World leaders had dramatically underestimated the effect of the decimation of the Amazon until it was too late. Respiratory diseases reached alarming levels, triggering a global war over the issue, which made matters worse. Fortunately, the re-seeding and regeneration project progressed well, so the forest expanded rapidly.

"I will send the dishes to the steriliser," said Ilya cheerfully. He would want a three-player chess game on the virtual board before begging for an old-fashioned movie from the central archive and popcorn from their treat allowance. Ilya's latest obsessions were Charlie Chaplin and Harry Potter. They could indulge in entertainment at the end of the week because they didn't have work in the morning. Ilya's grandparents often popped in on their day off, so they shouldn't stay up too late. Julia worried about so many indulgent adults surrounding Ilya, but it didn't seem to affect him. He was polite, helpful and caring to those around him, which meant lots of friends and an active social and sporting life.

Ilya's Algorithm test was scheduled. The test usually spikes parents' anxiety levels, and Julia and Alex are no exception. However, as a scientist, Julia's mind tells her Ilya is perfect and he will score well. Probably much better than her if her theory is correct. Alex and Julia try not to worry about the testing, reassuring each other that Ilya will do fine. Ilya decided to forego the chess if they could watch a longer movie, so they snuggled together on the couch. Each clutched a portion of popcorn and lost themselves in the fantasy of someone else's life in another time.

The following day they slept late and chose their favourite breakfast, showered and dressed. Julia's parents were the first in a succession of people to arrive at the apartment. Ilya bounded to the door to be scooped up by his grandad, who swung him around, pumped his hand and gave him a bear hug. Grandmother, Ming Song-Rodin, waited patiently for her turn to embrace her grandson.

Julia loves her mother's name. When a child is delivered, parents can choose the last names for the baby. They can select a combination of names from parents and grandparents. Her parents named Julia, Stryker-Rodin, and when Ilya was delivered, Julia chose Song-Petrel. Ming had, however, urged Julia to retain the Stryker name to please her powerful grandfather and secure his support for Ilya, just as she had for Julia. Parents preferred to share one of their names with the child, so Alex and Julia chose Petrel so Ilya would have a name from each of his parents.

Leo Hussein-Rodin's meetings with Ilya are enthusiastic, but his grandmother loves him dearly. She manages to find him the most thoughtful gifts. Ming is a ground-breaking neurosurgeon, psychologist, the daughter of a Council member, and Leo Commander of the Southern Military. Their work affords them opportunities to earn privileges, which they lavish on their grandson.

Julia once had a younger brother. The QCB terminated him at three years of age. The loss of Sebastian was an enormous blow to them all, particularly to Ming. QCB investigators found that the fertilised egg wasn't Ming's but a reject that medical staff should have destroyed. The faulty egg was responsible for Sebastian's behaviour defects. Nevertheless, the loss of her son was traumatic. Ming refused to have any more children after Sebastian. Leo could have chosen another partner, but he loves Ming, and she loves Leo fiercely - he's everything her father wasn't. They stayed together, grateful to have seven-year-old Julia, who exhibited early signs of brilliance.

Perhaps the personal loss attracted Julia to genetics and drove her to strive for perfection in science and process. When her parents found out Julia and Alex were going to have a boy, they were ecstatic. Ilya brought joy back into their lives. It was as if he filled the enormous void Sebastian left. Julia felt the same and could see how happy Ilya made her parents. Her biggest issue was preventing them from spoiling him mercilessly. Ilya showed his grandparents the glass cube of flowers he made for his mother, explaining the process proudly. Grandma Ming drew a package from her bag with a flourish.

"What is it?" asked Ilya, eyes shining with excitement.

"Open it up and see for yourself," Ming replied, shooting an amused look at Julia. It was an outdated microscope no longer used at the hospital, abandoned in a supply room. It still worked, so Ming organised a trade. Ilya could use it for his botany and science projects. He loved it, so

Ming showed him how to use it, and the two examined several subjects. Leo hovered and encouraged Ilya asking him lots of questions.

Leo was always a positive influence in Julia's life. He was the father who let her parachute from an aircraft without telling her mother. Thanks to her father, Julia grew up disciplined, fit, adventurous, assessed risk and made strategic decisions. Julia saw why he ranked in the military. Leo was an authoritative, decisive, intelligent, and likeable natural leader. She observed her parents and felt she won a gene lottery but was fortunate to be raised in a home filled with love. It was what she and Alex wanted for Ilya. They both grew up in healthy, happy homes, which allowed them to flourish.

Alex's parents weren't together anymore, but his father Dmitry visited every week with his new partner. His mother, Monica, holo-called every couple of days from Antarctica and hoped to join them on holiday after her scientific expedition. Dmitry was also an engineer in charge of the city's logistics and supplies. In short, he had access to everything. If Ilya needed anything, grandfather Dmitry could get it for him. As Ilya was named after Dmitry's grandfather, who he had adored but died during the black years, spoiling was an issue from both sides of the family. Dmitry was more conservative by nature, less demonstrative, but he and Ilya bonded from the first time they met. When Ilya clasped Dmitry's finger in his tiny fist and smiled, his grandfather lost his heart.

Julia was sure all parents thought their child was special, but these grandparents made it worse. They all worshipped Ilya with complete devotion. She was pouring the tea when Dmitry and Claire arrived, so she pulled out extra cups and let Ilya entertain his grandparent fan club. Alex raised his eyebrows at her as she bustled about the kitchen before sneaking up behind her, grabbing her backside and whispering in her ear.

"We need to apply to have another child."

Julia turned, wearing her inscrutable smile, batted her eyelashes and whispered, "meet you in the shower after our hike, and you can audition for the role." Alex laughed as she shimmied out of reach to pour tea. She loved the fact he laughed a lot. He had inherited his mother's vivacious personality and offbeat sense of humour, not his father's serious nature. Alex was handsome. When the RD first matched them, Alex stunned Julia with his good looks. Sandy coloured hair, chiselled features, grey eyes with darker brows, and a gymnast or swimmer's body. Tall and muscular but slim. At first, Julia thought it was a mistake and that Alex wasn't her match. But he was, and Alex was as nervous as her. His sense of humour and hilarious self-deprecation soon had her laughing, which banished her awkwardness, allowing a sharp wit and cheeky side to emerge.

The first meeting was so successful, they went to his apartment, tore each other's clothes off, had fantastic sex and decided to move in together the following week. It was the kind of impulsiveness that surprised their parents. However, they all wanted to be grandparents, so their parents didn't ask many questions - apart from those vital to selecting candidates for a Parental Permit. Their parents' desire to see their family continue amused Julia, and professionally, she marvelled at the drive for gene survival reproduction in humans.

Leo had exhibited protective issues in some of Julia's developmental relationships. Especially once she achieved the age of CSA (Consented Sexual Activity). Julia knew her Dad loved her, and Ming patiently explained the genetic programming of the dominant alpha male in the family unit, which made sense to her scientifically. When Leo and Alex met for the first time, they got on famously, and Julia felt slightly left out. As they were both in the military, they had lots in common and seemed to share beliefs and values. She had to give the PD credit, as they selected a partner her overprotective father accepted.

Once Ilya was born, Leo adored Alex even more. When they applied and were approved to cultivate a second child, Alex could do no wrong.

Life was perfect in many ways, but as a scientist, Julia appreciated perfection as a rare and often illusionary state that didn't last. Perhaps her research made her notice things she wouldn't have otherwise. She observed Ilya and his friends scientifically as well as a mother when they played or worked on projects. Her observations tallied with her research data. Humans have been evolving quickly since the introduction of the Goodness Algorithm and genetic testing. They were more intelligent, healthy, secure, kind, confident, and intuitive emotionally.

Children possessed a natural symbiosis with the earth, the universe and their place in it. Julia anticipated some of the results but was surprised by evolutionary acceleration. Basically, they were breeding superior beings. A bigger shock for Julia was discovering Ilya was doted on and adored by friends and neighbours. Ilya attracted other students like a magnet. He treated everybody kindly, was always helpful, loved working on projects, playing, and discussing various subjects. Julia was alarmed to notice people sought his guidance, deferred to his opinion, and seemed to love him. He made everyone feel great without any effort at all.

Julia was home this week, preparing for the arrival of their new baby, so she noticed more than when she worked at the lab. She assumed her mother's goggles made her elevate Ilya to the most special person in the world. It was unexpected that unrelated people would feel the same. Ilya's superb testing scores were a source of pride for Alex, Julia and the family. Could she be reading too much into this, she wondered? The motherhood implant pumped Julia with the maternal hormones she would need to breastfeed and nurture the new baby. The baby was growing in the incubation unit, where it underwent constant monitoring and testing.

On the other hand, Julia was a born scientist, and anomalies stood out. The behavioural response of people toward Ilya was abnormal. She examined her own behaviour and Alex's. Were they deferential, she mused? They let Ilya decide what they would do on their day off, and he wanted a younger sibling. Granted, she and Alex had already discussed it. Ilya's friend Xian had a younger sister Chinta who Ilya adored, so they applied for a baby girl permit. Julia frowned in concentration, saw Ilya look up with concern at her expression. 'Work,' she mouthed at him so he wouldn't worry. Ilya flashed her a grin; he knew his mother's thinking face and returned to the workgroup project. Julia decided to discuss her observations with Alex and look at Ilya's reports. His results were fantastic, or they wouldn't have received a child permit. She was particularly interested in any observations or comments from Ilya's tutors and examiners.

Alex convinced Julia not to blow her observations out of proportion. A popular boy, Ilya was kind, which resulted in people treating him well and loving him. In the whirlwind of baby preparations, including moving to a larger apartment, Julia put her concerns aside for the moment. However, in the testing and tutorial reports, she noted constant references to Ilya's kindness, how well-liked he was, and his natural leadership. Ilya's tutors believed his future would be exceptional.

Tamara arrived, and the family-focused on settling the baby into their home and lives. They were besotted with the latest member of the family. For the first time in his life, Ilya asked to stay home rather than attend lessons. With Alex on paternity leave, Julia applied for Ilya to have two days off. As Ilya was ahead of the learning program, his tutors approved the application.

Institutions gave important family occasions priority over non-critical tasks. The baby basked in the attention lavished on her. Tamara was ready to pod to the nursery in her second week of life while the family returned to their duties. Julia zipped to the nursery at feeding time. The baby carers took care of everything else until Tamara's pod was delivered to the apartment when Julia or Alex finished work. Julia spent less time at the lab and more time working at the apartment, so she and Tamara had time to form a maternal bond. Ilya enjoyed time with his baby sister, reading, playing and studying beside her while she slept. Julia wasn't surprised, but she was moved by how sweet and caring he was. Ilya never shirked with helping her, even when it involved vomit or poop.

2

Testing Times

When the shock happened, it disturbed the equilibrium of life. Ilya came home from lessons rushed into Julia's arms, tears in his eyes, chest heaving with emotion. She had never seen him this distressed, and it upset her greatly.

"What's wrong, Ilya? What's happened to you?" she asked, holding him at arms-length to see his face. While she held him, the tears rolled down his face as he tried to compose himself to speak.

"Xian's sister, his little sister, Chinta, was... was terminated," he sobbed.

Julia enfolded him in her arms again, closing her eyes. These situations were never easy on the family. She had lived through it herself. Chinta wasn't a young child either, and Julia wondered what transpired. Children studied the screening and testing process at school. However, it was confronting for Ilya to face the reality of losing somebody he was close to.

"Why do things like this happen, Mama? Why do they have to be so mean? Is termination the only answer in this day and age? I couldn't stand it if anything happened to Tamara. It doesn't make any sense at all!"

He howled, racked by sobs once he vented his pent-up frustration. Julia continued to hold him, not sure what to say. She didn't want to state the obvious, the topics he learned in lessons, but wanted to provide some comfort. In the end, she held him close, stroked his hair and let Ilya cry.

"We need to change this, Mama. It's barbaric. After everything we've done to make the world a better place, how can we surrender our humanity, compassion and kill children? Why don't we save them?"

Julia knew they were on dangerous moral ground. A strict set of laws governed society, rules that pulled the human race from the brink of self-destruction. Ilya's eyes reflected his pain. The reverse blade to his kindness was the inability to view subjects in a cold or logical context without compassion. He was questioning the fabric of the community where they flourished as a family, society, and their existence. Julia needed to work through this carefully.

"Do you know what was wrong with Chinta, Ilya? A termination is a distressing event. You know I experienced this with my brother Sebastian when I was young. Talk to me please, tell me what happened?" she asked tearfully.

She wanted him to express his feelings, to show him empathy, and not judge his opinions or emotions with her scientific logic.

"Xian said Chinta was having tantrums. Sometimes she wouldn't do what her tutor asked. She became angry or irrational, and she stabbed her tutor's hand with a pair of scissors. Violence isn't allowed; I know that, Mama, but Chinta was uncomfortable with that tutor. He always wanted to be alone with her, and she... she didn't like it. Chinta told me she didn't want him to touch her or be alone with him. She didn't tell her parents because she was afraid something bad might happen to the tutor, but instead, she forfeits her life. It hurts so much, and I feel so helpless. I should have told you or her parents because I am older. What should I do now?" he asked.

Julia was alarmed by the nature of Chinta's termination and what she confided in Ilya. The ED scrutinised anyone who came into contact with children. Violent outbursts were highly unusual, especially in such genetically screened offspring. Chinta might have been one of the chosen five per cent, as she came from a good home and her brother Xian a model child.

"What I can do, is request Chinta's genetic records to see if we missed anything concerning her behaviour. I will also request a report, and monitoring of the tutor involved, from the Education Authority (EA) if you can give me the tutor's name," Ilya nodded. "They will determine if the tutor contributed to the outburst," said Julia earnestly. The ED would remove the tutor from duties if he were at fault, but if Chinta overreacted, the investigation would exonerate him.

"Thanks, Mama. Why didn't they investigate before the termination? Nothing will bring Chinta back. Who made that decision? We must change this," he said, deadly serious. Julia held her arms out, comforting him with her love and support. It wasn't the moment to discuss politics or society.

Ilya toyed with his dinner, then asked to sit with Tamara and retire early. Julia acquiesced to his wishes, he had had a terrible day, and she wanted to fill Alex in on their discussion.

Alex raised an eyebrow in question. She went to the cool box, took a bottle of beer and poured two glasses. The action signalled a serious conversation. Alex noticed how subdued Ilya was and couldn't recall him asking to go to bed early. Julia conveyed the details of Chinta's termination, Ilya's thoughts on the process, his determination to change things, and what she would do to support his grieving process. Julia asked Ming to come over to discuss the issue with her in the morning. As the daughter of a Council member, Ming grew up immersed in politics and decision making. There was no room for discussion or dissent in the quest to save the planet.

Society's rules bound them rigidly together and ensured only the fittest survived. Squandering resources on people who failed in the system wasn't an option. After the failures of justice systems that fostered appeal after appeal, social welfare and politics generated one inquiry after another with little result; tolerance was low. It was a fine line between supporting Ilya and encouraging criticism of the life that rebuilt the planet. Ilya asked intelligent and valid questions of his mother. Julia felt responsible as a parent to offer him reasonable answers. Alex agreed with Julia that they must learn from the termination. It could have been one of their children. He didn't want to see Ilya losing faith in them, the community or experience emotional harm from the loss of his friend.

Ilya's future was bright, and his Algorithm test was fast approaching. Julia requested the records for Chinta. It wasn't an unusual investigation for her department as they strived to understand every factor that led to termination and incorporate learnings into the screening. Chinta was of an age predating Julia's appointment, so there was much to learn from the failure.

Tomorrow, Julia would speak to Ming's friend in the ED and instigate a discreet tutor check. They finished their beer, feeling uneasy about the termination. The circumstances were strange, and Ilya's involvement brought them closer to the issue. Life was going so well. Tamara and Ilya were everything they dreamed of, but Chinta was a reminder that others could take it all away.

Alex tidied the kitchen while Julia fed Tamara, and they checked on Ilya, who was sleeping fitfully, before retiring early themselves. They held each other close while sleep eluded their grasp. Every demon that haunted parents' nightmares in their world flitted in and out of troubled minds.

Tamara awakened them early in the morning, and they looked tired as they ate breakfast.

"Ilya, do you feel up to going to lessons today?" Alex asked gently.

"Yes, I think I will, just in case Xian is there and needs me. He may not want to be home at the moment. I imagine life is difficult for his family," Ilya replied. He placed his hand over Alex's to thank him for his concern and smiled bravely. Alex regarded his son. Even now, with emotions in turmoil, Ilya noticed and acknowledged the subtle gesture. Perhaps Julia was right in her observations - she usually was.

"Ilya, your mother, has stuff to do for you today, but you can contact me if you or Xian need anything, okay?" Alex clasped Ilya's shoulder and gave a reassuring squeeze. The boy nodded his thanks, eyes letting Alex know he was grateful. Julia observed the exchange between them, loving Alex more for his sensitivity and thoughtfulness. Maybe Ilya got his kindness from his father. Ilya had pulled himself together to be at his friend's side. The records on Chinta were awaiting Julia in her office, and it was better to view them privately, so Ilya going to lessons was a blessing. Her work required security and discretion. She would take care with Ilya, no matter what she found. The rest of the family took pods to work, lessons and nursery, leaving Julia alone in her office.

Julia combed through Chinta's records one by one, methodically following her journey from selected ovum and sperm sample to a high standard embryo. She perused the full genome spectrum reporting in incubation, infancy, and early development monitoring and testing to her latest formal reviews. Julia could see that there was nothing in her genetic makeup to indicate emotional instability or violence.

Genetically, Chinta was close to perfect. Julia frowned, her thinking frown. She hoped there would be something obvious, but the research led her to social and environmental influences, a more complicated path. An enthusiastic researcher, Julia relished diving into the data. She was working backwards from the termination event and regressing through the tantrums, the minute indicators in testing or behaviour, following the thread to identify where the near-perfect child diverged from the path of normality.

The signs were subtle. To a less experienced scientist or researcher, they may have gone entirely unnoticed, but this was Julia's world. She cross-referenced her data sets to find a point of origin. The deviation into abnormal behaviour had started somewhere, after such a promising beginning to her life, and there it was. When Chinta commenced her tutorials, her behaviour started to change. That didn't necessarily mean the tutor Chinta didn't like was the problem. Julia needed to look at everyone Chinta was in contact with - tutors, students, family, friends and how they interacted with her behavioural pattern. Good scientists didn't jump to convenient conclusions. They examined as many facts as they could gather before forming any hypothesis. Before her mother arrived for tea, Julia isolated a recurring factor in Chinta's outbursts and deviating test results. The facts didn't lie. There was an issue between Chinta and one of her tutors. Julia meticulously saved the mapping and data sets methodology, as they could be refined and run as a preventative diagnostic by the ED.

A chime sounded, alerting her of a pod arrival. Julia secured her workstation and greeted her mother.

"Good morning, darling," said Ming cheerily as she stepped into the apartment, "how are my grand-children today?" She kissed Julia on each cheek, noticing dark smudges under her eyes. So unnecessary to put up with that these days. It told Ming her daughter wasn't interested in her appearance but absorbed by other things - family, work or both. Ming was committed to helping Julia and Ilya and remaining as positive as possible, so she maintained her light-hearted demeanour. Julia looked serious enough for both of them and looked like she was going to a funeral or being crushed under the world's woes. Julia told Ming she would make tea before discussing what was happening, and she wanted some advice.

Ming raised an eyebrow at Julia. Her daughter rarely asked her for advice on anything. Julia loved the challenge of working things out her-self - had done so since she was a child. It was a trait that made her an ex-cellent scientist and a self-sufficient person. At times Ming longed to be needed a little more, but Julia was a product of her parents, practically born standing on her own two feet. Ming drew a package of macaroons from her bag. The treats were Julia's favourite, so Ming brought them to have with their tea. She wasn't disappointed with Julia's enthusiastic reaction to the goodies, only surprised Julia hugged her and thanked her for remembering how much she loved macaroons. The demonstrative emotion was ringing alarm bells for Ming - something had upset Julia.

Once seated with their tea, Julia nibbled thoughtfully on a macaroon, organising her thoughts before launching into a thorough account of events. Without going through the science with Ming, Julia outlined her research and what she learned from the data.

"I was thinking of contacting Camilla this morning and asking her to take a look at the tutor. It may be nothing more malicious than a clash of personalities, or it could be something more. What do you think, as Camilla's friend, my mother, Ilya's grandmother, and as a psychologist?" she asked, reaching for a second macaroon. Ming smiled, as this was more like the Julia she raised, so many questions in one sentence.

"To answer your first question, contacting Camilla and giving her a brief verbal account of your findings is a good idea. She will make swift and discreet inquiries without causing any alarm. As a psychologist, it is highly probable the conduct of the tutor, malicious or otherwise, was a critical factor in the child's behaviour and therefore contributed to the termination." Ming wore the same frown as Julia did when she was thinking. "As your mother, I want to support you, and your pursuit of the contribution of the tutor is both responsible and admirable. It will also comfort Ilya to know you and Alex care about his friend and what he thinks. Ultimately this will build his confidence and trust in you as parents." Ming paused - how best to approach Julia on Ilya's views.

"It's okay, Mummy. Please don't sugarcoat your advice. You grew up around Council members and politics. I know, you know, how they think, understand their attitudes and views. It's one of the reasons I want your advice. You have sheltered me from that world. Our visits with your parents were and are infrequent, especially after we lost Sebastian," she said quietly, reaching for Ming's hand.

"I am glad you raised Sebastian with me, Julia. The Council is extremely intolerant of any suggestions to modify the Algorithm's termination protocol. They see safety in the rigidity of a tried and trusted system, and they view change as a threat to their power. I understand this from personal experience, as do many parents who have lived through the trauma of having a child terminated. We ask ourselves if the termination was necessary, or could someone have found an alternative? The Council responds that we shouldn't divert resources to save the weak. Society must continue to invest in ensuring the healthiest people flourish. I'm afraid we will need to be honest with Ilya because the Council will interpret his views as dissent. Ilya is an unwanted and undesirable voice for change and a threat to the rule of law. I agree with his sentiments, but as his grandmother, I want him to live. That means he shouldn't be publicly critical, or he could place himself in danger. He is yet to undergo his Algorithm test, and we cannot afford to be naïve," she said gravely, holding Julia's gaze firmly. Julia swallowed, she was expecting caution from her mother but not such an honest assessment of the threat Ilya's views might pose.

"He is a child, and surely they won't consider such a young boy a threat? I'm sure Chinta's brother and every other sibling must feel the same way," said Julia searching her mother's face. What she saw in Ming's face didn't comfort her at all. Perhaps she was blissfully ignorant.

"Shall we speak to Ilya together?" Ming asked.

"Maybe that would be a good idea," said Julia. "Alex and Dad are both in the military, and involving them won't provide any better out-come. Ilya is wise beyond his years. He will be disillusioned, but he will understand. Can you come back after lessons?" Julia asked. Ming nodded, sipped her tea and took a macaroon. It was a distraction while they mulled over the conversation before contacting Camilla.

As a close friend of Camilla, Ming had her private secure-communication channel, so she initiated the contact. They exchanged pleasantries and news. Then Ming briefly outlined why she was calling before letting Julia take over.

Camilla was whip-smart, had known Julia a long time and respected her scientific work. She asked Julia to give her some time, and she would be in contact as soon as she could. Julia and Ming thanked her, but Camilla only shook her head and said she was grateful they brought the issue directly to her so that it could be dealt with swiftly.

Julia buried herself in work for the rest of the day so she wouldn't keep thinking about Ming's words. Hours had elapsed before she knew it, and she heard the chime. Ilya, she presumed. Ming checked when

Ilya's lessons finished and decided to arrive before he did. In her experience, young people were impulsive when emotionally stretched. If he had a difficult day, Ilya would immediately download to Julia. He loved and trusted Julia as he should. Ming was acutely aware she had sheltered Julia, who was now unaware of the mechanisms of government.

Without scaring Ilya too much, Ming must ensure he understood. He shouldn't voice his opinions as criticism of the Council. Power remained as attractive and desirable as ever. Despite all the improvements made to the environment, their way of life, and the human race's continued survival, human nature hadn't changed.

Ming was a perpetual student of the human brain from a neurological and psychological perspective, and she understood the strong drive for dominance and power in some people.

Her father was an example of it, and that was how he gained a seat on the Council. They had lived in an opulent home with the best of everything and no rules. Ming grew up without time or affection from her father, merely a novelty to show off at parties.

The one time Ming asked Stryker for anything was when Sebastian failed his test. She didn't plead for his life, only for time to understand what caused the failure. She wasn't surprised when he declined to make an exception for her. To do so could have compromised him politically, but his lack of compassion and cold dismissal was unforgivable.

Ming ensured they saw little of her parents after Sebastian's termination. They occasionally communicated because she wanted them to support Julia in her studies and career aspirations. Ming wasn't naïve, and she didn't want to make an enemy of her father. So they maintained as little contact as they could within the bounds of social acceptability.

It was enough for Ming's father, who didn't notice but disappointed her mother. Her mother remained with Stryker for the lifestyle, even though he flaunted the many live-in mistresses he called Assistants.

Ming embraced Julia and explained why she had arrived early. She didn't want Julia to deal with the issue on her own. Julia was grateful her mother would be there as she was in tune with people's thoughts.

The chime signalled Ilya's arrival, and they greeted him as he tubed into the apartment. His face lit up when he saw Ming was visiting again, and he ran to hug her before throwing his arms around Julia.

"How was your day?" Julia asked, searching for an honest answer in his face.

"It was difficult, Mama. Xian is understandably miserable and doesn't say much. We ate together in silence today, but he knows I'm there when he feels like talking."

"That is thoughtful of you," said Ming, nodding her head in approval. "You offer compassion and support without any pressure. I can't imagine anything better you can do for Xian right now."

Ilya looked at his grandmother gratefully, he knew she was a respected psychologist, and her approval meant a lot. The entire day he'd been seeking the appropriate words or actions to support his friend, but in the end, his silent company was enough.

"Your mother told me how you feel, Ilya. We understand how frustrating it is when you can see an alternative to taking irreversible action. We lived through it and survived, so we know how hurt Xian, and his parents are. We are extremely proud of you and the empathy you feel for your friend. You are a good person Ilya." Ming smiled at him, and Julia admired her ability to find common ground and deliver genuine praise before tackling the issue at hand. "You are a smart young man, and I know you want to change the world, but please listen carefully because I love you more than anything."

Ming put her hand on his and looked him straight in the eye. "I'm going to be very straightforward. The Council doesn't tolerate criticism of their policies at all. If you publicly oppose the Council and our current system, you will place yourself and our family in danger. I don't agree with them, and neither does your mother, but this topic is so sensitive that we haven't even discussed it with your father or grandfather. You know that your great-grandfather is on the Council. I grew up in a world where holding the reins of power consumes the minds of the strongest people. There are many benefits of the current system but also major flaws. Our society isn't as flexible as it could be. Do you understand?" Ilya nodded his head, eyes serious and thoughtful as he processed the information.

"If I oppose them openly, do you believe I could be terminated or fail the Goodness Algorithm, Grandma?" Ilya asked quietly.

"Yes," replied Ming, impressed he grasped the issue and identified the severity of the repercussions. "Or your father could be posted to Antarctica, your mother replaced in her position, or the whole family put on an experimental, exploratory space mission." She held his gaze, knowing she stripped away his childhood, but determined to save his life.

Julia paled as Ilya asked the question. She went to him as Ming responded, placing her arm around his shoulders protectively. Part of her wanted to scream at Ming to stop, that he was just a boy. Deep down, she knew her mother wouldn't be doing this if it wasn't essential. Her heart ached as Ilya consigned his childhood naivety and trust to the past, knowing he viewed the world through adult eyes. Ilya turned to Julia, pain written on his face.

"Don't worry, Mama, I won't let any harm come to you or our family," he said, comforting her. That was so 'Ilya' to consider everyone else before himself, and Julia's love for him surged. How could anyone this wonderful fail the Goodness Algorithm? She also chastised herself for her gullible nature, as she could see Ming's worry was more than a grandmother fretting for her family. Ming rarely talked about life with her parents unless it was positive. Julia realised Ming's effort to allow her to live a carefree, happy life. To Julia, Ming's upbringing, close to the seat of power, sounded awful. That perfect world was at least partially an illusion.

"Ilya, if you want to discuss what we have talked about today at any time, please speak to your mother or me. We love you more than we can ever express," said Ming.

"I love you, Ilya, for being kind and compassionate, not just for being my son," said Julia. "Shall we have Tamara sent home while grandma is here?"

Ilya nodded his ascent, the thought of seeing his baby sister bringing the first smile to his face since he told Julia about Chinta. They fed and played with the baby, which was a welcome, uplifting relief after such sombre conversation. Ilya read stories and sang nursery rhymes to Tamara as Julia said goodbye to Ming. A bell sounded in Ming's bag, and it was Camilla.

"Hi, I'm glad you two are still together. I have an update. Do you have time to talk, and can you activate your privacy encryptor?" Camilla asked. Ming nodded, and they moved to Julia's office and commscreen. Camilla's worried face appeared on the screen, so Julia and Ming closed the door.

"After your call this morning, I ran a thorough background check on Chinta's tutors, and they have excellent credentials, which makes sense, or the ED wouldn't have appointed them." Camilla switched languages and spoke to them in old fashioned Mandarin, a language hardly understood by anyone in the new order but a shared hobby with Ming and Julia. "I also checked the surveillance data for two weeks before the stabbing incident to look for anything unusual, and I found an issue. There is a storeroom in one of the tutorial rooms, and a tutor sent Chinta in there on more than one occasion. The tutor followed her in, and there were no cameras. So I checked the tutor, James Kitchener, more thoroughly. He is respected well-liked by his students, parents, colleagues and department heads, with an exemplary teaching record that could get him an appointment anywhere." Camilla paused for a moment.

"None of this made sense, so I decided to run a series of data checks on him. Nothing stood out, but when I ran the blood on the scissors to check his gene profile testing - it wasn't a match. That seemed ridiculous, as he is identified by the facial and retina scanners every day when he enters the building. I asked my records expert Karl to look at the employment history files in the central repository. Karl couldn't tell me how they did it. He thought it was impossible to do, but someone recoded the data in the tutor's file. The tutor is not James Kitchener. James Kitchener lives in Perseverance City in southern Chile, where the ED posted him five years ago. The file has been duplicated then manipulated to replace the identifiers with new data, giving somebody else an excellent profile - but of course, you can't replace blood. The access level and skill required to achieve this deception are astounding. I will change channels and call back."

The screen went blank before signalling an incoming comm from an unidentified number. Camilla switched to Turkish, another uncommon language they spoke fluently. "Sorry for the additional precautions, but there is more. The termination team mobilised wasn't official. They were impostors. I cannot tell you who took Chinta, whether she was terminated or kidnapped, but she has vanished along with the tutor, who isn't James Kitchener. I wasn't expecting to find illicit criminal activity, as it doesn't exist in our world these days, but that is what it looks like."

Camilla returned to the common language. "I have alerted the Behaviour Investigation Authority (BIA), the Central Record Repository (CRR) of the security breach and the QCB of the issue. Nothing like this has happened in many years, as far as I know, and I'm not entirely sure how matters will proceed from here. I feel for the girl's family, and I seek feedback on the correct procedure. It's just so much to take in." Camilla nibbled on a fingernail as she paused to let Ming and Julia absorb the information she offloaded. Her head was spinning all afternoon as the situation lurched from concerning, to troubling, to unbelievable. To Camilla, the issue landed in the shocking and sinister baskets.

"Thank you, Camilla. I don't know what to say. Best this remains confidential for now," Ming responded casually. "Let's keep in touch, shall we?" Camilla nodded, said goodbye, following Ming's lead, keeping the conversation light. Julia's face was white, and Ming grabbed her hand to squeeze it in reassurance, although the unexpected report also rocked her.

"We may never find out what happened to Chinta, but I'm sure the investigation will be thorough, and Camilla will update us. The authorities will keep the breach in security confidential, and Camilla has kept our exchange private. Together we must decide what to tell Ilya. Based on his quick grasp of our conversation earlier this afternoon, I'm inclined to tell him the truth, but you are his mother. Whatever you decide is the course we will follow," said Ming gently. Julia closed her eyes in pain as she thought. Part of her longed to have Ilya grow up as carefree and naive as possible, just like her. At the same time, she didn't want to shield him with lies or risk losing his confidence by withholding information.

"We need to tell him the truth," she sighed.

They told Ilya they were taking the baby for a walk outside in the park. While they were walking, Ming and Julia told him everything they had learned. Ilya's eyes registered his disbelief as the story unfolded, but he turned to them both when they finished.

"Thank you for being honest with me. I know I am young, and apparently, I am extremely naive. I will never mention any of this to anyone ever. Love you both." With that, he took Julia's hand and turned to walk home. Ming looked at Ilya with tears in her eyes. He was an exceptional young man who would walk into his future with his eyes wide open, just as she had.

Life at home settled back into a routine. Ilya betrayed few signs of his ordeal. Julia was surprised, as she often found her thoughts drifting when she fed the baby or showered. Ilya continued to be as supportive of Xian as possible. The young man was often over, working on projects or playing chess now that his Goodness Algorithm test was over. Xian achieved a fantastic score. Julia and Alex were so pleased for his parents, and they invited them to dine out together with the boys to celebrate. They all enjoyed the evening immensely, although Julia glimpsed the sadness lurking in Xian's mother's face. She and Alex made every effort to keep the mood light and buoyant. It was Xian's night, and they wanted him to enjoy his moment of triumph.

Ilya would be sitting his test in a couple of weeks. He spent a lot of time revising all his lessons while sitting with his baby sister. Tamara never tired of Ilya reciting information or reading to her. She fixed her grey-eyed gaze upon him and observed until sleep or hunger overwhelmed her. Ilya often anticipated what Tamara wanted. He fetched Julia when she was hungry or carried her in his arms to be fed or changed. Julia teased Ilya that his sister would be ready for her Algorithm testing as soon as she left the nursery. Ilya laughed and told Tamara she would be a genius.

Alex was more nervous about Ilya's test than he had been about his own, so Julia frequently massaged the tension out of his neck and shoulders. The grandparents also fussed and fretted, trying to maintain an air of confidence, but betrayed their worrying in many ways. Ilya was the only family member beside Tamara, who remained calm.

Julia dived into her work in an overzealous frenzy. She had three excellent research scientists working on her Escalating Evolution (EV) theory data. EV progressed rapidly beyond a theory. There was a substantial amount of evidence indicating leaps made in every generation.

Health, security, and education increased emotional development in previously undeveloped brain regions. Children were now able to work cohesively in large groups, without conflict, to achieve common goals. The non-verbal communication skills had evolved to such a level that Julia was now exploring whether they were sharing or reading body queues or thoughts. She felt she was living in an experiment every day with Ilya, his friends and Tamara, who didn't cry.

Genetic selection and methodology weren't only eradicating undesirable behaviour but enhancing the development of new skills. Could Ilya's ability to understand Tamara's needs be due to a developed sense of emotional receptivity or perhaps, some other form of communication, Julia wondered? The further Julia delved into the project, the more complex her questions became. The research was fascinating, often uncovering new pathways of thought to follow. Julia was sure the generation of children developing in their midst would surpass previous generations of human beings in every way possible.

When the appointed day of the test arrived, Ilya kissed them all goodbye with a smile and took a pod to the Academy of Assessment

(AOA) without a backward glance. The Goodness Algorithm testing would take the entire day. Julia and Alex worked to take their mind off worrying. The AOA would analyse his results, and they would be available in the evening, so the family hoped to be celebrating. It was early afternoon when Julia received an incoming request from the Head of the AOA for a holo meeting.

3

The Shift

Julia's heart beat an erratic pace as she accepted the call, and she thought she might pass out from a spike in anxiety.

"I know you must be worried, so I want you to know Ilya hasn't failed. I am Thomas MacArthur, Head of the Academy of Assessment." He sputtered, possibly because he noticed Julia's blood-drained face. As the words registered, Julia inhaled to get some oxygen circulating in her stressed body. She recognised the physiological reaction and counteracted it with deep breaths.

"Is something wrong with Ilya?" Julia asked as her brain jumped to another possible reason for the call.

"No, nothing is wrong with him. He is physically fine. The reason for my call is he's completed his test already, which nobody has ever done. And I can't begin to explain his results. May I call you Julia?" he asked.

"Of course," Julia replied.

"Julia, Ilya's results are off the charts. He hasn't just passed. Ilya has redefined the boundaries of the Goodness Algorithm. One of the monitoring scientists alerted me this morning of anomalies in the test results. He initially ran diagnostics, suspecting a glitch existed in the testing program. He found no errors, no differences in Ilya's testing methodology or equipment to any other participants. The central computer analysed Ilya's results twice because it couldn't comprehend the data. Some of Ilya's responses are ground-breaking leaps in many fields.

His problem-solving skills display a depth of thought and complexity we have never encountered. You are also a scientist, so I'm sure you grasp how fascinating Ilya's results are. We want to explore and understand more about the way he thinks. He has so much to teach us for one so young," he stammered.

Julia digested Thomas' information, one fact at a time, ensuring she grasped critical data elements before forming conclusions. Not so easy when the subject was her son, the person she loved most. Julia prioritised her questions. She wanted as much information as possible.

"Thank you for calling me Thomas and alleviating my concerns Ilya had failed. What will happen now?" she asked. Julia deliberately posed her question to invite him to vocalise how he saw the future.

"Ilya can pod home once our post-test analysis is complete. I would like to have him return to the AOA as soon as possible, but I must discuss this with the ED. His test results will garner interest from the Central Academy, and they will want input into how we proceed," he said with a frown.

Thomas had ideas on how he wanted to approach Ilya's results, but his superior or another department might overrule him. There was no question in Julia's mind, having Ilya's results assessed locally in New Zealand was the most desirable outcome for the family. Her maternal instincts wanted Ilya's life to carry on as it had, but that was an impossible outcome.

As a scientist, her point of view would be different. A scientist desired the best facilities, the most brilliant staff - as the Head of Genetics, that's what she wanted.

Julia wondered if being Ilya's mother would prevent her from executing her professional role or if her unique position to scientifically observe Ilya in his natural state could enhance her input. Her team's work was highly relevant to improvements in testing.

Ilya and his friends were driving segments of empirical data analysis, and the lab facility was the world's best, thanks to the generous funding for genetics.

"It will take some discussion to decide where we go from here, Julia. So, I would take Ilya out to celebrate his results. He can return to lessons until we make a decision. Ilya is a gifted, wonderful child. You and your husband must be proud, and I truly want to be part of his future," said Thomas sincerely. His comment struck Julia as heartfelt but unusual for an analytical scientist. Still, she was aware of the 'Ilya effect', as she had dubbed people's reaction to him.

"Would you like me to speak with Ilya's father, or would you prefer to do that yourself?" Thomas asked. He was affording Julia a lot of professional courtesy, from one Department Head to another, and she was grateful for the offer to brief Alex.

"Thanks for your consideration, Thomas. I would like to share this news with Alex in person," she said. They agreed to keep in touch before terminating the link.

Julia sat quietly for a moment, calming herself, deciding how to break the news to Alex. She sent him a message that Ilya had passed and asked him to pod home early. He would be surprised she knew the result, but Julia was resourceful.

Julia ordered herbal tea and poured a cup each as Alex's pod arrived. She embraced Alex, and asked him to sit as she had news. Alex's eyes searched her face, she never asked him to come home early, and his thoughts immediately flitted to the children.

"Ilya and Tamara are fine. Ilya performed exceedingly well in his testing." Julia repeated everything Thomas MacArthur told her verbatim, what she asked him, and his responses. Alex ran busy hands through his hair, betraying his worry to Julia.

She let him digest the information while she sipped her tea and held his hand. They sensed the seismic shift in their world where Ilya was concerned. Both agreed to call Ming and gauge her thoughts on the situation before Ilya returned home. They were glad they involved her, as she wasted no time getting on the front foot.

Ming suggested they, as a family, should formulate a plan. A plan designed with Ilya's well-being at the centre, with his input, that incorporated their society's guiding principles. The positive influence of the stable family unit and community in the new order was a factor in every child's development.

While Ilya would be studied and tested, they must ensure they remained involved. Ming, like Julia, considered what she could contribute professionally. If she couldn't conduct brain activity mapping and psychological analysis herself - she would select the team. It was inevitable experts in every field Ilya excelled in would be consulted. They must try to keep Ilya's life stable by conducting tests at home. When Ilya travelled, a family member would accompany him. The family would minimise Ilya's separation from his parents and Tamara.

Julia and Ming were sure the authorities would closely monitor Tamara's development. Society must protect Ilya's social and sporting activities or they risked inhibiting the environment that had allowed him to flourish. Ming's arguments were sound, affording Julia and Alex some comfort that Ilya's destiny wasn't out of their hands. Waiting for other people to make decisions about their son wasn't palatable to either of them.

One of Alex's childhood friends, Yoshi, a sports training partner, was a specialist in civic rights and child law. Alex knew Yoshi would help them, as he was fond of Ilya, and they were often at the gym together.

"One last thing, Julia, you should call your grandfather. Tell him you don't need him to do anything, but let him know your plan. It's a courtesy call. As Ilya's grandfather, you don't want him to be surprised when Ilya becomes a topic of conversation. You are a brilliant scientist, and he is proud of you. He will also be proud of Ilya and grateful to hear the news from you directly," said Ming.

"And he'll be impressed I have saved him any embarrassment and more likely to help if we need influence. I'm lucky to have a clever mother who understands power," finished Julia with a grin.

When Ilya arrived home, Julia and Alex felt calmer, but Ilya noticed something was amiss. The crushing hugs probably didn't help either, but he knew they would be anxious. All parents worried.

"Ilya, how did you find the testing today?" asked Julia.

"It was interesting, not what I was expecting. The dynamics and parameters were different to anything else I have done. I believe I did well. I finished the program faster than everyone else, and now I'm so hungry." Ilya's hands gripped his stomach as he dramatically rolled his eyes in the air. "Please tell me I have earned a huge dinner after today's brain activity. Can I have some snacks?" he begged.

Julia and Alex laughed at the amusing boy they had created. A budding genius, or evolution at work, but just a hungry child for now. Julia told him what happened after completing his test once Ilya was seated, devouring his allocated afternoon snacks. Ilya continued munching on his food and looking thoughtful but took the information in his stride.

"So now I suppose everybody will want to study me, to understand why and how I think differently," he stated while contemplating his apple slices. "I hope you and Dad are coping with this. Sorry to be the source of worry for you. I can feel how anxious you are. I don't want to be away from you or Tamara, and I assume it's logical to study me in the environment where I developed. The authorities will blend my lessons and other studies, I imagine. Minimal disruption to my everyday life until they understand what shaped my brain development. Do you think you and Grandma Ming will be involved, Mummy? Perhaps I will request you are. My rights as a child, to access the best possible care and security, can be exercised," he said before taking a bite.

Alex and Julia looked at each other. Julia made an effort to keep her features neutral, while Alex was less successful and wore a bemused look. Ilya's rapid assessment of the situation eclipsed their reactions markedly. Two well-educated adults, Julia, a world-leading scientist, and Ilya, made them feel like children who hadn't quite grasped the question.

Julia wondered how she missed this side of Ilya. Why hadn't his tutors jumped up and down for joy? She pondered if the Goodness Algorithm testing was responsible for stretching the way Ilya used his brain. He mentioned it was different to anything else. Ilya had always been intelligent, intuitive, but he now seemed to be functioning at a completely different level. Still the same child in some ways, yet somehow subtly altered.

After Ilya dealt with his hunger, he put his hands on top of theirs, smiled and told them not to worry. It would all be okay. Julia experienced an intense rush of love and warmth for Ilya. Every cell in her body was surging towards him as a flower turned to the sun. She felt bathed in happiness, flooded with light, and wanted nothing more than to look after Ilya. His eyes reflected how she felt. No wonder he challenged the Algorithm! The goodness inside of him shone outwards. They hugged each other. Content that they loved one another, and they would deal with the future together. All they needed now was Tamara, so they had her sent home.

It was only later, when Julia was showering with time to collect her thoughts, that she questioned, replayed and analysed the emotions of the afternoon. She was Ilya's mother, had loved him his whole life with all her heart. Yet this afternoon was different, abnormal. Julia tried to put her finger on exactly what she had experienced. Magnetic adoration was the description she chose. Was that how Ilya made people feel, Julia asked herself? She recalled, with eyes closed, how other people looked at Ilya when she first noticed his influence on others. When Julia thought about it, she couldn't recall anybody who didn't like Ilya. As a mother that filled her with pride, Julia questioned the odds as a scientist.

They were going out tonight to celebrate and eat burgers at the Rock 'n Roll Diner. Meals at this restaurant were a rare treat, as it imposed limited reservations, customarily saved for Ilya's birthday. While the meals were healthier than in the twentieth century, they were still substantial. The diet planners adjusted energy input and physical output throughout the week to accommodate the nutrient-dense meal. Julia spent an extra half an hour exercising on the day so she could share a chocolate milkshake with her boys. She selected a soft pink dress with a full skirt, a letter sweater to fit in with the restaurant theme and distractedly applied makeup as her mind ticked.

"Tonight is for Ilya," she told herself in the mirror, "lighten up, Julia." She slicked gloss on her lips, pinched her cheeks and put on a cheery smile before heading into the living room with a twirl. Alex gave a wolf whistle as he moved to catch and dip her, making Ilya laugh.

"You guys are the silliest parents ever. I'm the luckiest kid in the world," he said, slicking his hair back and giving them his best leather-jacket clad, bad boy look. They wanted to take Tamara with them, but Ming claimed 'Grandma time.' In some ways, it was fun and felt right to focus on Ilya. The Goodness Algorithm was a rite of passage for all youngsters, and it was time to celebrate.

When they arrived at the restaurant, Ilya began chatting with the host, also wearing a leather jacket, and the family were upgraded to a coveted red-leather booth. Julia raised an eyebrow at Alex, who shrugged his shoulders, trailing behind the host and Ilya, who were talking like long lost friends.

The Diner atmosphere was festive, as only people celebrating special occasions ate there, but everyone seemed to know Ilya tonight. As he skipped off with a friend to say hello to her parents, Julia quipped to Alex, "this must be what it was like going out with a celebrity."

Alex took her hand under the table and whispered, "more alone time to be naughty." Julia threw back her head and laughed. Alex loved to make her laugh. It transformed his clever, pretty wife into the beautiful, exotic creature he fell in love with on their first date.

While they were waiting for dessert, Ilya played pinball with friends, who celebrated passing their test. After ten minutes, they looked up to find a group of young people surrounding Ilya. Even the host and waitress were there. Ilya was talking and smiling while people stared at him adoringly. Finally, their dessert arrived, and Ilya bounded back to the table like a happy puppy, anticipating the taste of his strawberry sundae.

"How did your game of pinball go?" asked Julia. Ilya had already shovelled a spoon full of ice cream into his mouth and savoured its taste with his eyes closed, but he grinned at Julia.

"It wasn't as challenging as I remember, so I taught some other kids how to watch the ball and anticipate its movements to improve their scores. Then we talked about kid stuff," he said, loading his spoon again.

"Even the host and waitress wanted to listen to kid stuff?" she asked with an indulgent smile.

"Well, I believe they were interested in our discussion too. Most of us consider how we will shape the future when we're adults. How we will become better people, live in harmony with nature. Many of us want to focus more attention and resources on returning our planetary environment to how it once was. These are issues we are passionate about, Mummy. We also want to laugh and love more, be creative, push the boundaries of how we perceive the world. We were all incubated in a laboratory, so sometimes, the world we live in seems pretty black and white. But we are fascinated by the colour of life and nature," he said with an Alex shrug. Julia and Alex regarded each other over dessert.

"Wow, evidently, I am completely out of touch with today's youth," said Alex. Julia nodded her agreement while sipping their milkshake. They gave over the rest of the meal to enjoying their hard-earned desserts and teasing each other about who licked their spoon or bowl cleanest before joining in the dancing.

The Diner screens would show an old film clip, run a tutorial, then the participants tried to emulate the dance moves. It was a lot of fun. Julia and Alex were always competitive. Ballet and gymnastics were in Alex's DNA, but Julia's athletic grace and analytical mind were formidable. It was always Ilya who danced best, thanks to both their genes and his youthful learning ability.

Ilya drifted off to dance with his friends to burn off a bit of fructose, so Alex and Julia popped into the slow dance section to enjoy a romantic moment. When they returned to the main area to look for Ilya, most of the diners were clapping and cheering. A group of children put on a synchronised dance display of the jitterbug, with Ilya dancing in the centre, mesmerising the crowd. The twelve participants took a bow and bounded off to their parents, breathless, happy, and with eyes shining.

Ilya hugged his parents and told them it was one of the best times he had ever had. Julia felt her heart pang - he was growing up.

They all wanted to see Tamara, so they said goodnight to everyone and took a pod home. Laughing hysterically at Ilya's animal imitations on the way, Julia decided he wasn't too grown up yet.

Two days later, the family received an invitation to a meeting chaired by Thomas MacArthur to discuss Ilya's results. Several Department Heads would attend from education, child development, civic rights, and various scientific and medical research organisations. Ironically this included Julia and Ming in their professional capacities. Julia, Alex and the grandparents were apprehensive, but Ilya remained calm and good-natured.

They had discussed the many possibilities or consequences that could stem from this meeting with Ilya. He steadfastly steered them back to the most logical outcome - what was best for him. They decided to let Ilya speak for himself, and they would support him where required.

Thomas introduced Ilya to everyone. Ilya was charming with his friendly nature, consideration of others, and genuine interest in their roles. When they finished introductions and refreshments, everyone wanted what was best for Ilya.

The head of the AOA provided a detailed brief on Ilya's test results, which included new formulae in mathematics, quantum mechanics, a theory on the evolutionary design of cells, medical cures - complete with supporting scientific explanations. Ilya had proposed potential alternative approaches to psychological treatment, an essay on the developing function of the human brain at an advanced level, philosophy, environmental connectivity and symbiosis. Thomas explained the outcomes had arisen from a desire to help others in hypothetical situations, which explored the boundaries of the individual for positive emotions and attributes. Ilya's capacity for kindness, compassion, empathy etc., manifested in ground-breaking problem-solving and unique thinking at an evolved level that pushed past the boundaries of the program. Initial analysis of Ilya's physiological state revealed Ilya was utilising neural connectivity in brain areas that were traditionally inactive.

"We want to understand more about you, Ilya, and the advanced knowledge you offer society is vital. I am also conscious that you are young and, therefore, still developing. We shouldn't interfere with or inhibit that growth," said Thomas addressing Ilya directly but making a point to everyone else.

"Thank you for your consideration, Department Head MacArthur," said Ilya with a nod and a bright smile. "May I have your permission to address the assembly?" he asked politely. Thomas MacArthur acquiesced to Ilya's request, opening the floor for him.

"As the subject of this meeting, I have digested the test results and what they mean. It is my civic duty to contribute to society, the natural environment which sustains humanity, as much as I can throughout my lifetime. I am also evolving, and there is much I don't yet comprehend as well as I might. For my brain to continue to develop on its current trajectory, it would be optimal to maintain my current environment and habitat. To enable the necessary scientific and medical study, I can organise my schedule to encompass lessons, sports, social activity, and testing to best understand my results. My learning curve for lessons is above average, and I can work harder to free up more time. The family unit is an integral part of my emotional development, so I should remain within that familiar and nurturing environment for now. My mother should oversee my genetic testing, and my maternal grandmother Ming can oversee the required psychological and neurological profiling. Their involvement will comfort me that I'm not about to become an old-fashioned lab rat. My family members cannot conduct any research or tests under the Scientific Study Accord Ethical Code. However, they are leaders in their field and have the unique opportunity to observe me regularly in my natural state. We can achieve the perfect balance between research and continued evolution while respecting my legal right to a supportive childhood," said Ilya with his trademark winning smile.

With a few simple sentences, Ilya determined the outcome of the meeting. His reasoning was sound and logical. Legally the rights of an achieving child to a stable home were absolute. The discussion shifted to accommodating the program Ilya proposed. There was jockeying amongst the participants to obtain priority in accessing Ilya, but again Ilya came up with a solution. If the ED granted him a short absence from lessons for a week, he could engage with each department. The offer seemed to satisfy everyone.

The participants noted that a brilliant adolescent chaired the meeting, with an agreed plan achieved in record time. They couldn't wait to spend time with Ilya and analyse how he functioned. Scientifically, he was fascinating. The group appointed Thomas MacArthur as the scheduling coordinator, and he closed the meeting, thanking Ilya for his input.

Julia breathed a sigh of relief and shot Ming a look of stunned disbelief. Ming's face was inscrutable, for she hid her emotions well. Julia noticed Ming's now relaxed flowing movements compared to her slightly stiff body when they arrived. Alex was an open book, his face advertising his pleasure that Ilya would remain with them. Leo was much the same. Dmitry, like Ming, kept his emotions in check, but he squeezed Ilya's shoulder and shook his hand in approval. For the moment, their world rocked but was only shifting.

Professionally, Julia was just as excited as everyone else about understanding how Ilya had made such a leap. If her theory was correct, Ilya wasn't the only child who would manifest advanced skills. They hadn't mentioned Tamara today, but all the departments would monitor her at every level of development to detect if she possessed Ilya's abilities. Julia's maternal instincts wished Ilya hadn't tested off the charts and could just have remained their boy. It was the vain hope of a mother who didn't yet comprehend the cult-following forming around Ilya.

Julia went to work straight away, and the lab analysed Ilya and Tamara's coding. The ability of Ilya and Tamara to communicate was intriguing. In collaboration with Ming's neurological department, they fitted them with sensory caps to visually measure their responses to one another. Ilya thought it an excellent idea and was as curious as everyone else to understand how he and Tamara communicated non-verbally.

Ilya sat at the dining table, surrounded by visual display units to record his brainwave activity. They would show inactive brain areas and comparative mapping to control group studies. At the same time, Tamara was alone in her cot in the nursery as Julia observed her on a monitor. Gerard, who worked with Ming, was a brilliant neurological scientist, and he jumped at the chance to conduct research in Ilya's home. He set up the testing equipment and had just replaced Ilya's cap as it seemed to be malfunctioning. Only it wasn't. The second cap was streaming the same data as the first, so he summoned Ming to take a look. All of Ilya's brainwaves were displaying extraordinary levels of activity. The theta and beta waves particularly, and the right parahippo-campal gyrus was lit up like a city at night on his brain map.

"Ilya, are you communicating with Tamara?" said Ming. "What are you thinking?"

"I am soothing her, telling her to be calm as Mummy and I are here if she needs anything," he replied. Julia could see Tamara lying there, quietly content on the monitor, and her brain was showing activity in the same region. They appeared to be communicating telepathically.

"Ilya, can you make Tamara laugh," asked Gerard. Ilya nodded his head enthusiastically, and sure enough, Tamara began cooing, then chortling, waving her fists.

"How did you do that, Ilya?" asked Gerard with a smile.

"I am making images for her of colourful bubbles bursting and tickling her face; it's one of her favourite games." Tamara quietened again, and Ilya explained he was sailing boats in the air for her, which she found relaxing. Gerard ran through a series of tests he had devised. Everything from tickling her feet to checking if Tamara was hungry, thirsty, lonely, happy, hot, or cold. There was no doubt they could share thoughts and emotions. Ilya could project images to her and stimulate her senses to react as he had done with the bubbles. These were only the first tests Gerard performed, and already they had uncovered so much new, exciting information.

"When you are working with the other children on projects, Ilya, do you share information in a similar way?" asked Julia, thinking back to her observations while on maternity preparation leave.

"Oh yes, we do. It's not the same as with Tamara, but we can share thoughts to shape our projects, reach a consensus and understand what we each have to do. Not everyone can share images, so sometimes I show the others how our project will look," he replied.

"Are you able to share something with me?" asked Gerard. Ilya frowned in concentration before explaining adults weren't as easy to communicate with as Tamara. He felt like he was yelling at somebody who couldn't hear him, and then he grinned mischievously. Gerard yawned suddenly, shaking his head before looking at a smug Ilya.

"Did you just make me feel sleepy, Ilya?" The boy nodded and giggled aloud, making Tamara laugh again as she shared his joke.

"Just one more question, champ, and then how about we let you get back to being a kid?" As Ilya nodded in agreement, Gerard asked if he could hide or stop people from feeling his emotions. Ilya explained he could. For example, Ilya didn't want to bombard his parents with Tamara and his thoughts. Ilya did, however, let them know he loved them often.

It was the same with his friends and study group. They connected when they needed to, but it was similar to ending a conversation. They just disconnected once they finished. You couldn't share with some-body else unless they wished to communicate with you, or you had an ambient connection like he did with Tamara. When Ilya was attending lessons, he wasn't sharing with Tamara, but she could reach him. Each answer posed another series of questions that Gerard should ask to test the boundaries of their abilities. Gerard was, however, sensitive to over-loading Ilya. Aware he was in Ilya's home as a guest, with so much data to analyse. He stuck to his word and declared the testing over for the day. Ilya shook his hand.

"I look forward to our next session Gerard. It was fascinating." Ilya loped off to scoop Tamara up and rock her to sleep as she was tired. Gerard believed Ilya was gifted. He wanted to do right by Ilya and his family, to protect his good nature from exploitation. As a researcher, Gerard hoped each department would approach the boy carefully. Scientifically, he wondered if Ilya would achieve that outcome through his abilities. Gerard pondered whether Ilya influenced him during the testing. Next time, he would monitor himself as well. Gerard efficiently packed up the equipment, thanked Ming, then Julia for the unique opportunity and took a pod straight to the lab.

"Gerard seems nice and talented," Julia commented to Ming.

"He is an exceptional scientist, and this was an interesting afternoon of research. Julia, do you think Ilya has maintained his connection to Chinta? Or that her brother Xian has? I wonder whether distance constrains their ability to communicate. Perhaps we should ask Ilya discreetly," she suggested in a whisper, using a bizarre mixture of obscure languages.

"Do you think it's important?" asked Julia, mirroring her mother's hushed tone. Officially, they tracked Chinta to boarding a transport to Chile via Australia, but she disappeared without a trace.

"We also asked Ilya not to speak of the matter publicly, but I know my grandson. He cares for people deeply under that sunny exterior," Ming whispered the words in Julia's ear as she hugged her daughter to say goodbye.

They wondered how they could best protect Ilya, who was far superior in many ways but perhaps naive to the brutality of human nature when it came to power and survival.

The more Julia thought about Ming's comment, the more convinced she was Ilya wouldn't give up trying to find Chinta with Xian. Whether he spoke about it or not, he believes society perpetrated a grave injustice upon Xian's family. Ilya's strong inclination to pursue a righteous course would prevent him from accepting Chinta's fate. Julia decided to ask him but would do so carefully. Society monitored everyone ordinarily, and they were now people of interest. Ilya wasn't the only person to have his childhood stripped away when Ming spoke to him. Julia discarded her sheltered youth as clinically as if surgically removed with a scalpel.

This morning, Ilya reported for a medical diagnostic examination and, in the afternoon, for psychological profiling. Today he was accompanied by Ming and Alex so Julia could continue her research. Ilya and Tamara provided critical evidence underpinning the data her researchers had compiled to date. While Ilya's algorithm score was astounding, there was an escalating trend in scores over the past two years, with a sharp spike in the last eight months. The scoring indicators pointed to rapidly increasing levels of empathy, compassion, consideration, and the result was an evolving, innovative, problem-solving skillset.

When the subjects found solutions, their thought processes were far-reaching—examining cause and effect, the consequence of actions that could occur in the future environment resulting from any decision. They didn't make impulsive, emotional decisions or attempt solutions that would create undesirable outcomes. For example, when faced with saving somebody from a hungry beast, they wouldn't kill the beast and risk leaving the beast's family without a provider. Recently, the participating students would examine how best to tame it, offer it other food, trap it, utilise a tranquilliser etc. Then they would look at how to avoid people getting into that situation again, how to solve any food supply or environmental issues for the beast, the role of the beast within the ecosystem.

The complexity of the solutions some of these youngsters came up with was impressive, and Julia surmised they were probably utilising similar skills and thought processes to Ilya. She wanted to substantiate her theory with meaningful observations and as much data as possible. Julia felt compelled to understand the depth of evolution of Ilya and his peers and never imagined her son would be her career's most important scientific find.

Scientist and mother warred in her mind. The rational mother admitted if she wanted to protect Ilya, she needed to be the first to comprehend the metamorphoses. So Julia worked hard, pushing herself mentally and physically, indulging her voracious appetite for scientific knowledge.

When Alex and Ilya arrived home, Julia was in her hiking attire. They discussed the medical examination procedures of the day. Doctors crammed in multiple physical tests, scans, bone, blood, and organ analyses. Ilya joked he was sure the medical team measured, prodded, probed and de-constructed every cell in his body. Ming would brief them on the psychological profiling when she came for dinner, as she understood the process.

"I need some fresh air to clear my mind," said Julia shaking her head from side to side with a maniacal grin. "Want to come to look after your Mama Ilya?" She made puppy eyes and pouted, practically begging him to go. Ilya agreed with a roll of his eyes, followed by bouncing up and down, making Dash yap. Boy and dog bounded off to change, giving Alex and Julia a few minutes together to catch up. Julia peeled herself reluctantly away from Alex, promising a back rub later before she and Ilya raced out of the building.

Ilya was getting faster, and she was becoming older, so it was a tightly contested race these days. It often ended with each person claiming victory over the other. Julia broke into a run, sprinting along the path into the park, with Ilya nipping at her heels, determined to catch her. They ran side by side, revelling in the freedom of the outdoors, basking in the endorphins their bodies created. Mother and son felt the easy companionship of their love for each other, flowing freely, like the blood pumping through their veins. Julia treasured these rare, fleeting moments with Ilya, just the two of them. She wondered if they were linked.

Was Ilya sharing his feelings with her? How receptive was she to his emotions? Perhaps she was sharing her feelings with him. A bond created by their love, these triumphant moments, or were they communicating telepathically? She wanted to test the possibilities. Ilya turned his head her way, raising his eyebrows at her - did he know what she was thinking? Julia pumped her arms, picking up the pace again and veered left sharply, turning into a side path. Ilya was right there with her, without missing a step - interesting. Julia jerked to a stop at a park bench, dropping to the seat, breathing hard. Once again, Ilya was right there with her, grinning, his face pink from their mad dash. She took his face in her hands and kissed his forehead gently before looking into his eyes, conveying that she wanted to ask him a question. At first, he looked confused, but then he smiled and inclined his head in agreement. Julia tried to clear her mind with a few calming breaths, closing her eyes to focus on just thinking the question.

"Can you talk to Chinta?"

At first, Ilya's face looked back blankly, then his brow furrowed as he looked at her intently. Finally, he blinked and gave an almost imperceptible nod. He placed three of his fingers lightly over his lips to ask for silence. It seemed he could read her thoughts, but she was telepathically deaf to his responses. Julia placed her arm around Ilya's shoulder and hugged him close. His world was far more intricate than the world they shared, and that scared her.

"Race you to that tree over there!" he shouted. Already bounding away from the bench, he laughed at Julia's startled look. Now it was Julia's turn to sprint after her son, and as she spotted the surveillance monitor near the bench, she applauded his timing. They reduced their pace to a jog when she caught up with Ilya, wending a path through the woods—moving away from the surveillance that kept them safe by watching them constantly.

It had never bothered Julia before, and she grew up feeling secure and protected. She pursed her lips in concentration. It was sometimes difficult to throw off the shackles that constrained her social programming, but she needed to be creative and more scientific to acquire privacy. Ilya had spent the day at the medical research facility. If she were a doctor trying to understand him, she would want to know everything.

Ilya's blood, his organs, would be full of bots. They would track everything he did and everywhere he went. As far as she knew from scientific journals, the ability to read thoughts hadn't yet evolved past reading body cues, facial expressions, propensities, physiological reactions, and brain activity. The human race had back-pedalled hard, away from Artificial Intelligence (AI). People realised AI would be superior in every way, eventually dominating and eradicating humankind. She needed to communicate with Ilya utilising thoughts on sensitive matters and trust that Ilya was smart enough to develop a way to communicate with her. Ilya graced his mother with a satisfied smile, his eyes beaming approval at the direction of his mother's thinking.

"Race you to the hilltop," yelled Julia over her shoulder, already accelerating. Their spoken communication and external body cues must stay on point. To any observer studying them, an afternoon of physical activity would appear normal if they stuck to their banter and trademark competitions. Julia powered up the hill, sucking air into her lungs to fuel her limbs, exhilarated by the sheer physicality of the climb. Ilya fell behind halfway up, but he surged forward on youthful legs pursuing his mother as they neared the summit. They crested the top of the hill together, raising their arms in victory as if they had just won the National Endurance Championship. Both collapsed on the ground, panting from the exertion and claiming the win.

"You're an impossible child, and I definitely won!" claimed Julia. She tickled Ilya mercilessly until he begged her to stop, ceding the win to her. Their faces were hot-pink from the running and the laughter, but Julia looked smug.

"I love you, you know my dearest Mummy, even if you are the biggest cheat in the whole world," shouted Ilya before rolling down the hill to escape her wrath. The journey home was full of similar shenanigans, as they let go of serious thought, living in the moment and confusing the crap out of whoever or whatever was monitoring them.

Ilya began training Julia. She sometimes found a picture of a chocolate milkshake popping into her mind and experienced Ilya's mirth infecting her. The more they practised, the more receptive Julia became, and her neural connectivity expanded.

Ilya's test results began to plateau. The Goodness Algorithm test provided enough exciting data to keep researchers and scientists busy for years. Further developments, however, weren't occurring at the accelerated level Ilya had previously demonstrated. The spikes and anomalies in his physiology settled or returned to a more normal level. Tamara wasn't displaying any testing out of the ordinary other than the connection to her brother. The departments searched for a relationship between the test brain-storm and Ilya's actions or environment. Logic dictated something caused his advanced neural activity, so Julia pored over the scientific reports, devouring every word and theory.

"Are you doing this, Ilya? Do you have control of your bots?" Julia asked silently.

"Yes, and yes. If I am too advanced, the establishment will devour Tamara and me. The problems consumed me during the testing, and I failed to consider the repercussions. It was a childish error and one I don't intend to repeat. The telepathic communication between myself and Tamara is interesting enough, and I want to live with you for as long as possible."

Grabbing his afternoon fruit snack, Ilya grinned cheekily at his mother. Dash yapped at his heels as he ran off to see his sister. Julia sighed. He was in control of everything, but she had no idea what was going on in the silent world he inhabited with his friends. She was like a toddler, standing dumbly in proximity to a group of brilliant scientists pondering communication and thought-leadership.

The research revealed how much evolution had advanced without anyone noticing. It was a hallmark of a significant mutation when it recognised the need to hide - virus-like behaviour to overtake a system by stealth. Could that be the reason Julia wondered? Was the next generation seeking to oust the current regime and implement a new way of life? Julia had learned to mask her thoughts. Ilya insisted she must know how to protect her privacy before he would teach her how to share. Julia hadn't realised how grateful she would be for that gift. Just as Ilya was doing with his testing, his mother was steering her research findings in a particular direction. The approach slowed progress, which meant she did a lot of the sensitive work herself. She also hid information inside other pieces of research and committed critical data to memory. Only Julia possessed all the puzzle pieces, the roadmap of evolution's latest leap, and the overarching quest for survival.

Three more years slid past. Julia and her team won a prestigious award for the watered-down EV research they presented. It was uncomfortable for her winning accolades while withholding critical data, but her team was ecstatic to receive recognition.

Ilya was lauded for his intelligence and contributions to society but was permitted to live the childhood he claimed as his legal right. Departments jockeyed to entice Ilya to join them in their work. It amused him that they all believed their function was the most important. His relationship with his sister remained close and fascinating in its complexity. Once she began to speak, Tamara could converse on a wide array of topics due to her connection to Ilya. While superbly engaging, the researchers' observations failed to identify or understand the underlying depth of the siblings' communication. Ilya was teaching Tamara everything he knew at an accelerated rate during her early brain development period, including how to store the knowledge without revealing it.

"Happy Birthday!" Tamara jumped on Ilya's bed, squealing, as Alex and Julia jumped into the room with party horns. They clapped and sang to Ilya, who smiled happily while wiping the sleep from his eyes. It was early, but traditionally they all ate a leisurely breakfast together on birthdays.

"I can't believe you are 16 already. Geez, that makes me feel ancient," moaned Alex.

"You are ancient, Daddy," said Tamara. Her sincerity made Ilya snort with laughter, and Julia's hand quickly covered her smirk.

"Thanks for your support, loving family." Alex gave a throaty growl tickled Tamara and Ilya, whose feet were as sensitive as ever.

"It's so difficult to choose a gift for someone who is such a grown-up Ilya, but we have tried to create something special." Julia unveiled his present, suspended in the air, covered by layers of virtual wrapping. The outside shell played scenes from Ilya's favourite movies, so he wanted to examine it before ripping it off. The next layer was equally entertaining, with old footage of colourful fish swimming about a teeming reef. The next layer was a montage of cells dividing to create a new person.

"Underneath is your gift. We hope you like it." Alex squeezed Ilya's shoulder.

It was a floating, spinning crystal orb. The orb was multi-faceted and refracted light in a luminous halo as it turned. Inside the sphere were holograms of Julia, Alex, and Tamara, beaming their love for Ilya.

"We love you, Ilya," said his family in the orb. Ilya blinked back tears. He adored the gift and loved his family so much.

"I couldn't have asked for anything more perfect. I love you guys too," he paused to compose himself. "Can someone tell me how this works? I would love to make one."

"We can talk about it over breakfast Sir Grown-up. Your mother is starving, so birthday or not, get dressed, champ!" Tamara giggled at Julia and reached for Alex's hand, as impatient to eat as her mother. For a child, Tamara's appetite was impressive. They assumed she had inherited Julia's fast metabolism as she was slightly built, lacking any cherubic features. The reality was her brain was burning energy at an unbelievable rate. Fortunately, the fully automated nutrition system recognised her needs and simply allocated more nutrient-dense food. It wasn't unusual as some children were more active or grew faster, so the nutrition monitor raised no alerts.

Dieticians allocated a menu to make birthday meals a treat. Ilya chose buckwheat pancakes with low-sugar synthesised maple syrup, natural fresh fruit, probiotic yoghurt, fresh juice and coffee. Ilya had never tried coffee (a decaffeinated substitute), but he knew Julia loved the bitter taste, so he committed his tastebuds to the experience. Julia usually ordered coffee on her birthday and was touched by Ilya's thoughtfulness.

It was one of those magical days to be retained and treasured, enshrined in their memories.

Dinner at the Rock' n Roll Diner, Tamara's first, was joyful family time. The dancing was energetic as they strove to burn off the day's excesses. By the time they arrived home, Tamara was asleep, and Ilya claimed the privilege of tucking her in for the night.

"It is my birthday," he teased his parents. Julia claimed mother time to tuck in Ilya.

"I know when I have been side-lined and out-ranked at every turn. But I insist on having extra hug-time, and your mother owes me ten kisses before she goes to sleep," said Alex.

"Ugh, Dad! You start to sound like a creepy old man," giggled Ilya. The ensuing playfight took a while, but Alex loped off to prepare for his kisses.

"I love how we are as a family. We are jolly silly," said Ilya in a posh accent. "I will never forget today as long as I live. Thanks for making it so great." Once again, he was Julia's little boy. Her eyes misted as she re-membered the day they brought him home. Now he was a young man, preparing to embark on the next stage of his life. They hugged, with eyes closed, feeling complete as they restored the mother-child bond. Julia began to feel a bit weepy, her whole body tinged with sadness. The emotion was out of step with the beautiful day they had shared. She recognised that it wasn't her sadness. Ilya was sharing his feelings with her.

"Why so sad?"

"I have to leave you." Ilya pulled his mother closer and stroked her hair, trying to calm the angst those five little words created for Julia. He had thought and shared a life-altering sentence.

"When?" Julia did her best to contain her panic.

"Soon. It's not safe for you to know more, and you can't say anything to the rest of the family – even Dad. They will worry and may even believe I am dead. You have to let them experience authentic emotions as the authorities will scrutinise you. There are things I must do."

Tucking his hair behind his ear, just as she used to, Julia kissed his forehead and prayed he would be safe.

"I will be safe. You know that I'm not alone, so I need you to trust me without question."

Ilya snuggled down in his bed as his mother closed his sleep pod gently. A chapter was ending, his childhood lay behind him, and he had work to do.

4

Vanished

Ilya's disappearance caused a furore. It was as if he evaporated. Julia filed a report when Ilya didn't show up for breakfast the following day. The Personal Security Authority (PSA) reassured Julia it was too early to panic. Kids behaved randomly, lost track of time, and he was probably at a friend's house. Alex and Julia were insistent that Ilya had never missed breakfast in his life or failed to tell them when he was going somewhere. The PSA representative said she would track Ilya's movements from the building if he had left and report back to them.

Alex was perplexed by his son's behaviour because it was so out of character, which worried him. Julia didn't share information with Alex. The more authentic they were, the better for them all. Ilya had entrusted her with a scrap of information, and she intended to keep it to herself. The ED filed a report when Ilya failed to arrive for lessons, as did the Academy Head when he missed scheduled research. The entire city looked for Ilya, but the PSA found no trace.

A forensic analysis team arrived at the apartment to investigate. The PSA had reviewed all surveillance without finding anything. They saw the family leaving, having dinner, Julia tucking Ilya into his pod, but there was nothing to report. The pod hadn't opened, Ilya hadn't left the apartment or the building. Alex went to Ilya's pod when he was late for breakfast and found it empty. The PSA checked the surveillance technology and the data analysed due to Ilya's outstanding abilities, but everything was in order. It was a mystery, and the PSA didn't like the unexplained, so they called in forensic experts. Forensics didn't find anything of interest either. There was no blood, no struggle, no chemicals or technology that shouldn't be in play – another dead end. The Head of the PSA raised her hands in frustration, her face blank on the commscreen.

"There has to be some explanation. I am a scientist, and what you tell me doesn't make sense!" Julia tried not to express her frustration but failed.

"I know my son, and he is dependable. We appreciate you are only reporting what you have - or haven't, found. What are the next steps from here? What can you or we do?" Alex took a calm and logical approach, although he was as frustrated as Julia.

"The PSA is doing all it can." She sounded slightly defensive. The failure to locate Ilya, a person of intense interest to many, reflected poorly on her and her team. "We are playing screen broadcasts everywhere, so when Ilya surfaces, he will be recognised. He hasn't boarded a transport out of New Zealand. That means he's still here somewhere, and he will show up. The only item of interest in his records, besides his Goodness Algorithm result, is his link to the disappearance of the child Chinta Katone. That was also unusual, but I have no evidence to suggest they are related. The circumstances are completely different."

"Is there anything we, Ilya's family, can do?" Julia didn't try to hide the desperation in her voice.

"Your grandfather ensures the PSA utilises all its resources," she replied curtly. "I will notify you of any progress immediately. Please accept my sympathy for how upsetting the situation is. Now I must return to my post. I will be in touch." The screen went black.

"I think my grandfather is flexing his authority. The PSA probably doesn't receive many direct requests from Council members, and she looks like she is under pressure. It can't hurt in the search. I will send Stryker a thank you message." Julia ran her fingers through her hair. A clear indicator to Alex, she was feeling stressed. Alex wrapped his arms around her and kissed the top of her head tenderly.

"We need Tamara," said Alex.

Days passed in worry. Then weeks turned into months, and still, there was no sign of Ilya. The Council suddenly replaced the head of the PSA, but her successor made no further headway. Nobody dared to tell Ilya's great-grandfather the PSA had reached a dead end with the investigation, but to Alex and Julia, it appeared they had. Julia experienced pangs of guilt as Alex stumbled hollow-eyed to breakfast every morning, but she knew Ilya's safety was also his priority. There was nothing more convincing than distraught parents, and while she said all the right things, the spectre of Alex would elicit sympathy from the most hard-hearted investigators. She was aware the PSA viewed them as suspects.

An element of joy faded from Alex and Julia's life with Ilya's departure. Tamara learned to talk and often asked, "Mama, when is Ilya coming home?"

Julia tried not to crumple in pain in front of Tamara. Alex was less successful at hiding his distress. A kind and sensitive Tamara defaulted to asking her grandparents questions instead. It wasn't a bad outcome when your apartment was under covert surveillance. The entire family was under no illusion the PSA had cleared them. Ilya was too significant to too many people. The medical breakthroughs alone earned him accolades of the highest order, and the establishment had identified Ilya as a future Council member. The family dogged various departments with ongoing barrages of questions, demanding to know how they fared. They threw themselves into work, exercise and lavishing love on Tamara.

Tamara was a well-balanced child who wasn't exhibiting any early signs of genius, but neither had Ilya. It was a relief to her parents when all of Tamara's tests returned results in the higher echelon but normal result range.

After the initial flurry of publicity to find Ilya, the PSA suppressed the story. The new order liked failure and the inexplicable, even less than anomalies. They couldn't risk causing doubt, panic, or a loss of confidence in the system to the general population. The high profile of Ilya's extended family made it worse, as the public knew them in society. If the PSA couldn't keep the child of such people safe, others might question who they could protect?

At the highest level, Prime – Head of Council harboured questions surrounding the motives of Ilya's grandfather Stryker. Always an ambitious man, it was entirely plausible Stryker had orchestrated Ilya's disappearance to shake confidence in Prime's leadership. If Stryker had managed to remove the boy without a trace, he wielded a formidable network and power. The extraordinary boy might have contributed to the deception of vanishing. Perhaps he was providing Stryker with advanced intelligence. The Council had discussed Ilya's potential to be weaponised by malign factions, and Stryker argued against the possibility at the time.

The issue facing Prime was Stryker's similarity to himself – completely ruthless, addicted to power, corrupt to the core. Absolute power required total control of the Council. When his staff acquired a beautiful, talented young girl to groom as his assistant, they had inadvertently crossed paths with Stryker's family. He had terminated the planning supervisor for his carelessness, but Prime was apprehensive Stryker would join the dots.

While all the Council members indulged in privileges to alleviate the boredom of long life and service, they were cautious. The outside world couldn't have visibility of their lifestyle or excesses. Stryker's child Ming was on the outside, which worried Prime. What did she know, he wondered? It was unlikely she would expose her father by discussing the life she had led, but it was still a risk. Perhaps he had grown too complacent.

5

The Ilya Movement

Ilya simply opened his sleep pod and walked out of the building. He took over the surveillance system, so the data flowed seamlessly through and around him, rendering himself invisible. It was the same with the transport he used. The surveillance showed everything in place the whole night, with no record of any movement in any of the instruments. Ilya had reinstated a retired model transporter in an old hangar, constructed an effective stealth mode, and flown away. The support and wishes of his closest peers echoed in his mind as he winged into an uninhabited area. Ilya executed the first step in their plan.

The telepathy started in his incubator. As he and other babies metamorphosised into beings, they linked minds, shared thoughts and comforted each other with emotions. It was as natural to them as breathing. New abilities emerged with each batch of incubations without much external detection. There was increased brain activity, but this followed a steady upward curve since implementing the Goodness Algorithm.

There were two catalysts for Ilya's transformation. The first was the kidnapping of Chinta, an event that triggered a flood of hormones, which kicked his survival and fight mechanisms into overdrive. Ilya rejected the injustice and lack of logic in terminating a child and friend. The loss of contact with Chinta telepathically confirmed the worst for him and Xian. Devastated, the boys were emotionally shredded, bewildered, disbelieving – until anger reassembled their tattered parts.

The second change occurred in the Goodness Algorithm testing. A chemically altered Ilya rapidly increased his neural connections in a sustained-stress environment as he searched for solutions to previously unsolvable problems. When he exited the Academy, he wasn't the same boy who entered but an Evolved Being (EB).

The issues with their world were glaringly apparent to a superior being, so Ilya resolved to change society and the planet for the better. He was angry, disillusioned, and sorry for the majority of the population who worked a six-day week believing they were creating a better society – like his parents. The reality of the imbalance of power, the interference with nature's evolution of the human race, was like a bucket of icy water in his face. Julia was unwittingly compressing the evolutionary timeline, and Council scientists were covertly skewing human nature toward passivity.

Nature always found a way to restore balance. When the planet was on the brink of destruction, the Council emerged. But while the Council had rescued Earth, they were now tampering with genes and engaging in exploitation. Ilya wondered if the EB skills were nature's way of expressing displeasure with the status quo. It was up to the EBs to champion change.

As Ilya shared his thoughts and what he learned with his peers, they began to transform. A revolution was born, silently, in the minds of children. They worked on swelling their numbers and became more robust, armed with increasing amounts of information.

Ilya separated from what he knew to design a strategy and vision for the future. He couldn't live the sheltered life his parents had or pretend to be ignorant of the injustice and control prevalent in society. The EBs had to transform the false world they inhabited, or the Council would exterminate them.

They wouldn't rush the process but hypothesise and plan in nano detail. In past revolutions, the changes often failed to meet the high ideals that caused them. What followed wasn't what people imagined, especially when living conditions worsened. Brutal regimes replaced each other with more of the same, and at the centre of it all was the propensity for corruption, fuelled by a lust for power. How to control the self-serving drive prevalent in some humans without resorting to wholesale slaughter, he pondered? Ilya wanted to focus his efforts on the plan, and his life didn't allow him enough free time for the task. He knew his departure would be difficult for his family, but the stakes for humanity were high. The future was opening with possibilities if they could usher in positive change. It was a calculated risk saying goodbye to his mother, but he needed her skill and support - in the war of minds to come.

The benefit of being the subject of many tests across multiple departments was that Ilya had slaved their systems to his brain. Technology was inferior to the advancements in EB capabilities. It was fortunate that artificial intelligence was no longer in play. He couldn't have risked teaching it evolved thought without conscience or compassion to counterbalance logic. As it was, Ilya could gather information and take on new identities with all the correct history and authorities. His blood bots, which he now controlled, would modify his readings to mask his identity or take on a new one. The responsibility was as mammoth as his task, but the sweetness of freedom was almost worth it.

Ilya planned to infiltrate the echelons of power to understand the Council better. After the acquisition team abducted Chinta, they let the drugs wear off when they arrived at their destination. Eventually, Ilya and Xian were able to reconnect with her. Their search for Chinta expanded and built the worldwide EB network as EBs relayed her image and story to each other. It was the beginning of a thought superhighway with brainwave boosting stations, expanding the reach of telepathic communication. For the first time, EB communities united. They established continuous telepathic streaming with their collective problem-solving skills, enabling a long-distance person to person connection with ease. It didn't take long to locate Chinta, but the reconnection with Xian and Ilya came just in time.

Chinta's life was horrific. Groomed as a plaything for the wealthy, Chinta worked every day, never left the mansion, and was subjected to the brutal whims of her trainers. Beaten into submission, drugged, and abused, they prepared Chinta for a life of service. What kept her sane was the ability to escape through her mind. Resilience, willpower, and her peers' love helped her survive, but a desire for revenge on her abusers also played a part. Chinta acknowledged her bitterness as an undesirable trait, but the burning heat of anger was a light in the dark of her despair.

Now, she supplied copious amounts of data, allowing Ilya access to their systems. Chinta marched in the vanguard of change.

But, behind the technology, the Council operated in an old-fashioned manner – a cell disconnected from everything and everyone else. Their decisions were debated and made verbally in a sealed, communication-blocked room. They were meticulous in their habits regarding security, and nobody outside the Council was privy to their discussions or decisions. Their power was absolute. On the surface, citizens were equal and existed in a fair and equitable society. Scratch the surface, however, and what lay underneath was a brutal dictatorship dedicated to serving the needs and desires of an elite group.

The Council pulled Earth back from the brink of destruction, but their reasons for doing so were entirely selfish. Like the ideals of communism, socialism and democracy before them, it was greed that drove the new order Council. Ilya once read Animal Farm by George Orwell and enjoyed it immensely. He had naively viewed it as commentary on a historical era, never expecting to live through unrest or find himself a character in 1984. The man had been a keen observer of human nature - a genius even - Ilya thought wryly.

Ilya planned to obtain an appointment as a catering manager in the capital Nirvana, on the island of Sanctuary in the Pacific Ocean - formerly known as the Cook Island of Aitutaki. It wasn't easy to choose a position that would offer proximity without being overtly in the realm of the Council.

Chinta indicated that elaborate food, the more exotic and rare, the better, was firmly entrenched as a sign of status in Nirvana. It had become an ongoing competitive game for people who could have whatever they wanted, whenever they liked. Leading citizens overindulged and artificially removed anything they consumed over and above their needs later.

The vanity of Nirvanans knew no bounds, and they cloned themselves with impunity to maintain the illusion of youth. Cloning eroded their emotional intelligence and compassion, but they simply viewed this as maturity.

The wasteful lifestyle made Chinta's eyes water with frustration, but her minders assumed they were tears of gratitude for being plucked from life as a peasant. Although she was young, her childhood ended. Put to work immediately, to learn the arts required of Prime's Assistants, Chinta became both prisoner and enslaved person. A dispensable puppet in the depraved household of the most powerful man in the world, she relied on her telepathy for silent escape. A link to life outside Nirvana and people she knew who cared about her and a reason to survive.

Ilya spent years researching and planning. To supplement his identity change, he transformed his physical appearance. Some of it occurred naturally, as his shoulders broadened and his height increased dramatically. He worked on his physique, pumping up his muscles with exercise and dietary supplements, genetically altering his colouring to fit the ideals of beauty in Nirvana. Bored Councillors and bureaucrats constantly looked for new amusements, so Ilya intended to be one of them and meticulously researched his creation.

At 195cm tall, he would be an arresting figure but wouldn't tower over everyone else. The melanin activation of his Polynesian and Scandinavian heritage rendered his skin a burnished gold, while his hair was a fascinating array of colours from honey to platinum. His eyebrows and long lashes were dark, framing eyes of a unique design – hazel irises shot with intense green and blue. Ilya looked like a Greek God of old, so perfect he would be irresistible.

He hadn't stopped at appearance, Ilya possessed detail about anyone who held power in Nirvana, and he intended to wield his cerebral charm like a thunderbolt. Julia and Alex might not recognise their little boy anymore, which was a good outcome. Chinta could see him under the glamour, recognise his mind, and that comforted him. The other EBs provided Ilya with data, suggestions, proposals, recipes, fashion trends, and anything else they believed could help him. If anyone had been able to map the flow of telepathy, they would have observed streams of data lines from all over the globe converging at Ilya. A generation of beings was empowering their champion to take up their cause.

The climate-controlled sky around Sanctuary was intensely blue as the ocean sparkled in its pristine brilliance. Sanctuary itself was verdant with lush tropical foliage. Nestled in its centre was the ultra-modern settlement of Nirvana. The Council spared no expense or resources in the creation of Nirvana. Its buildings shimmered with radiance, breathtaking to behold, epitomising the creativity of the human race. Beneath Nirvana's aesthetically pleasing exterior was a formidable fortress, defended and armed with weaponry left after the Black Years and any arms developed since. Nirvana was a fortress that an enemy could only take from the inside.

Ilya stepped confidently off the transport, hidden from sight by his alter-ego.

"Viking Argos, I presume?" The redhead woman's lips parted slightly to appreciate the man she came to greet. His reputation and talent in the culinary arts preceded him, but his magnetism and sexuality hadn't.

"Charmed to meet you. You must be Flame Santander." Ilya took her hand and brushed his lips across her knuckles as he had seen people do in old movies. "I must say your hologram doesn't do you justice. Your hair is simply stunning." He bathed her in his smile, and she basked unashamedly in the compliment. Flame invested considerable resources in her brilliant locks, and Viking's attention assured her it was worth it.

"Well, I must say, your profile didn't prepare me for how lovely you are either. May I call you Viking?" Ilya inclined his head, holding her gaze with his. "I have been appointed to show you to your quarters and give you an orientation tour of Nirvana. Is this your first time?"

Ilya gave her a slightly carnal smirk before replying. "This is my first visit to Nirvana, yes."

He held her hand captive in his for a moment longer, letting his eyes wander over her shapely form with amused sparkle. Flame was flustered. Her body was flush with desire for this man, but someone as beautiful and enigmatic as Viking would be off-limits to her. She chewed her lip before taking his arm and leading him to a quaint antique golf cart.

The island's ambience was more holiday resort than the seat of power, reflecting the hedonistic lifestyle favoured by the Council - when they weren't busy ruling the world. Ilya took it in his stride, flirting shamelessly with Flame while they drove to his quarters. His objective was to ensure she would do anything for him by the end of the orientation. Flame's area access card was impressive and could be a valuable asset, potentially offering a disguised Chinta more freedom in Nirvana.

Viking seized every opportunity to bring his body in close contact with Flame's, overwhelming her with his presence. He baited her into taking him to a non-surveillance area, a tunnel between two city sections, where he pulled her into a steamy embrace. They were barely out of sight for a few seconds, but it was long enough for Flame to take leave of her senses and fall madly in love with the reckless Viking Argos.

Ilya had memorised the layout, construction, living quarters of citizens, service areas and supply stores of the city, so Flame wasted her tour on him. It was also an opportunity to practice using his new identity and influencing skills. He would play back the interactions in his head later and determine if he needed to be more or less subtle with the Councillors.

The exercise was beneficial for Ilya, who had interacted with the same group of people his whole life and only socialised with family or other EBs. His developing body, and increased hormone levels, created reactions, and he needed to control new emotions. The kiss with Flame was his first and a technique he had studied. However, the physical response to each other was a surprise. It was probable some Councillors would try to seduce him, and they would be highly experienced sexual beings, occupying youthful cloned bodies. Some members had been Councillors for over 100 years, and although he was confident in his studies, he recognised experience would be helpful.

Unlike other cities, the PD didn't govern Nirvana's citizens with restrictive pairing rules, so moral responsibility was unusually relaxed. When Flame returned Viking to his quarters, he determined to start his research.

"Thank you, Flame, that was an enlightening tour." Viking's eyes crinkled in appreciation. "May I offer you a drink?"

"It was my pleasure, and I am quite thirsty," she replied huskily, entering the living space.

It all happened very naturally. Ilya's instincts and extensive knowledge bank accounted for his inexperience, while Flame was no stranger to random assignations. However, after a few hours, she wasn't used to feeling like a love-sick teenager. If Viking asked her to move in, she would do it. The man was magnetic, and she already imagined how beautiful their children could be.

Flame's feelings were out of character, and they scared her, especially when she knew Nirvana's elite would desire Viking. They showered together before Flame tore herself away to catch her breath.

Ilya found the fling enlightening for his part, and he analysed all his physiological data with intense interest. Unlike Flame, he wasn't besotted or emotionally involved on any level. She didn't wield the arsenal of brainpower or physical glamour Viking did, and he couldn't connect with her like an EB. The relationship was shallow for him, purely physical. He understood it was considered normal in Nirvana to dally sexually, so the depth of Flame's attraction to him wasn't something he anticipated. Ilya realised he should tread more carefully and be more sensitive to the emotions he created. Chastising himself for his clumsiness, he decided to befriend Flame and treat her with respect. Chinta was more familiar with these people. He would ask for her advice from a feminine perspective.

His quarters were sumptuous and far too large for a single person. There was a masculine feel to the apartment, with clean lines stone and metal finishes, but rich fabrics and colours were also in the furnishings. Ming and Julia would love it, he thought wistfully.

He was surprised to be afforded such lavish living quarters, even though he knew this was the Nirvanan way. The bedroom and living area featured floor-to-ceiling windows that looked over Nirvana to the cerulean ocean beyond. There was an extensive walk-in closet packed with garments, shoes and accessories. The bathing room was luxurious, with a sunken bathing pool and a sizeable multi-jet showering area made of pale stone. His bed was vast and covered with soft pillows in calming hues. Above the bed was a burnished metal plate attached to the ceiling, reflecting the bed and whoever was in it.

The living area provided several comfortable chairs, divans and couches, with a series of low tables scattered with attractive bowls, vases and curiosities. Behind the living room was an enormous kitchen, sporting every gadget and convenience known to humanity, in Ilya's opinion. Somebody had designed the apartment superbly for entertainment, with the kitchen a nod to the importance of his craft. Someone had filled a walk-in cooling unit with more foodstuff than Ilya had ever seen.

"Well, Viking, you have arrived," he laughed. "Don't mind if I do." He stayed in character by pouring himself a glass of vintage champagne and sipping it in appreciation. Ilya reached for Chinta, but she wasn't accessible to him, so he enjoyed the view while considering what to create from his extensive pantry. Tonight he would host ten bureaucrats, including five assistants to Councillors, for drinks and a late supper. It was critical Viking made a favourable impression on these people, as they would usher him into the inner circle of power. He would have a large staff for food preparation in his new role, but tonight was a test of his skills and creativity.

Ilya prepared his own meals in exile. He practised extensively, tapping into the exotic recipes of chefs from the past. The practical dining of his era did not inspire, but the greedy obsession with food throughout history provided a plethora of ideas.

"How is your first day in Nirvana, Ilya?" Chinta connected with him telepathically, and her timing couldn't have been better. Ilya was standing in his wardrobe, trying to decide what Viking should wear.

"It has certainly been interesting. I have a lot to learn, Chinta, and I could certainly use your help choosing what to wear. What do you think?" Ilya shared the image of his flamboyant wardrobe with Chinta before walking to the mirror wall to reveal himself as Viking to her.

"Goodness, Ilya, Viking is sex on a plate! That's the kind of phrase they like to use in Nirvana, but seriously, you are beautiful. Your eyes are enchanting; I particularly love the gold radiating from your pupils. It makes the blue and green stand out. Did you design those yourself?"

"Yes, I did, so thank you. A few years of living physically by myself offered me plenty of opportunities for creative design, and you did tell me to come up with a unique glamour. According to my research, I am desirable to 94.4% of the population."

They fell comfortably into the banter of friendship shared since childhood. When Prime abducted Chinta, they began to link more frequently, with and without Xian.

Chinta was brave for her brother as she didn't want to distress him, so she shared her trials and fears with Ilya. Ilya gave her a purpose and the strength to manage whatever her captors inflicted on her. Whenever she was overwhelmed, she detached her mind from her body and sought Ilya.

"What an over-achiever you are, Ilya. Looking like you do, Viking will be the toast of Nirvana in no time. You could probably serve them toxic sludge on dry bread, and they will still worship your skill." Chinta's infectious laughter bubbled in his head, and he couldn't help but grin at her sense of humour.

"Appearances are everything here, however, so we must kit you out, so you are uniquely fashionable. Unless, of course, you want to serve them naked?" Her giggling started again.

"Come on, Chinta, you are supposed to be helping Viking – focus."

"I'd like to help him alright, and that wouldn't involve dressing him," she purred. *"Are you blushing, Ilya? That will never do. Control yourself at once,"* she scolded.

"We have been friends forever, and you are teasing me like your latest conquest, so you will need to forgive my shyness, saucy coquette."

Having satisfied her penchant for making Ilya feel awkward, Chinta moved on to choosing his outfit with ruthless efficiency. Chinta was now Prime's favourite Assistant, so she attended banquets, dances, parties and events almost every day. Prime required her to look her best for each outing, and Chinta was considered a fashionista in Nirvana.

Ilya submitted to Chinta's decisions without question, knowing she cultivated skills over many years. Chinta opted for chic sophistication. They wanted to incite curiosity, pique interest, and leave Viking's guests with a desire to see more. She also wanted her friend to be comfortable, confident, and concentrate on his food and hosting.

"You look delicious, Viking."

"Why, thank you, madam. I have an amazing stylist who has an innate sense of fashion." He admired his reflection. Viking wore biscuit, soft-suede pants that hugged his muscular legs and slim hips. A cream silk shirt hung off his broad shoulders, showed off his tan and its sleeves became fitted below his elbows so they wouldn't trail in food or drink. Around his neck was a simple antique gold choker, with a polished turquoise stone set in the centre and a matching band adorned his wrist. A pliant pale-leather cummerbund wrapped his torso while elegant sandals of the same material graced his feet. Chinta eschewed the use of cosmetics for his first outing, preferring to let his natural beauty shine. She was confident they would all be smitten. As jaded as she was by the insatiable appetites of the Nirvanan elite, Chinta found herself strangely attracted to Viking. It didn't feel right, as this was her friend,

but her body didn't lie. She wondered how much was visual and how much Ilya was exerting telepathic attraction.

When Viking's guests arrived, their reactions told him his efforts were not in vain. Regardless of age, gender or sexual preference, they were all enchanted by their host. Unlike he'd done with Flame, Ilya exuded a more subtle magnetism and only used his appearance to stir desire. It was more than enough.

The food was delicious, the drinks were divine, and the music was pleasantly unusual, but Viking Argos captivated them with his witty charm. The evening was a raging success and resulted in a flood of catering invitations for the people they served. There was also a bold personal invitation from an Assistant to a Councillor. She cunningly excused herself while everyone else was taking their leave.

"Well, Viking, it seems we are alone at last. Thank you for a wonderful evening."

"It was my pleasure, Maya. I must admit I was a little nervous before everyone arrived, but I believe I will enjoy Nirvana."

"You will receive a catering request from Councillor Shand's household tomorrow, but I would like to extend a more personal invitation to join us for drinks and a swim." Maya lowered her lashes, and the corners of her mouth moved upward in the slightest of smiles before she raised intense violet eyes to his. She was gorgeous, with shiny dark skin, long coppery curls and a statuesque figure. Maya propositioned Viking, Ilya thought. The second time on his first day.

"How could I possibly refuse such a kind invitation, Maya. Here I am, a nobody in a new city with no social connections, at the mercy of strangers. You do me a great honour, thank you." Viking took Maya's hand and lifted her fingers to his lips, brushing them with a kiss, locking his eyes on hers. The chemistry between them was palpable, and it was Viking who drew away from her. Maya's heart was pounding with arousal, but Shand would be very generous if she brought this prize home to play. She departed already anticipating their next meeting and decided to use Shand's clout to reorganise Viking's schedule so they could meet tomorrow. If Maya hesitated, the vultures would descend on the spoils quickly, and they might miss out. There would be entertainment at Shand's mansion when she got home, and Viking had put Maya in the mood for sport.

Ilya shared access to the evening with Chinta, so she could drop in whenever her schedule allowed. Fortunately, Viking's was an early event, so Chinta spent a ridiculous amount of time on her grooming and dressing for the evening of gambling she would attend with Prime. Her activity enabled Chinta to watch proceedings, offer silent advice and observe everyone attending closely. Ilya hadn't skimped on his study, and he was faultless in his role as Viking.

Chinta broke their connection when Maya manoeuvred Viking into being alone. She didn't want to spy on Viking's assignations if that was what it turned into, but Chinta experienced a hot stab of jealousy. It was a strange emotion for her, which Chinta found unsettling and confusing. Prime had many Assistants, frequent dalliances, and she never minded that he enjoyed other people – often, it was a relief. Perhaps because Ilya was a friend she cared for, her feelings differed. Chinta checked her perfect appearance in the holo-mirror before leaving to play her part in the Nirvana charade. The dewy beauty of her natural youth was an aphrodisiac in Nirvana. Youth was a commodity out of reach to all but the most powerful. Inadvertently, she was the most perfectly placed spy.

Viking's staff adored him as much as everyone else did, especially the EBs, who he marshalled into a supportive community. Many of them were unaware of their skills, just assuming they were intuitive or heard voices in their head. Most of the EBs were acquired similarly to Chinta, but the few children created in Nirvana were also evolving.

The Councillors were addicted to creating new life in their image and spawned a ridiculous number of children during their long lives while denying permits to everyone else with impunity. In the Councillor's offspring, Ilya found like minds utterly frustrated with their parents. He was careful not to reveal his identity as Ilya or Viking, but he became their leader and champion. The EBs found their voice, and Ilya listened. They thrived and grew under Ilya's patient tutelage, testing the boundaries of their thoughts and power. Linking to the EBs in Ilya's network outside of Sanctuary opened their eyes to the outside world and an alternative reality. A movement seeking significant social and political change blossomed in the heart of Nirvana, in the bosom of the Council.

6

Risk

It was dark, but Julia was absorbed in her research, so she didn't notice. She was working offline on an outdated computer with a redundant operating system. It protected the information she was unearthing. Ilya covered her tracks and allowed her visibility of data unavailable to anyone else. Caution was prudent, and Ilya edited information about himself. The fight-flight reaction and the resultant alterations within Ilya's brain were plain to see. During the Goodness Algorithm Test, the participants were subjected to continuous high stakes decision making and weighing risk and trauma to others. Each year the Algorithm was altered and recently the impact on brain function had escalated. The other EBs displayed similar developments if you knew what to look for, but Ilya's transformation was on another level. Her unique child was the link at the apex of evolution, creating a pathway for the future of their species.

Julia pondered how that pathway and future might look. The EBs would be able to topple those in power and take over the planet. Forecasting the most probable scenarios wasn't Julia's forte, but as the data was exclusive, she felt driven to do it. The core of her research was mapping the DNA of the EBs and Ilya to overlay them against generational control groups. It would allow her to identify and chart the precise course of genetic mutations contributing to the massive increase in cerebral expansion.

It was a fascinating task, but she also wanted to understand the shift in thought and change in perspective it was driving. The EBs, from what Julia could ascertain, were better people in the simplest terms. Their emotional intelligence, compassion, and ability to balance conflicting needs of multiple species or environments, were like breathing. They possessed natural powers previous generations could barely comprehend, and Julia was sure the Council wouldn't empathise with their views. Her analytical mind snagged on this point. It would become the crux of impending conflict.

Conflicting ideas, morals, vision for the future - would lead to what she pondered? Social uprising, a struggle for power, or perhaps another global war. Their son was at the centre of the approaching unrest, which terrified her. Ilya was her baby.

It was enough for one day, she decided. Julia encrypted the work with her self-designed codex before storing it in a secure facility only she or Ming could access by a regular live-brain scan. It was an innovative technology developed to prevent access under the influence of drugs or duress, during the high-stakes espionage era, before the dark years. Any detected anomaly in the brain, breath, or facial scan, would render access invalid. Julia routinely used the facility for her genetic research, as she utilised enormous quantities of restricted personal data.

Tamara squealed when her mother arrived home. Alex had embroiled her in a tickling fight, which she was losing and, therefore, happy to abandon. A sensitive child, Tamara never cried or moaned but made every effort to fill the void left by Ilya. Of course, she could still speak to Ilya. Tamara did so every day until recently, and that was because he was busy working. Young she might be, but Tamara had a purpose, supporting Ilya's labours on behalf of the EBs, humanity, and the planet. She devoted herself to making Alex happy, knowing Julia was aware Ilya lived.

In contrast, her poor Daddy was ignorant and must remain that way for now. Tamara couldn't communicate with Julia the way Ilya did. She could influence Julia and share emotions, but her abilities were not yet fully evolved. One day, she hoped to follow Ilya's circuitous neural pathway into Julia's otherwise closed mind - when she matured. They were fortunate their mother possessed the ability to link with them at all, as they hadn't found anyone else her age with any latent telepathic capability.

"How is my wonderful girl today? Hungry, I am guessing. Mummy is sorry to be home so late." Alex tried to entice Tamara to eat when Julia was working late or had appointments, but she staunchly refused as she preferred to dine with her parents.

"Famished, just like her Dad, but we love eating together, so we waited." A shadow passed over Alex's face, but he hid it quickly. Julia knew he thought of Ilya every day and couldn't imagine how empty he must feel. She constantly wavered regarding telling Alex, it seemed so unfair and deceitful not to, but Alex's pain remained Ilya's most effective shield. Tamara took Alex's hand and came to the table they set together.

"Can you sit by me, Daddy?" Her grey eyes, a carbon copy of his, pleaded with Alex and won a smile.

They tried to maintain the element of fun which had been part of Ilya's life, but try as they might, they had transformed into more serious people. Consequently, Tamara laughed less than Ilya, so they felt they were failing her as parents.

"I am happy you are my Mummy and Daddy. I love you, and you love me. We are all sad I'ya (her pet name for her brother) is gone, but we have each other."

Tamara took a mouthful of food before placing a hand on each of theirs. She was astounding and shared Ilya's thoughtful, kind nature. How blessed they were to be gifted, two such children. Alex placed a tender kiss on Tamara's head, and Julia squeezed her hand to acknowledge her words of wisdom, smiling to herself.

"Now, Julia, if you have thought of anything remotely funny, I order you to share it!" Alex clicked into silly mode.

"Well, how many parents get a pep talk at the dinner table from someone six years old? You are one of a kind, Miss Tamara. Absolutely, fantastically, amazingly, stupendously, wonderfully, marvellously, wise beyond your years, to the power of google!" blurted out Julia in one breath, making Tamara giggle.

"I'ya and I have the silliest parents ever." She shovelled more food into her mouth, eyes shining with contemplated mischief. The voracious appetite never diminished. Tamara was a slim, walking-talking, bottomless stomach with the metabolism of a trainee spacecraft pilot.

There are days in your life that shatter the peace like a hammer blow to a mirror. Julia tubed Tamara to her early learning facility when an urgent tone sounded from her commscreen. Alex left early to install a significant engineering project, so Julia put her bag down to take the call. It was her father, Leo, and he looked distraught.

"Dad, what's wrong?" Julia was a little freaked out. Leo was a rock in the direst situations.

"I- I don't know how to tell you, Julia. Your mother is.... Ming is gone." A sob escaped him, and he scraped tears from his eyes. He desperately wanted to be strong for Julia, but it was too much. "There was a freak accident with a pod," he sucked in air to calm himself. "The braking system failed, and she didn't stand a chance. There will be an investigation, but your mother inserted a 'No-Clone Clause' in her will. I wanted to come over Juli (his pet name for her), but I was afraid you would hear about it before I got there." Every communication device Julia owned was blinking or making a noise, so he was right. She didn't know what to say or do - she felt numb, disbelieving, her mind rejecting the news. Julia placed her hands over her face and began to cry. Surely, this couldn't be happening.

"I am coming over, Juli, and Alex is on his way too." The commscreen went blank as Leo raced to comfort her. Ilya arrived before anyone else did, at least in her conscience.

"I'm so sorry, Mama. We all loved her." Ilya flooded Julia's mind with beautiful memories, feelings of being loved, warmth, calm, thankfulness and images of himself, Tamara and Alex.

"Thank you, Ilya. I need to comfort Grandpa Leo, and I can't do that if I fall apart." Tears trickled down her face, drawing a trail of wet grief in salty drops.

"I love you, Mama, and I need you more than ever. Can you please give the flower cube I made for you to Grandma Ming, and I will create you another?"

Ilya understood Julia needed tasks to occupy her and give her time to process Ming's sudden death. A death that shouldn't have happened. Life snuffed out at the whim of a power-drunk individual whose suspicions were justification enough to enact an Erase Order. If Ilya had required any reinforcement of the necessity for change, this heinous act would have provided it. He was grief-stricken, white-hot with anger, but he masked his feelings to protect his mother.

"I will also comfort Grandpa Mama, Tamara knows already. Know that I love you all, with every cell in my body."

Julia sat on the floor, trying to gather tattered thoughts and emotions. She sent her Research Coordinator a communication. Ash would cancel her appointments, brief her team, and respond to Julia's many comms. To Camilla, however, she sent a personal encrypted message and asked her to come to the apartment when she could. Ming and Camilla were best friends, and she would be devastated by Ming's death. A chime announced Alex's arrival. Julia ran to the comfort of his arms and snuggled into his familiar shoulder, allowing her tears to flow again naturally. Knowing she was fortified emotionally by Ilya, she would focus on supporting her father and Alex. Julia would take Tamara's lead and lean heavily on Leo and Alex. The needier she was, the more needed they would feel, comforting them both. It wouldn't be difficult because her family was disintegrating around her.

The family were in shock. Alex's Dad, Camilla and Julia's best friend Diana arrived at the apartment to support them. Julia and Leo took a comm from Ming's father. He couldn't be there physically, but he would be virtually present for Ming's carbonisation ceremony. Stryker was angry, not grief-stricken like the rest of the family. In reality, he barely knew his daughter and couldn't understand why she chose not to clone. He based his knowledge of Ming on her family association with him and her many professional achievements. Stryker boasted of Ming's accolades. The people who knew her, her wonderful personality traits, quirks, and endearing characteristics, lamented the callous disinterest of her self-absorbed father.

They cut solemn figures, all attired in black, as they arrived for Ming's carbonisation. The Last Rites centre was packed, testimony to Ming's popularity and the professional respect she commanded. Julia was serenely numb. Ilya surrounded them with his unique gift of love and calm. Ming's close family knew she believed in reincarnation. It was one of the reasons she didn't choose to clone. She aspired to reach the next plane of existence and return to the next life evolved. Ilya created pictures for Julia and Tamara of sunflowers turning to their namesake, tiny amoeba recreating themselves in the volcanic depths of the ocean, and the birthing of stars in other galaxies. He didn't believe the beauty of Ming's energy was at an end. She was only transforming.

Julia delivered a pre-recorded holographic eulogy, revisiting Ming's many achievements - expressing the love and affection Ming inspired in her family and friends before Camilla sang Ming's favourite song. Leo read a poem she loved before Ming's remains were carbonised, compressed and handed to Julia as a diamond. Sparkly, beautiful even, but there, the similarities to Ming ended. The diamond was enduring and cold, reminding Julia of Stryker, whose bored countenance occupied the dignitary commscreen. He hadn't shed a single tear. Julia couldn't bear to look at him and admired her mother more for refusing to hate him. She wasn't sure she would be up to that task, so she let Ilya soothe her with his empathy and kindness.

Alex held her close, Leo squeezed her hand, and Tamara stood in front of them, leaning back so her body warmth suffused them. Tamara turned her face into Grandpa Leo's legs periodically, distracting him, reminding him he was alive and that she needed him. It was lovely of her, and Alex clasped Julia's hand, letting her know he had noticed.

In this day and age, carbonisation ceremonies are unusual. For many of the guests, it was the first one they had attended. The ceremony moved people, and tears flowed as they placed remembrance tokens for Ming next to her stelae. Alex and Dmitry placed Ilya's flower cube prominently in the centre, where roses would bloom perpetually for years to come. They both would have loved that. Dmitry pulled his son close, blinking his eyes rapidly, and Alex knew he mourned Ilya's loss along with Ming. Tamara materialised next to them, taking their hands in hers and pulling them insistently toward the refreshments.

Shutting the door to their apartment behind her, Julia closed her eyes in relief. It was over. She just wanted some time alone with her family, to mourn her mother in private. Her Dad needed them, as the bottom had just dropped out of his life. The flipside of the love Ming and Leo shared was the pain he was now experiencing as the one left behind. It was the kind of relationship Julia had aspired to find, and she didn't want to imagine losing Alex. Just thinking about it distressed her, but it helped her understand what Leo was going through. He was going to stay with them for a couple of days. Tamara asked him to sleep in her room, to keep her company, because she felt sad Grandma Ming was gone. They found solace in comforting one another, looking at memories together, sometimes crying, sometimes laughing. Julia and Alex joined them when they were free from other tasks, and together they began the process of grieving and healing.

7

The Powerful

The depravity and waste in the halls of power would have shocked the outside world. The banquets Ilya prepared were extravagant, reminding him of texts he had read on ancient Babylon, Rome and the Imperial Courts of various dynasties. He rapidly became the darling of the Councillors. His creativity was incomparable, and Ilya delighted them with novel ways of entertaining them with food at every outing. From the turn of the 21st century, an old book by Heston Blumenthal had captured his imagination with its gastronomy. Ilya disguised food to fool the senses and presented dishes theatrically, using his mind to make creations fly in formation before landing in front of guests. They adored him. In record time, Prime's staff invited him to cater an event for their master, a Greek-themed picnic.

The amount of time the Council and bureaucrats wasted entertaining themselves was ridiculous. Their world revolved around parties, picnics, fashion shows, cocktails, gambling, theatre, music, art and banquets, while the masses slaved like busy ants. The excesses supposedly left in the past were well preserved for a privileged few. The Council, like the Gods in Greek mythology, sat atop Mt Olympus, randomly interfering and dictating how ordinary people would live their lives.

Ilya planned the menu and beverages with studious attention to detail. He was nervously excited about seeing Chinta. While they communicated daily, it was years since they played in Xian's apartment. Twice he caught a glimpse of her, from a distance, in a cluster of people. As Prime's favourite Assistant, Chinta occupied a position in the most privileged inner circle of the elite. Access to Prime was rare. Prime excelled at plucking and grooming his genetically superior Assistants while they were young as part of his security regime. It was dangerous enough having to contend with Stryker and the other ambitious Councillors without creating attachments to outsiders. Staying in power was Prime's obsession, and it was no coincidence he was in his position.

The caterer to the elite, Viking Argos, outdid himself. Divans and couches were shaded under whimsical draping fabric, scattered throughout a field and the beach. An army of servers, scantily dressed as slaves, fanned guests, filled wine cups from amphorae, and strolled about with platters of fruit, nuts, olives, cheese, meats, cooked dishes and sweets. Olympic sports contests entertained, with guests able to compete or watch the discus, javelin, wrestling, or running races. Many chose to participate enthusiastically in the medal ceremonies while overtly admiring the oiled bodies of winners.

For the dignitaries, Ilya concocted a cocktail he called ambrosia. While the ambrosia was delicious, he laced it with a powerful surge of brain stimulation which transformed it into a nectar fit for Gods. Mermaids and Poseidon circulated with delicacies from the sea; caviar, oysters, and crustaceans, all grown and harvested in the morning by Ilya. The food was a triumph, and the Councillors devoured delicate pastry-wrapped oysters, surrounded by whipped lemon mayonnaise, quail eggs injected with caviar, tomato and garlic confit jelly shaped like tiny apples stuffed with lobster. At the end of the meal, mechanical butterflies delivered desserts fashioned into narcissus flowers or Leto's frogs.

Each morsel tantalised the tastebuds, the eyes, and the spoiled company were impressed. A theatre set welcomed a troupe of players who entertained with Greek tragedy and comedy. They were compelling, as they tried to catch the eye and find favour with the powerful. Costumes were a study in extravagance as each player vied for attention, flaunting both talent and attraction. The merriment and flirtation would inevitably lead to intoxication and fornication as the day wore on. With this in mind, Ilya ensured the guests could lower the drapery to form private tents or pavilions with a click of the fingers. He reserved the most sumptuous of these for the important guests, who preferred clandestine assignations or discrete orgies to protect their preferences from prying eyes and each other. The Councillors' minions circulated throughout the day, selecting entertainment they believed would please their benefactor to the strains of Pan's pipes. Everyone except the Councillors was working.

The Councillors dressed as various Gods, Prime as Zeus, Stryker as Ares, Shand as Athena and together, they formed the pantheon of Olympus. While his position was necessary, Ilya knew better than to dress as a god and risk competing with anyone important. He would be the only guest dressed as the unfortunate warrior Achilles. Chinta thought the choice amusing as he was fighting a war and would prove to be the Achilles heel of his masters. She chose Helen of Troy to complement him – although she preferred to think of herself as the Trojan horse.

Chinta schooled Ilya in the art of cosmetics to complete his outfit and look. Ilya buffed his skin with glittery oil, eyes outlined with metallic bronze, lids shaded with the blue, green and gold of his eye colours. His lips shone bronze, his brows threaded with glittering jewels in topaz, smoky quartz and jet, while his face was air powdered with light-refracting lustre. Resplendent in gold armour, Viking Argos radiated fashionable, youthful beauty like the sun-pounded earth in the midday heat. Applause greeted him as he showed Chinta his mirror image, and with a wry chuckle, she said, *"I can hardly wait to see the reaction to you, my dear."*

Fortunately, Julia and Alex enjoyed dressing up with him as a child, so Ilya was reasonably comfortable in his costume. He followed Chinta's instructions, and people stared at him wherever he went. Viking had taken the liberty of inviting Flame to participate in the games, which allowed him the opportunity to cool her attraction to him and build a mutually beneficial friendship. Brain impulses were not the only cause of Flame's infatuation with Viking. Switching it off wasn't as easy as he thought it would be. Flame's feelings toward him were surprisingly tender, and Ilya smarted with guilt. She also attracted attention to them with her flaming locks and piqued curiosity – were they lovers or not, people wondered?

Although Viking was busy supervising and marshalling his army of staff, he found time to exchange pleasantries, making new acquaintances. Charm oozed from Viking in waves, his ready laughter bubbling forth as he chatted with guests while he directed his people. "More food over there, Phoebe. Serve the wrestlers, won't you, Kenji, and Delilah - please ensure the ambrosia is flowing in the Blue Zone. Lovely job, everyone. You are doing wonderfully for a bunch of love-starved slaves."

They basked in their manager's humorous praise, smiles and giggles escaping as they rushed off to do his bidding. He was a fantastic teacher and manager who fuelled their ambitions as he built new skills. The catering and events teams were exuding newfound confidence under Viking's tutelage. Viking made them feel they could do anything, so consequently, they excelled every day, coming up with unique ideas and creative concepts. In a few short days, people found they loved their job with a new passion.

"I would say you have created another resounding success. Congratulations, Viking Argos," Maya purred. Lips close to his ear, her breath tickled. Maya was flirting while Flame immersed herself in gossiping with an acquaintance and she wondered if Ilya and Flame were together. Shand might be interested in a private exhibition. Just because Prime was the host didn't mean he would grant Argos an audience. It was unlikely. While there would be competition for Viking's presence, he had already worked for Shand and Maya had ensured his experience was intensely pleasurable.

"Thank you, Maya. You are always so charming," he said, taking her hand and brushing it against his lips, a fashion taking hold due to the trend-setting Viking. "It is a privilege to cater for Prime. I was surprised to receive the invitation so early in my contract, and I want this event to be memorable." He constantly scanned, underpinning his words with meticulous attention.

"I extend an invitation to you, and anyone you may care to bring, to Shand's pavilion once you fulfil your duties for Prime. Maya raked her eyes over a sensuous-looking, well-muscled male server before raising an eyebrow at Flame in appreciation.

"You are too kind to me, Maya. I have no idea when we will finish, that will depend on Prime, but if I'm not required this evening, I would love to join you." His eyes twinkled with mischief, recalling their last encounter, while Maya experienced a tingle of anticipation. The food, drink, and distractions were merely a colourful backdrop for the elite's favourite sport – seduction.

The crowd became raucous as the games came to a close. Jests were ribald, and the flirting turned to dalliance and the pursuit of pleasure. Ilya was relaxed, Viking's supervisors were doing splendidly, and Prime's coordinator Xenon had already visited to express his master's satisfaction with the event.

Xenon dressed as Perseus, Zeus' demigod son, carved in bronze, or so it appeared, with every muscle perfectly defined in his lean body. He observed Ilya from a distance, intrigued by his affable nature and effortless magnetism. The man was even more beguiling in person. When he returned, he would speak to Prime's Assistants regarding extending an invitation to Viking Argos. Prime was fussy about who entered his household, let alone his presence. However, Xenon knew his master would want to start screening him. He would volunteer to escort him in personally. There would be competition and pecking order to consider, but he sought Ilya out, and he wanted him. A sexual tension built between them as they spoke. They could have been the only two people on Sanctuary as their eyes met, and Xenon was almost as obsessed as Flame. The new Catering Manager spiced up the day with more than just culinary treats.

"I will return. Perhaps you will be able to join the post picnic debrief with Prime's key household staff if he is amenable."

"You honour me, Xenon, with even the suggestion. I will be here at the event centre for some time yet. Thank you for inviting me to cater and coming in person to alleviate my apprehension regarding Prime's response." Ilya's eyes were clear, sincere, penetrating and took Xenon's breath away. They looked so innocent, without artifice, scheme or malice. He was gorgeous. Xenon turned on his heels to tear his eyes away from Ilya's, and many watched his graceful form appreciatively as he stalked from the field.

"Be careful with that one, Ilya. His intelligence surpasses Xenon's physique, and he wants you. His desires are dark, and there are reasons he enjoys Prime's favour at his advanced age." Chinta sounded a little concerned.

"I wouldn't fret, Chinta. You know as well as I do that Prime will choose an Assistant to vet me. My belief is he will choose you."

"That could prove awkward, Ilya. While I am a Nirvanan and jaded beyond belief, I have never dallied with another EB. Have you?"

"No, never, Chinta. To our kind-" Ilya paused, thinking, *"we are both virgins."* They giggled with each other without ever blinking or moving a muscle.

"After what I have seen and done here, Ilya, I find that supposition hilarious, but I love it. Perhaps I will see you later."

The tents and pavilions were abuzz with gossip and conjecture about Viking Argos. Prime's party was no exception. Xenon arrived with a report for Prime's Assistants but was surprised when Prime wanted to hear it first-hand. Chinta knew of Maya's catering and personal invitation on Shand's behalf. With a little snooping, prying into a mind here and there, she whispered the most salacious gossip to Prime in graphic detail. She would never be so rude as to invade Ilya's privacy by asking him to share. Prime's eyes were gleaming with arousal at Maya's inventiveness in entertaining the new arrival - how he loved Chinta's ability to ferret out dirty detail. Her face and body might be that of an angelic fourteen-year-old, but it was her devious mind that made her his favourite.

Prime was considering keeping Chinta as his permanent partner. She was someone he could trust, his creation, fashionable, envied, smart enough to produce intelligent children, and she captivated him like nobody else. The games she came up with to please him made him quiver like a teenager. Prime had no idea how subtly Chinta influenced his brain, thoughts, reliance and need for her. Ilya taught her how to inveigle her way into his affections, and she was an excellent pupil.

"I am intrigued enough by Argos to introduce him to the household myself if it pleases you, Councillor Prime." Xenon finished his report with the offer, hoping Prime would accept it. Prime noted Xenon's enthusiasm and recognised his suppressed desire for what it was. An interesting turn of events.

"Your interest is noted, Xenon, but I'm in a cautious frame of mind. Argos is new to Nirvana, so it's too soon to bring him home. Chinta, dearest, I am intrigued. I'd like you to screen him. Meet me in my chambers after you have dressed for the evening." With a wave of his hand, Prime dismissed everyone, retiring to his private dressing room where he could see his Assistant's getting ready to bathe and dress. It had been Chinta's idea. Prepare him for the evening by spying on dalliances, self-pleasure, bathing, dressing, and primping. He didn't go out afterwards, especially if Chinta planned the entertainment. Sometimes she was a participant looking directly at him on camera; other times, she was a bystander or a voyeur with him. He couldn't wait to hear her plan.

Chinta blew Prime a kiss and signalled to the surveillance camera that she would join him in his suite. Her evening attire was still in the character of Helen of Troy. She cut an arresting figure in a diaphanous white gown sewn with crystals that showed off her taut young flesh but left enough to the imagination. Her throat dripped with amethysts. A stunning teardrop stone nestled seductively between the voluptuous breasts she had convinced Prime she must have. It surprised him that he gave in to her plea for enhancements, but she rarely asked for anything.

They made her appear older and more acceptable in society, but generally, he preferred young girls.

"My darling Prime, I have the most delightful plan!" Chinta bounced into the room, face lit up like the child she was, clapping her hands together in glee. "Oh, dear Charlaine, not that dress tonight. It screams girl for rent." She frowned momentarily at the screen, clucking her tongue and alerted the Wardrobe Manager of the impending faux pas. "Now, where was I – yes, the plan! Viking Argos is delectable, almost good enough to eat. Like one of his canapes, but what lies inside, I wonder? It's too soon for him to be near you, a ridiculous level of risk. The anticipation of waiting will be deliciously unbearable for us."

She flopped down on Prime's gigantic bed, and purple lips parted in an ecstatic sigh. "I don't want to have him before you, so Xenon and I will lure him into a pavilion with an invitation. I have handpicked four of your favourites and set up a VR holo on them so you can participate safely. Xenon and I will watch, and we can play, but we won't interact with Argos, so we save him for you. I don't want Xenon scaring him into Shand's arms or thighs. We will decree him off-limits to all but your household, which will send everyone into a frenzy for him. Tonight I was thinking," Chinta whispered in Prime's ear, what she was planning. It was Prime's turn to clap his hands. She was planning to outdo Maya and Shand.

Chinta despatched a messenger to Viking Argos, the invitation bore Prime's seal, but it wasn't an invitation to his mansion. Chinta shared the plan with Ilya while she came up with it, so he knew what to expect. He even added a few suggestions. They needed to proceed cautiously, step by step, bringing Ilya closer to Prime without arousing suspicion.

If they wanted to avoid a bloody civil war, they must find a way into the minds of the Council to understand them. They needed data and visibility of what created the problem to solve it.

The EBs knew they could solve whatever it was, and they had to, as their existence depended on it. There would be only one opportunity. The current regime would dispose of them mercilessly if they believed anyone threatened their power. Ilya was a force to be reckoned with, but he was one person and couldn't change the world on his own. The global EB network which had grown up around him would be the harbingers of change, opponents of the Goodness Algorithm and every-thing it represented. He also needed his mother. Julia's science could help unlock the data puzzle, but she required more time. Equations determining a person's right to live or die was a giant step away from humanity - it had to stop.

8 |

Genetics

Recovering from Ming's loss was a slow process, so Julia did what was best for her – she worked. So close now to uncovering the information Ilya wanted. It was a voyage of discovery for Julia. She understood the interactions between genes, amino acids, proteins, hormones and the neural capacity of the brain better than the most advanced medical researchers. Having Ilya as an assistant had its benefits. Her hunch, then theory, was spot-on.

The genetic selection escalated the abilities of off-spring to produce and utilise building blocks, expanding brainpower every generation. It created a snowball effect. The more proficient they were, the faster they improved. Their increased brain capacity allowed them to learn new skills, such as telepathy and multi-dimensional problem-solving. There were multiple changes in the limbic system - the brain's emotional centre - expansion in the prefrontal cortex, new connections formed between the amygdala, thalamus, hypothalamus and hippocampus, driven by complex chemical alterations and hormones.

Julia herself was part of the evolution process. Exceptional, she discovered when analysing her biological, chemical, and genetic data. Stryker's access to genetic enhancement may have impacted her and Ilya's genetic profile. Unfortunately, it was a likely scenario, and that scared her.

There was commonality in the most transformational leaps, predominantly during puberty. The key that turned the brain into overdrive was trauma, particularly emotional trauma. It triggered primaeval flight or fight. For Julia, it had been losing Sebastian, but for Ilya, it was Chinta's abduction. She wondered if losing Ming so suddenly would affect Ilya now that he was past puberty or her. Julia would request Ilya's data so she could find out. Part of her, the maternal Julia, hoped it wouldn't alter him further as he was already the most evolved human on the planet. If he advanced too far ahead, he could become isolated, and nobody wanted that for their child.

"I adore you for worrying about me, even though I should tell you not to," Ilya teased.

"Well, you are a little late, so you can't blame my overactive, fertile imagination," Julia quipped. Their telepathy had advanced from their early efforts. While Julia liked to think she was improving, she suspected Ilya was rewiring her brain. He had created a path into her communication centre, perhaps aided by the active maternal bond and a latent but undeveloped ability. A result of regular telepathy with Ilya was that Julia often anticipated what people wanted. She wasn't sure whether she was receiving thoughts or her intuition had sharpened, but she hoped to explore the concept when time allowed.

"How is your research going? I am impressed with what you sent me, including your formula to eliminate maternal bias! The data is aiding me in educating fellow EBs on self-improvement, which improves our odds of an altered future."

"Glad you approve, boss," Julia teased. *"I have made some discoveries in the Council data, but there remains a lot to explore. The methodology is similar to the EB overlays, but there is a level of complexity in isolating what drives them. I suspect multiple combined factors and generational genetic manipulation – some intended, some consequential and much of it unplanned. They share unusual markers or genetic variants that drive a need for dominance and power. There are unusually high levels*

of hormones and chemicals which feed optimal performance, similar to athletes doping in the 21st century, but for problem-solving. They created most of these dramatic increases through gene manipulation or external stimulants.

On top of that are the changes wrought by frequent cloning, youth therapies and cosmetic enhancements. The Council are experiencing the opposite effect to the EBs. Their emotional centre is shrinking, while dangerous levels of synthesised testosterone fuel increasingly erratic behaviour. The Councillors aren't young, some have served for 100 years, yet most appear to be 25-35 years old. Their youth comes at a price, Ilya. Wily and cunning they may be, but their cognitive abilities, decision-making, and bodies decline. It makes them more dangerous than ever, as they are aggressive, unpredictable and focused on self-preservation. Be careful, Ilya. You do well to flatter them; their vanity is an Achilles heel." Julia quirked a lip at her joke as Ilya had told her of his costume choice.

Julia hadn't mastered control of her facial expressions while communicating with Ilya, and sometimes Alex stared at her quizzically. Usually, she went to her office to work, but occasionally Ilya reached for her while they were enjoying family time. Tamara never indicated anything out of the ordinary was going on, but Julia would often pause mid-sentence or gaze into space, leaving Alex perplexed about her behaviour.

"Don't fret, Mummy. You will get used to tasking and conversing. Maybe just let Dad know you are preoccupied with work. Your research is fascinating and offers me insights into the psyche of the Council. How much longer will your research take?"

"It could take up to four weeks, Ilya, but if I'm lucky, maybe one or two. I feel in my gut that I am close to understanding the interplay between the common traits and variants." Julia tried to suppress the professional excitement from her face.

"You are spending a ridiculous amount of time at work, so I suggest you and your team provide more ground-breaking research. I know it will slow you down, but you have access to my knowledge, and your researchers will

go wherever you direct them. Select something of current interest that will improve the world, and I will provide you with information. Although I doubt you require my assistance."

"Flattery will get you everywhere, Ilya – you smarty pants! It's a good idea. Another accolade will be a great distraction for our Dads. I have something in mind."

"I love you and miss you all. Until next time," said Ilya.

"Wait! I found something else. We - you, me, and Tamara – have unique genetic traits. They could be inherited from Stryker and may be the product of genetic enhancement. I am looking into it further, and I am studying the impact of the trauma of Grandma Ming's death on us."

"You are concerned one of us could become another Stryker, and Grandma's death will trigger another emotional-stress transformation?" Ilya asked.

"I am uncertain of either of those eventualities, but I'm aware they are scientific possibilities. You also need to be aware. Now off you go. I love you."

Always buoyant after speaking with Ilya, Julia felt extra guilty that Alex missed out. Keeping anything a secret from him was difficult for her. He was, however, a military man, and he didn't deserve to be compromised. Tonight, she would order some favourite meals for tomorrow and spend time talking over dinner like they used to. The ongoing work, her distraction, losing Ilya, and Ming's death took a toll on them, and Alex seemed distracted lately. They clung to Tamara like a lifeboat in a storm, and she was terrific, but the ache of loss dulled slowly. Julia worked from home the next day, sowing the seeds for another Genetic Department triumph, and was surprised when Alex arrived home early.

"Hi, you're home early. What happened?" Julia put on her surprised face but greeted Alex with a sultry kiss.

"Careful, Julia, or you will also be finishing work for the day." Alex tilted her chin and pulled Julia hard against his body, claiming a kiss. "I need you to finish what you're doing right now because I want to go hiking. No arguments. Just once, play hooky on your work and run away with me." Alex's face was merry, but his eyes looked serious.

"Will there be more kisses for me on this hike you are planning?" she asked.

"Now, that would be telling, but I assure you your presence will be well rewarded." He smacked her bottom playfully and pushed her in the direction of her office to finish up. "Let's rendezvous at the front door in 10 minutes. Two kisses if you are on time." Alex raced off to the bedroom, blowing Julia a kiss as she giggled her way to the office.

It was brilliant, Alex at his unpredictable best, and he wanted to discuss something. Private conversations happened on hikes, away from interruptions, children and surveillance. Julia hadn't thought about it in their early years together, but the security surveillance must have concerned them, why they hiked off into the middle of nowhere to talk. She secured her work and shut down comms. The team was changing gears, stimulated by the latest project. Alex was stowing supplies in his carry-pack in the kitchen, so Julia raced to the bedroom to change.

"Right, I am one minute and 35 seconds early, Alex, so give me my kisses." Julia pouted and made cow eyes until Alex paid up.

They left the building hand-in-hand, like a couple of teenagers sneaking out on a date. Alex led them to one of their favourite self-made trails, complete with climbing, abseiling and creek crossings, really off the beaten track. They kept the mood and conversation light, but Julia sensed tension in Alex. Her intuition and instincts felt so enhanced lately that she thought he was waving a red flag. Halfway up a cliff, they stopped on a plateau.

"It's beautiful up here, isn't it?" He turned to Julia and put his arm around her shoulder.

"It certainly is a fantastic view. Want to tell me what's on your mind?" She took his hands in hers and looked up at his face. There it was. Worry etched in his handsome features, face tinged with sadness.

"I asked for a copy of the report on Ming's accident, and I got it, but it wasn't as comprehensive as expected. Dmitry received the crashed pod in logistics. The report and the pod wreck don't match up, Julia. The pod was tampered with, and the accident was sabotage." Julia covered her mouth with her hand.

"Are you sure it's not a mistake, Alex," she whispered.

"You know Dmitry well - he is thorough. He examined the wreck because someone hid it, so nobody would notice they sent it to recycling. Ironically, Dmitry looked for anomalies, and the pod didn't follow the correct protocol. Dmitry believes somebody assassinated Ming, and with the absence of evidence, it appears to be an Erase Order." He took Julia in his arms and stroked her hair, devastated to be sharing such terrible news. Julia rested her head on his shoulder, feeling numb. "Say something, Julia. I know this must be a shock."

"Perhaps not as much of a shock as you think, Alex. My mother exposed my ignorance when Ilya came home upset about Chinta's termination. Ming enlightened us on the Council's position and her life with her father. She was blunt with Ilya and me regarding how much danger we would be in if he chose to oppose the Council. My mother advised us wisely, cautiously, in secret, much as you have done today. Alex, Ming, grew up in a different world, so she possessed information that could threaten Council members or the Council itself. It could even have been Stryker."

"Oh God, do you think they erased Ilya as well?" Alex ran his fingers through his hair, speaking the words constricting his throat.

"No, no, no – I'm sure Ilya is fine. That isn't just my position as his mother. Ilya's disappearance reminds every investigating department in New Zealand that they failed. We live on an island, so locating someone shouldn't be difficult. It would have been public and tied up neatly with a bow if someone had erased him. Maybe an accident, a test failure, or a threat to the population. Trust me, Alex, Ilya is out there somewhere. Have you ever heard Tamara speak of him in the past tense or express sadness? They are telepathically linked, and she knows he's okay." Julia took Alex's face between her hands, desperate to convey reassurance without placing him in further danger.

"I love you, and I want you to be right so badly. Everything you say makes sense, but I miss our boy. I want him to come home, Julia, hold him, see him smile. If he is alive, he grows into a man without us, which hurts."

"I know Alex, and I feel the same. However, my conviction that he is alive and thriving has never wavered. We raised a super-intelligent, highly evolved child together, and I'm confident in his abilities. Abilities fostered by us." She paused, hand cradling his face, trying to influence him, and give him confidence. Alex rewarded her with a smile.

"Dmitry and I can run a discreet investigation into Ming's-"

"Please don't, Alex. The matter needs to be left alone, or you will expose us to a ruthless enemy. The Council's power has grown after years of ruling unchallenged, never having to explain decisions, and they are an elite dictatorship, Alex. The rules we live by don't apply to them. Above all else, my mother would want us to protect our family. Do you understand?"

"Yes, difficult as it is, I do. I'll speak to Dad, although leaving loose ends isn't his strong point. He doesn't trust anyone. Our family history as agents during the Black Years haunts him." Alex frowned and thought about convincing his Dad to drop the investigation.

"You need to be compelling, Alex. Neither of us wants to lose another parent. He is a smart man who understands the rules of engagement. Your heritage, the knowledge of life under a ruling class, will be useful." She searched his face, and he nodded silently before turning to finish the climb.

They ascended as fast as possible to cover the time they spent on the ledge. While Alex and Julia were in the wilderness, both harboured an acute sense of caution. As they climbed, Julia tried to focus and not dwell on Ming's murder.

9 |

Ruling Council

The Council completed the elaborate security process that precluded every meeting. Sentinel computers scanned their bodies and tested blood for nanobots. They changed clothing in a sterile environment, as eyes, brain images, bone structure, and teeth were data-checked to formalise identities. Protocol increased over time as technology advanced, and nothing from the outside ever entered the Council Chamber. Once they were in, security sealed the room, and they were the safest people on the planet.

Unless the chamber descended into magma beneath the Earth's crust and couldn't find a place to emerge within 48 hours, the Council would survive. The Council commissioned the construction of the chamber from the best materials the space exploration industry had to offer. The exterior was encased in nuclear pasta, patiently mined in minute quantities from neutron stars. The material was so dense transporting it was a logistical nightmare, even in space. Internally the chamber was kitted out with a life support system, biological hazard scrubbers, and enough supplies for the Council to survive for a year. If that wasn't enough, a thick layer of tiny spheres, which could absorb the shock of being hit by any known bomb or a meteor strike, surrounded the exterior. Finally, a magnetic repulsion shield enveloped the compound the chamber resided in, and a weaponised defence system sat at Prime's fingertips.

Prime could snap the repulsion shield tightly around the spheres in an emergency. Ruling the planet was serious business, and the Councillors didn't tolerate interference and planned for the worst scenarios.

The meeting covered the usual topics of global production, finances, discoveries, exploitation of other planets' resources, population, propaganda and any decisions they needed to discuss and debate.

"There is an issue with a critical mining venture on Wolf 1061c," said Councillor Wei.

"Please elaborate, Councillor," asked Prime.

"The manager sent me an encrypted comm last night. They detected advanced life forms in the topographical and environmental mapping program."

"There is enough Rossinium on Wolf to power our space fleet for the next seventeen years and huge deposits of valuable metals. What's more, the deposits are accessible, and mining is a simple and cost-effective operation. Who else knows of the life forms?" queried Stryker. Experienced in mineral exploitation, he had already calculated the potential value of the mines. Stryker wasn't the only one calculating profits, and Prime inclined his head to Shand, inviting her to speak.

"Our primary responsibility is to protect our people here, on Earth, and across the universe. Over the years, we have encountered several evolved life forms, and we have a clear precedent and protocol to follow. New life forms may carry unknown diseases or prove hostile to humans. I move that we maintain our security."

"I second," said Stryker.

"Let's vote," instructed Prime.

The Council voted unanimously to terminate the life forms that stood in the way of the mining venture.

"Councillor Montreaux, please eradicate anyone besides the manager privy to the life form information. Search all data and erase any publicly accessible records. Councillor Wei, organise with the manager to activate neutron cleansing of the exoplanet as soon as possible so the mining operation can commence," instructed Prime.

Montreaux smiled, and she and Wei bowed heads to acknowledge the tasks allocated to them.

"Councillor Shand, please update us on the PPS (Passivity Propensity Screening)," invited Prime.

"The revised settings, to render the general population breeding program more docile, will be uploaded tomorrow, placing the project two months ahead of schedule," reported Shand. Councillors turned their heads and bowed to Shand's efficiency.

'Other Business' was always the last item on their agenda because it could take five minutes or five days. Prime was impatient to return to his new distraction and hoped there wouldn't be any lengthy discussions. He was disappointed.

"There is a sensitive matter I would like to discuss," said Stryker silkily. The Councillors turned to him, intrigued. "My grandson Ilya, a person of significant interest, disappeared without a trace, and now my daughter Ming has been Erased." There was shuffling, and everyone was poised, fixated by Stryker's story. They lived for gossip.

"Surely, you must be able to clone Ming Stryker. It's the 22nd century, for Sanctuary's sake." Shand eyed Stryker for reaction, searching for weakness. Her appearance belied years and intellect. At first glance, Shand appeared unremarkable to people, which was the result she wanted. Shand was the girl next door - brown hair, freckle dusted nose, hazel eyes, and a suntan. Everything about Shand's appearance was benign and invited strangers to like and trust her. Many years ago, she and Stryker were lovers but discovered they were too alike to be compatible. Instead, they were rivals in a quest for power, but their former relationship meant Shand knew Stryker well. He was posturing for a strike. Who is in his sights, she mused?

"Ming left specific legal instructions, under the Life Choice Article, that we must not clone her. Although our positions offer many freedoms and privileges, I do like to suppose the Articles we live by are also observed by us. Under item 345 (d) of the Councillors Code, our families are supposed to be protected by law. Somebody violated my rights at least once and possibly twice. I demand to know who issued the Erase Order or Orders and why." Stryker leaned forward, dagger-eyes pointed at Prime.

"Now, Stryker, I know this must be emotionally difficult for you, but of course, I issued the Erase Order. Ming left Sanctuary before the new code requiring our children to remain here was implemented. She posed a risk to us, Stryker. Snippets of comm conversations in various languages were pieced together and delivered to me. After all the years spent outside, Ming finally spoke of her father's house and the Council. While we don't have all the details, it is my responsibility to protect us, and I always do my duty." Prime's tone was soft, righteous, slightly condescending as if explaining a complex issue to a recalcitrant child.

"I wonder why Ming was discussing anything about Sanctuary or her home? Do you believe the botched abduction of your Assistant Chinta, an acquaintance of my grandson Ilya, had anything to do with that discussion, Prime?" Stryker was challenging Prime, calling him to account, a rare occurrence indeed.

"We must retain our unity. That is our strength, Stryker. I freely admit the team assigned handled the abduction poorly, but it was dealt with swiftly and efficiently by me." Prime's tone was deadly now, laced with an implication that he dealt with issues clinically. "I had absolutely nothing to do with the disappearance of your grandson. He could hold the key to our future. It's a mystery, and I don't like the unknown. So, I am asking all of you, does anyone know what happened to Ilya Stryker-Petrel?"

In classic style, Prime shifted the attention from his misdemeanours to a different topic. The Councillors turned their attention to Ilya; nobody else wished to clash with Prime. Stryker lost the skirmish. Prime offered an olive branch to Stryker by engaging the entire Council in the quest for Ilya. While he wasn't pleased with Stryker's approach, the points he made were valid, and Prime's grip on power relied on the Council's cohesion. None of the Councillors had any knowledge or intelligence of Ilya's whereabouts.

"When was the last time anything on this planet happened that we didn't know about or couldn't find details on?" asked Prime with a frown.

"The hack and viral attack on the Goodness Algorithm in 2055. Of course, the surveillance systems of those times weren't anything like we have today. Only the people in this room possess the power to override external systems," said Stryker, looking grim.

"But if it wasn't somebody in this room who removed Ilya, then who did? The alternative presented is that an external force exists which can control our systems. I find the possibility unsettling," said Shand.

"Perhaps we haven't given enough attention to what appeared to be a puzzling disappearance. Shand is right. Stryker, you have a personal interest in Ilya. Would you take the lead on a more thorough investigation?" Again, Prime deferred to Stryker. The man was a natural politician. While Stryker was disappointed Prime deflected his attack so simply, he desperately wanted to find Ilya. His grandson could potentially deliver him Prime's authority.

"You honour me with this investigation, Prime, and I thank you." Two could play the political game of cat and mouse cloaked in niceties. "I request assistance from Councillor Montreaux on this project due to her expertise in technology." Stryker also knew his request would annoy Shand greatly, she had supported Prime in diverting attention, and Montreaux was her arch-rival. Montreaux was clever, unnaturally beautiful, creative, and competed fiercely with Shand for distractions and power. The slight pursing of Shand's lips indicated his success in riling her. The meeting was closed, and they commenced exit security procedures, as complex as the entry process. No data exited the chamber.

Chinta awaited Prime in his private bathing suite, and she filled the enormous, sunken bath with steaming scented water. She reclined naked, her hair piled with artfully-haphazard care, on top of her head. Prime was often tense after the Council meetings, and she knew how to relax him.

A snap of her fingers would summon the best masseuses on the planet to knead his muscles, oil his body and give him whatever he wanted. Now she rose to pour his favourite aperitif, ambrosia by Viking, and distract him from his worries. She never asked about the meetings, knowing he couldn't tell her anything. Her job as Prime's Assistant was to take care of him, which she learned exceptionally well from her predecessor.

The road to her position was degrading, humiliating, and painful. In return for surviving and learning without breaking, she received almost the best of everything. As long as she was amusing and compliant, Prime treated her well.

Sighing audibly, Prime stepped into the bath, took the proffered ambrosia, and submitted to Chinta's ministrations. She was excellent company.

"Oh, I couldn't wait for you to return. Have I got news for you on our favourite tasty morsel!" She giggled playfully, taking a sip of her drink. "You won't believe the attention Argos receives – it's unbelievable when everyone knows I'm screening him for you. That vixen Maya has been sending him messages carried by one of his staff, Xenon is mooching around like a love-starved pet, and Montreaux sent her Assistant Erik to try and seduce him when inviting him to a fashion show. Sacre bleu! Is nothing sacred anymore on this island?" Chinta was animated, obviously enjoying the gossip and that Viking was so sought after by the Councillors.

"You will be pleased to know I have almost completed the security screening for Argos. Security scanned his blood for malicious bots, double-checked employment records, and they have vetted his family health. Last night we administered the truth serum in a cocktail and questioned him extensively - I think you enjoyed that show." Her smile was mischievous as she placed her lips against Prime's ears. "Soon, you will be able to have him," she whispered. "Although I must say, intriguing as he is, the anticipation is delicious. It makes me feel aroused just thinking about it. And, I found this covert footage of Viking Argos' city tour."

Chinta queued a screen on the wall, lay back with eyes half-closed, back arched erotically, and Prime responded to her excitement with his own. There is no need for masseurs today, thought Chinta, whose insatiable appetite drove Prime crazy. She hadn't intended to spy on Ilya, but the surveillance popped up in her network, where she learned everything about everyone. The sight of Viking having sex with Flame left her breathless, panting, yearning, in a way the organised shows never did. The sting of jealousy seared her as Flame climaxed, and she knew she must show it to Prime. It was the most erotic titbit she had viewed for a long time. Ilya was her friend, she felt dirty, but Chinta admitted she wanted Viking like everyone else.

Life was hectic for Ilya and Viking. He had catering to do, staff to manage, a network of EBs to train, infiltration to work on, and juggling the jockeying Councillors and Assistants. Chinta was the highlight of his day when he could get time with her. There was no pretending or mentoring when they spoke, just two friends who had known each other all of her life. Of course, she teased him mercilessly but spared him the embarrassment of turning him into one of her play-things.

It was barbaric that Prime brought Chinta to Sanctuary as a child concubine. Ilya admired her adaptability for survival and courage as their primary source of information on the Council. Thanks to Chinta, he would soon be invited into Prime's presence. If Julia could help him with details, he would find a way into his mind and unlock the secrets it held.

Mind exploration was an untried form of espionage. Until then, Ilya trained the EBs to influence thought, gathered information from his many admirers, and brought Sanctuary's systems under his influence.

He coded stealth loops that fed their data into his brain, which meant he could issue the system commands by thought in return, without anyone knowing. Ilya could now move through the city utterly undetected by surveillance, alerted to other people, drones, bots or droids.

Slowly, he was testing his abilities, but he was cautious. There could be low tech systems in place, old-fashioned spying, or traps set to catch people out.

Assignation invitations were the perfect opportunity to push boundaries and bring him close to Council members. Tonight Erik had organised a tryst on the lagoon with Montreaux. Erik assured Ilya he would take care of the security arrangements so Chinta and Prime would never know about it.

Ilya knew Chinta spied on them all, so he was eager to see if Erik could elude her network. Montreaux was the latest Council member, younger than the others and highly engineered genetically. She replaced her father on the Council when he became bored and volunteered to lead a deep-space colonisation fleet to planet Terra Duo in the Cygnus constellation.

After disgracing her mother and assassinating any ambitious siblings, her father endorsed Montreaux as his successor. Unashamedly ambitious, Prime and the Council couldn't ignore her genius. It was also better to have her in their midst and not working against them or causing mischief. They never regretted their decision, as Councillor Montreaux was highly innovative, improving security, systems and profit. She was a perfect fit, better suited to the evolving world than her father, and devoid of morals or scruples.

Erik and another assistant arrived dressed in cloaks and masks. There was some exaggerated flirting before they whisked Ilya into the bedroom.

"I have black-zoned your room for a minute, Viking. Put on Kalin's clothes quickly, and he will get into your bed. Come, come, we don't have long." Erik walked to the entrance, tucking Viking's arm in his, before turning back to the bedroom.

"Thank you for receiving us at such short notice, Argos. The invitation still stands. It's such a shame Prime found you so quickly, but Chinta is rather greedy with treats. We will call again to ensure you haven't changed your mind. Divine catering at the fashion show, by the way. Montreaux loved the miniature accessory canapes. I nearly forgot to deliver a kiss from her." Erik walked to the bed and kissed Kalin's head before he and Viking departed, with Erik waxing lyrical about the entertainment he was organising.

Viking played along, nodding, laughing and making approving noises. They dropped in at a marquee crammed with people in masks, being entertained by acrobats and circus performers swinging from the ceiling. In a fortune-telling booth, Erik placed a long black wig on Ilya's head, a harlequin mask on his face and had him wriggle into a dark blue, one-piece circus costume. Erik left the tent with someone else in the cloak and urged Viking to find a clown at the entrance with curly purple hair in a pod.

It was a simple ruse, requiring no technology apart from the brief black zone in the apartment, which Ilya suspected Chinta would notice. The clown took him to the waterfront, helped him into a boat with a silent bow, and Viking was transported to a softly lit pavilion, floating in the middle of a silvery lagoon. Montreaux was flattering him with her elaborate effort to conceal their affair and possibly avoid Prime's displeasure.

Intellectually gifted and enhanced, Ilya needed to keep his alert levels high with Montreaux. This woman was also the architect of the systems he now controlled, undetected, he believed, but he wasn't taking anything for granted. Chinta advised him with much amusement, "Montreaux competes for everything Shand wants, and apparently, that includes you." She was more serious when she suggested, "Montreaux could be assessing you for herself or the Council. Your rise is rapid, be careful with this woman. She is cunning and cold." Those words echoed in his head because Chinta betrayed worry, tinged with fear.

The boat ride gave him time to consider his preferred strategies. Would Montreaux succumb to his charm without becoming suspicious, he wondered? Chinta was schooling him in her subtle tactics, and he needed to be agile and aware. Ilya hoped Montreaux wouldn't drug him as Chinta had. It wasn't that he couldn't dispose of chemicals or toxins, but it was an unwanted distraction.

Ilya was aware of a security protocol running on the boat, sampling his cells and breath, scanning his body, authenticating his identity, measuring his pheromones - interesting. Next to the Council Chamber, the world's best scanning system, but Ilya controlled all the data, so the results were perfect for Viking Argos. Montreaux was receiving the data she was expecting physically. The boat pilot ushered Viking onto a wooden platform.

"My mistress awaits within." The boat withdrew, leaving Viking alone with Montreaux. An unusual risk for a Council member to be alone with one individual. Security systems surrounded them, Ilya could read them all, and Montreaux was an avid combat student. Rumours circulated that she assassinated some of her rivals herself. It suited her to instil fear, and she might have organised the tales, or they could be true. Montreaux's thoughts exuded self-confidence, but there was also a glimmer of curiosity laced with triumph – over Shand, perhaps.

Viking drew back the silken drapes, ruffling in the breeze. He still wore his mask, wig, and costume to observe her without revealing himself. Montreaux was breathtakingly beautiful, aesthetic perfection personified.

Breath drawn in, Viking stood for a moment staring. She unleashed a barrage of potent pheromones, human, animal and synthesised. Maybe this was his effect on people. How poetic, he thought. Ilya recovered rapidly, organising his receptors and fine-tuning them to her.

She had attended the games as Aphrodite, and Montreaux looked every inch a Goddess. Montreaux's platinum blonde hair was tied in a high ponytail that cascaded shimmering waves across one shoulder. Her flawless skin allowed cerulean eyes, the same colour as the lagoon, to shine - jewels in the perfect setting. Thick dark lashes fringed her eyes under arching brows, and her lips were plump, inviting. Lilac chiffon draped over swollen breasts, exposing a deep decolletage, tiny waist, flaring hips and long shapely legs. Montreaux wore almost no cosmetics, and she didn't need them.

It was easy to become attractive when the cost was no object, but Montreaux was spectacular. No wonder Shand hated her with a passion. For Ilya, working furiously inside Viking's glamour, the view was less attractive. Chinta was right; she was cold and calculating. Also vain, selfish, greedy, lustful, emotionally deficient, and primitively unaware of the natural world. To Ilya she was repugnant. Viking would take the lead, and he was highly trained for this purpose while Ilya attempted to navigate the sewer into her mind.

"Step into the light, Argos. I want to see what all the fuss is about." Her melodious voice had an intriguing accent, but it didn't disguise the command. She threw back her head and laughed, "how delightful of Erik to gift wrap you."

Clapping her hands in appreciation, she rose from her divan with the grace of a hunting cat. "Time to unwrap you, I think." Gently she removed his one-piece costume, hands brushing against his muscular body as she disrobed him. Viking was wearing a fine lawn shirt and soft leather trousers underneath but felt naked under her touch. She teased the wig from his head and ruffled plastered hair into place.

Standing back, she admired him, he was certainly pleasing, but her eyes narrowed, a huntress ready to pounce. What's behind the mask, she wondered? Montreaux moved back to her divan, sipped her champagne and arranged herself to look alluring.

"Remove your mask."

Viking drew the mask upwards slowly, revealing his perfect features one at a time, before whisking it off with a flourish and bow. He hit her with the power of his smile and gaze, all at once. This woman would only crave the bold.

"Viking Argos at your service." His unusual eyes twinkled with mischief, but he didn't move a muscle as he directed a ripple of longing in her direction.

Montreaux inhaled a sharp breath as she looked Viking up and down. So, there was a reason people fawned over him, competing for his affections. No wonder Prime claimed him. Still, she was confident she could enslave Viking to her, then plead her case with Prime. A challenge, she loved a challenge, and Shand would be apoplectic with indignation – divine!

"As you see, I'm rather casually dressed. There is a robe for you to change into while I pour you a drink." Viking pulled off his clothes and wrapped himself in the flimsy robe before Montreaux waved him to the divan next to hers.

"What do you think of Nirvana so far, Argos?"

"Please, call me Viking. Would you like a safe or honest answer, Councillor?" Viking's eyes beamed merriment into hers until she snorted with laughter.

"Oh, so you are amusing as well as pretty! Please call me Darling, and let me see, I choose honesty." She giggled, enjoying spontaneity, such a relief from the predictable boredom of life.

"Darling, I'm wounded," he said, hand on heart, "you think me merely pretty. I've spent a small fortune and hoped to make a favourable impression on the fairest woman in the land." Viking raised pleading, sad eyes, begging for her approval before his face split into a mischievous grin.

He regaled Montreaux with a pithy assessment of Nirvana and the inhabitants of Sanctuary, inventing comedic names as he described a variety of known figures. Montreaux hadn't enjoyed herself so much in decades. Viking took a risk with his honesty, it ceded power to her over him, but she was used to adoration. It was more than drooling over her as men often did. He was familiar and intimate with her. Although he was respectful and observed proper protocol, he wasn't scared of her. Viking treated her like a woman and an equal. She could feign insult, but it was refreshing and made her feel young, which had become increasingly difficult.

Hours passed in conversation and banter as they dined and drank as if only the two of them existed.

"I'm sorry, Darling, I have been boring you with my frightful stories for hours. Tomorrow I must cater a breakfast Stryker is hosting, and I am determined not to outstay my welcome. The scintillating conversation exceeds your hospitality. And the fact you haven't tied me up, spanked me, oiled me, subjected me to every sex toy in the kingdom, fed me to hungry entertainers, or tried to seduce me is a pleasure." The corners of his mouth moved in the slightest of smiles. "Darling, I do love a woman who gets to know you before exploiting your body. The anticipation is delicious, don't you think?" His eyes crinkled in amusement.

"I did have plans to tie you up, spank and oil you before giving you to the circus performers, but as self-denial titillates you, I will try it. Besides, I wouldn't want to leave you too shattered to cater for Stryker's breakfast."

Montreaux gave him a beguiling smile, eyes wide with innocence as she displayed her assets, enticing him with what he was missing. "The boat awaits. You have only to don your disguise, and you will be back in your quarters in minutes. I hope you will lie on your back and think of what I might be doing to entertain myself."

"Oh, Darling, I'm certain I will. I hope there will be another invitation as I haven't enjoyed an evening so much for a long time." He projected sincere admiration and decided to plant a thought in Montreaux's head that she must see him again. Viking smiled and kissed her hand but found the idea already there, so he bid Montreaux goodnight.

Once in his quarters, Ilya reached for Chinta. It was akin to knocking on someone's door to see if you could come in to talk. For a change, Chinta was available and alone. A new trainee assistant had arrived in Prime's mansion, and Chinta dreaded being called upon to instruct her. It wouldn't happen immediately. The tutors only approached a favoured Assistant to teach advanced lessons if the child made the grade. If the tutor deemed the child unsuitable, they placed them in the household labour pool.

"You are alone, Chinta! And troubled, it seems."

"Contemplating a potential role in ruining the life of another innocent child, Ilya. I fear this may pose the biggest challenge to my carefully cultivated act. The kindest strategy would be to ensure she fails, but I only postpone an inevitable task that shreds my soul to ribbons." It was unusual for Chinta to express such despair, so Ilya wrapped himself around her, comforting her in her need. *"Sorry, Ilya, I'm being pathetic. We fight for the survival of more than one child. Please forgive my self-indulgence. You are a true friend and inspirational leader. How was your meeting with Montreaux?"* she asked cheekily, more herself. Ilya knew she suppressed her feelings of sadness but answered her query.

"As you are alone, I was hoping I could share the highlights of the evening with you and hear your opinion?" Chinta's reluctant embarrassment touched him. *"No, Chinta! It wasn't a physical encounter at all...I would never subject you to that. It was more chase and catch, a flirtatious liaison, but I wanted to know if I was the chaser or the catch? I also tried some of your techniques tonight, overrode her security systems and sneaked around in disguise with Erik. You are far more competent in Nirvanan culture than I am. Help me?"*

"Oh, Ilya, you are such a prude," she giggled, his Chinta again, *"I already stumbled across your 'tour' with Flame. I regret to advise you that my embarrassment is due to my invasion of your privacy. Not that I could see very much in the dark, but I confess I was excited and a little jealous. I showed it to Prime as a teaser."* It was Ilya's turn to emit the equivalent of a telepathic blush.

"Erik's black-out zone was an unnecessary anomaly which alerted other Assistants in Nirvana. He is either stupid, careless or did it on purpose. If it is the latter, there are several theories why Montreaux wants people to know she snagged you. I lost you somewhere between the shore and the pavilion but successfully hacked her surveillance. To be honest, I found it quite boring, so I filed it away for later. But, if you want to share the highlights, I will tell you what I observe," she laughed. Chinta's candid humour had always hit Ilya's funny bone. They were both resting with

eyes closed in repose to any observer. Behind their lids, a lively conversation, shared images, lots of teasing, and some astute feminine feedback occurred; two people, free to be themselves in secret. Both masked their brain activity, so surveillance would only detect sleep patterns.

"In summary, Ilya, I believe Viking chose the correct strategy with Montreaux. She is intrigued, and you have triggered her base emotions by offering a unique proposition. For a person who can take almost anything she wants, you are less accessible, more valuable - better sport. If you ratchet up your charm in small increments, she may eventually believe she is in love with Viking – or the nearest emotion to love she is capable of feeling. As your cultural tutor, I am impressed. I suggest we make Viking unavailable when the next invitation arrives. An invitation from Prime will see Viking reluctantly decline her invitation. Montreaux will elevate Viking to the desired toy she cannot have – perfect. Shand will find out, Maya is resourceful, and she will prod Montreaux mercilessly," she purred.

"Goodness, I'm glad you're on my side, Chinta! And thank you for the compliment. It means a lot to me. I felt Viking achieved his objective, but I find Montreaux so repulsive that I was afraid I would inhibit my glamour. Now I have been inside her mind, and I have to segregate my inner self from Viking. I don't imagine any of the Councillors will look any better than she does when I strip away their exterior.

I have put another critical experiment in place. Like Shand before her, I have rewired Montreaux's brain, hidden the change in the systems, and I will monitor the result. This time, I focused on stimulating the emotional area to develop feelings for Viking, which she was incapable of doing.

When they clone themselves, the neural receptors weaken and break down over time, making them incapable of many basic emotions. The cell scrubber-bots also damage reprogramming, so I have created shortcuts to repair and improve them. We need to understand how effective the reconnections are. If we can restore the Councillors to full emotional capability, our task becomes more straightforward. Once my mother finishes her research, we will understand if this is an option. In the meantime, Viking needs Montreaux to be malleable so that I can access her. There are no guarantees I will ever have the level of access to Prime we need, so Shand and Montreaux are essential, as they may be our way inside the Council. We should get some rest, Chinta. I can't express how vital our contact is to me; I can never afford to lose myself in all of this. Love you."

Chinta experienced a thrill of pleasure when Ilya described Montreaux as repulsive. Montreaux was considered one of the most beautiful women in the world, but to Ilya, she was ugly. How satisfying, thought Chinta! Viking was glamorous, but she understood Ilya's reaction, as Ilya's inner self was far more attractive to Chinta than his lovely exterior. Ilya appreciated her, her sacrifice, opinion, and he had told her he loved her so naturally - then he was gone.

It disconcerted Chinta, and she was confused. What did those two words mean? Did he love her as a friend? An EB or a colleague? Or did it convey something more? Surely, with all this advancement and telepathy, they could at least comprehend each other's feelings more clearly. The next time they were together and not working, Chinta decided to explore Ilya's feelings for her. Before then, it would be prudent to assess her own. Everybody, without exception, loved Ilya, and she would deliver him to Prime to achieve their mission objective. Now was an inopportune moment to develop an emotional attachment to Ilya but evolved as Chinta was, her heart wanted what it wanted.

10

Dominance Quotient

"Alex, I am completely obsessed with my current research." To prove her point, Julia shovelled food into her mouth at an accelerated pace, eager to return to her data.

"Strangely, Tamara and I noticed that already. We thought the two of us might go on vacation to Europa with your father."

"That sounds fun." Julia was formulating her next data wash - she was so close.

"Ok, you are miles away and not listening. I just suggested taking our daughter to the single adult entertainment moon with your father, and you said it sounds fun." Alex stabbed his fork in the air to make his point while Tamara giggled, finding her parents amusing.

"Oh, I'm sorry, Alex, Tamara. I know I'm distracted, but I am ridiculously close to making a breakthrough that could change our world! Forgive me? When I finish this project, we can take a vacation together, somewhere more child-appropriate, with swimming for Tamara." Julia tickled Tamara under her chin, making her laugh. She was such a joy. Considering how neglectful she had been lately, Tamara was surprisingly content. Alex was thriving. He stepped into the role of primary carer enthusiastically, and his bond with Tamara was adorable. Julia experienced a pang of guilt, followed by a stab of envy. Tamara took her hand and kissed it gently, "Mama, Tamara loves you." Tears pricked behind Julia's eyes, and she blinked to dispel them, studying her food so Alex wouldn't notice. Tamara gave her a mental hug, understanding the importance of Julia's work and supporting her with the wisdom of an EB. Dabbing her mouth with her napkin, Julia rose, gave Alex a peck on the cheek, and implored him to release her from dinner.

"You are incorrigible, Julia. You are excused, but – you owe Tamara and me a favour each. What do you think, Tam?"

"Yes! I want ice cream tomorrow."

"Is that right, ice cream – done. What about you, Alex? What's it going to cost me?"

"I am thinking about it, and I refuse to tell you until you have finished your work." His eyes narrowed, and the smirk on his face belied his claim he was still considering the favour. Julia was curious, so she hurried off to her office, happy Alex indulged her professional drive so patiently.

Julia picked up the analytics where she left them, running the data wash formulated in her head over dinner. The Council member data was fascinating. They were the most imperfect specimens she had analysed in a long time, perhaps since she was a student working with frozen old blood. The Councillors carried a gene mutation on their X chromosome, which produced an emotion inhibiting enzyme. Serotonin levels were abnormally low, while testosterone was 50-100% higher than normal indexed levels. The Councillors enjoyed sexual pursuits, favoured aggression, and pumped themselves full of the hormones they desired at will. The cloning they engaged in to stay young degenerated the amygdala and the prefrontal cortex receptors controlling aggression. The reduced emotional activation produced impulsive aggress. While the changes may have begun as a genetic design, each clone was more damaged than the last.

By the time the most recent clones were fifteen years old, most of the receptors had broken down, leaving them emotionally deficient. If that wasn't enough, the Councillors all deployed nanobot scrubbers that circulated in their blood to detect abnormal or deteriorating cell activity.

The job of the nanobots was to fix anything and everything before it became a problem. To these invaders, emotions they couldn't understand, anything illogical, was a problem. They repaired acts of decency, fairness or kindness if they were of no benefit to their host. By altering neural connectivity, the nanobots were eroding human qualities.

The collagen boosters, epidermis regenerators, and cell renewal therapies that maintained their youthful appearance functioned as a chemical cocktail that diminished their ability to empathise with others. It also affected their enzyme production and protein composition.

Brain scans, although uniquely individual, betrayed similar patterns across all eleven Councillors. Montreaux, the youngest, was gene-deficient and felt no guilt. Probably an unintended consequence of genetic engineering focused on physical traits and intelligence. She was also one of the five per cent, which made her a dangerous innovator.

Prime, however, was in the best shape of them all. He appeared older than the others and therefore subject to less manipulation, so his receptors were more intact. There were segments of Prime's brain, which he had cultivated exceptionally well, notably the areas of reasoning and negotiation. His serotonin and empathy levels were higher. No wonder he was an excellent politician. Prime possessed all the genetic markers of a born leader, mustering his dangerous peers into a community that could face down any threat. In his original life, he was a medical doctor, and Julia wondered if he engineered the changes. Perhaps he ensured he maintained an edge.

Stryker was fascinating to her. The similarities they shared were multiple, but the differences were also dramatic. Ming inherited less genetically and biologically from Stryker than her mother. What a stroke of luck for them both, or they could have been monsters like Montreaux.

Psychologically and neurologically, council members were supremely hard-wired to fight for survival, status, and resources. They were the product of paleobiology, generations of natural selection, and unnatural selection, wrapped in attractive packaging. Their ancestors almost destroyed the Earth, but they found a way to survive. The Council bent their intent on maintaining the status quo, a world they created, so they would always be ruthless and without mercy.

The Council effectively suppressed pre-existing culture, dictated societal behaviour, and crushed the population into a mould of their design. Julia paled as she thought of Ilya and his gentle, silent friends lamenting the damage to the planet and humanity. Was this analysis going to be enough for them? Could they find a way to infiltrate the seat of power and influence the future? Julia wondered what would happen to the telepathically deaf and mute in the EB world if they were victorious. She sincerely hoped she was making the right choice, but her research favoured the decision making of the EBs, and in her world, data didn't lie.

Saving and securing her research, pleased with the result and eager to share it with Ilya, she went in search of Alex. Feeling jubilant, Julia figured out what the favour might be and skipped to their bedroom.

Ilya knocked softly but insistently at Julia's unconscious mind, tugging her from dreams. Eyes fluttered in the dark, Ilya a whispering echo inside her head.

"I am sorry to wake you, Mummy, but developments in Nirvana make me eager to see your research. It isn't the kind of information we can share in any tangible way, even encrypted, as the surveillance here is layered. Could I look at whatever you have through your eyes? Dad is in a deep sleep, enjoying dreams of our camping trips, and he won't wake up."

"Good morning, I think. Of course, you can. I was hoping you would contact me last night, as I now have a comprehensive data set. I call it the Dominance Quotient. It is fascinating to research because the subjects are so different to us."

Julia was out of bed and trotting down the hallway, dying to hear what Ilya thought. She ran her security protocol with practised ease, chattering to Ilya as she went.

"The interplay between the many variants is the key to making the Council tick. They are the evolution of our prehistoric ancestors and regression, all in one package."

The research loaded as Julia navigated the multitude of blockades she had erected around the data. She didn't run her decryption code but provided it to Ilya to decrypt in his head. If anyone ever discovered her research, the Council would execute her. There was an overarching synopsis of her key findings, a report on each Council member, and reference data sets to support her conclusions. Ilya absorbed it, as intrigued as his mother. Merging his mind with Julia's, he consumed it in minutes.

"I have an important question. In your opinion, is it possible to reverse the variations, at the same time or in a short period, to render the Council more human? Can we make them more evolved people?"

"I doubt it. Unless you come up with innovative new methods, which you may be able to do. The dramatic changes involved in reversal could over-tax their physiology. Maybe over a sustained period, you could generationally reverse some traits. In general, we are talking about a personality transplant, Ilya. These are the elite cavemen and cavewomen who have survived everything since we became homo sapiens. Unravelling complex hard-wired behaviours which evolved over thousands of years isn't as easy as manipulating genes or altering chemical compounds."

"There must be a way to achieve the repairs. Nature maintains balance. After the Black Years, the Council had a unique opportunity to steer us away from exploitation and greed. Instead, they chose to remain selfish and enslave the population to fulfil their needs. We, the EBs, are nature's chosen method of counteracting the genetic tampering of the Council. The irony is that they have inadvertently helped create us while rendering themselves inferior. However, we cannot afford to fail because the Council will destroy us in the power struggle. There are other options available to nature, and one of them is to destroy us – perhaps let us kill each other. I perceive nature's grand design and the Council's flaws with their folly. Every species has its rise, fall and extinction."

"Perhaps you or the EBs will find a way. It is beyond my humble capabilities."

"I wouldn't describe your capabilities as anything but spectacular, and not just because you are my mother." Ilya's humour had the same flavour telepathically as when he spoke, which comforted Julia - he was still her boy.

"I concur with Ilya. Your research is spectacularly ground-breaking in its innovation and complexity." Tamara joined in the conversation, but her command of language telepathically was far superior to her verbal skills. *"I have to vocalise my thoughts at an appropriate level for my age, Mama, or I will attract unwanted analysis. My learning is accelerated, supplemented by Ilya so I can assist him. That's why I'm always eating because my brain requires the nutritional intake to work at night."*

"There are almost no barriers between myself and Tamara. Everything I know, she knows, except for the sexual sport in Nirvana."

"You are such a spoilsport, Ilya! I have to learn about reproduction and sexual behaviour at some point. I don't like to disconnect from you." Tamara was pouting telepathically, like other children her age, struggling with not getting her way.

"Thanks, Ilya. The last thing your Dad and I need is a precocious six-year-old sex kitten. So we three can have a conversation together? Can Tamara speak to me without you, Ilya?"

"No, she can't. I am the only one with entry into your mind to protect you. Besides, I can't have her nagging you all day for ice cream when you are supposed to be working."

"You have become so mean since you went away, Ilya. I would only use the most subtle suggestions to acquire what I want." Her tone was light and teasing.

"There is also Dad to consider, and grandpa Leo, you have important tasks at home, Tamara. I have to go, you two. Mummy, your work is outstanding and much appreciated. Love you both."

The void left when Ilya departed made them ache. Tamara was tucked up in her pod, having never moved a muscle, and Julia sat massaging her scalp while she locked up again. It wasn't unusual for her to be in the office in the middle of the night. If she had a brainwave, it was critical to capture it before going back to sleep. Alex usually slept through her nocturnal excursions, but Julia was grateful Ilya ensured his Dad got a good night's rest.

They missed Ilya terribly. His presence, his humour, the light he brought to their world. Julia's receptors were whirring again. Ilya was special, magnetically attractive in such an indefinable way. Why did people love him? What made them react to him the way they did? If she wasn't Ilya's mother, would she still feel compelled to help him? What drove his charisma? They were scientific questions to Julia, not just a mother's musing while missing her firstborn. She unlocked her work on the EBs and focused her attention on Ilya.

Using a similar methodology to the Council Member research, she began to wash and index Ilya's data more thoroughly against a control group. It was more work than she wanted tonight, but it was a start so that she could pick up the thread later. She was so tuned in to the hunt that her eyes snagged on anomalies and differences, and Julia knew she would leap out of bed in the morning. For now, she would snuggle up to Alex, try and get some rest, and give her hard-working baby Tamara some of her food in the morning.

11

Intrusion

Ilya discovered how right Chinta was - most of the Councillor's Assistants knew of Viking's tryst with Montreaux. It ignited a frantic round of invitations, events and attention. It offered Ilya an opportunity to meet the Councillors face-to-face, and he made incursions into their thoughts or explored brains while Viking flirted and charmed his way into their affections or beds. The ever-wily Chinta used the Councillor's lack of control to amuse her master and increase her favour.

"Look at them! They are practically falling out of their clothes before the poor man has even had anything to eat." She squealed with delight as Councillor Tigris and his Assistant Ksenia attempted to seduce him with a provocative dance. "What shocking manners, and so crass. See how he rebuffs them so politely. Tomorrow my background check will be complete, and if all is well, we could rescue him from this Prime. What do you think?" Chinta handed him a fresh drink and offered a plate of exquisite canapes.

She ignored the boy perched on Prime's lap and the couple amusing each other on a raised divan. They were household entertainment, therefore discreet. The penalty for gossip was death or banishment to the mines of Neptune - if Prime spared you.

"The fact they compete, ignoring your claim so blatantly, surprises me. Viking seems incredibly charismatic for a food creator, don't you think? Perhaps I will go over the surveillance myself. I suspect, however,

I will just want him more. Please promise me that he won't replace me in your affections?" Chinta pouted her displeasure coquettishly, looking younger than her years, face stripped of cosmetics. Prime adored youth, and when they were at home, he preferred the natural look. She was cautious, vulnerable, youthful, entertaining him with his pets and plying his mind with her need for his protection.

"My dear Chinta, I doubt anyone could ever replace you. You seem to read my mind and conjure up exactly what I need. Without a doubt, you are the best Assistant I have ever had," he chuckled as his lap-boy nuzzled his ear.

"You honour me with your praise, thank you!" Without humility, Chinta toasted Prime, eliciting another laugh from him.

"I'm sure your surveillance check was perfect, Chinta. No need to torture yourself. I'm not sure I can sit through his exploits again. As soon as you and security clear Argos, bring him to me. Time to assert my authority. We will save him – for ourselves."

Chinta danced around his chair, laughing, and shared kisses with the boy before pirouetting off to join the couple on the divan. While she cemented her place as Prime's premier companion, she divorced herself from her body and crowed success to Ilya.

"It worked, Ilya, and you could be in the mansion tomorrow."

They did it. Prime would invite Viking into his home. Even better, armed with Julia's research, when Ilya ventured into Prime's mind, he would be equipped with a map and signposts. The initial incursions Ilya made were for reconnaissance, although he conducted unique experimental rewiring on each Councillor to ascertain how effective it was. The only Councillor he hadn't fraternised with besides Prime was Stryker. It suited him, as his grandfather was the only person who had met Ilya. No matter how distant, the personal relationship could be more challenging, and Ilya had no desire to find out how kinky his grandfather was.

Ilya chose his glamour with care to appeal to most Councillors and Assistants. He was aware Stryker preferred buxom women. It was also possible Stryker didn't want to cross Prime, as their relationship was as tense as Shand and Montreaux's.

Viking politely declined any post-work invitations, including one from Montreaux, at the risk of offending. Instead, he invited Flame to share a meal with him. He had an ulterior motive. Ilya wanted to copy her access card. She took all maintenance staff assigned to security or surveillance on orientation tours under the city. Prime's security system and the Council chambers were shielded and separate from all the other systems on Sanctuary, and he needed access to them both.

If he disguised Chinta as Flame, kept Flame busy, and reprogrammed all the other systems, he could gain access to the off-limits area through Chinta. Once he was in, he could control everything, but he also needed an alibi to place him above suspicion. Viking would be the most recent entrant to Prime's mansion, so the least trusted unless he was with Prime. Chinta was above suspicion unless she got caught. She would be taking a risk, but they needed control of Prime's security to advance their cause.

Flame was flattered to be invited to Viking's quarters again. His status was above her station, the new darling of the Councillors, but here she was. She dressed with care, not an inch of skin showing, the opposite to what he saw every night, she hoped.

"How lovely to see you again, Flame! You were my first friend in Nirvana, and I feel we have known each other forever. Thanks for coming. I'm exhausted by the hectic work and social calendar. It's beautiful here, but there is no rest. A lovely evening at home with good company is what I'm longing for." Viking smiled at her, and Flame's bones melted. They hadn't seen much of each other recently, and she imagined her memories of him were overblown – but they weren't. As charismatic as the day they met, Viking was unlike anyone else. The problem was that everyone in Nirvana felt the same way, a ridiculous situation Flame didn't appreciate.

"You look lovely, by the way; there is beauty in simplicity and style." He raised his brows to the heavens and brought his hands together in prayer, implying an unfulfilled longing for those qualities. Flame laughed because he was naughty under his impeccable manners. She arched under his praise with a feline purr, the silky touch of the oyster sheath dress caressing her. He made her feel so....exotic, sexy and playful.

Viking served a sumptuous meal, new recipes he was trying, with accompanying beverages of his creation. Conversation flowed freely as he turned up the charm and entertained Flame with a barrage of amusing stories – no names mentioned, of course.

Early the following day, Flame was scheduled to conduct an orientation security tour for a new technology overhaul. Prime commandeered state-of-the-art developments as soon as inventors trialled them, so Flame needed to keep her wits about her. She intended to be cooler towards Viking, with no physical interaction, depart early, but they were having such a good time. Before Flame realised, it was too late. She was in Viking's arms, sighing with pleasure under his satin sheets.

Flame went to sleep. Lulled by drink and coaxed by Ilya, she dreamed. He felt guilty for using Flame's affections against her, but the sheets shielded them from view as he copied her access card. Copying the card wasn't as easy as he hoped it would be. Due to her access, somebody had built additional layers of protection. He carefully peeled them away, dissected the technology, then rebuilt them for Chinta. Flame would be safe here.

The sheets pulled taut above Flame, making the bed appear empty. Ilya reprogrammed the security system to show them leaving together and travelling to Flame's quarters. Only Viking left the building. On the way, he secreted the disguised access card at a pod station and telepathically showed Chinta where he hid it. Chinta would retrieve it on her way home. The surveillance systems would see Viking kiss Flame's hand chivalrously and wave goodbye. An image created on her arrival at his quarters, simply transposed into a new setting, undetectable as Ilya controlled high and low tech systems now.

It was critical to Flame's welfare that she appeared to be at home, exactly where she was supposed to be. Flame had been in Nirvana so long, performing the same role, that she wasn't a person of interest. She was a perfect accomplice with an alibi, captured on spy-tech, sleeping soundly in her quarters. The footage was a seamless montage of her regular evening routine. Chinta would become Flame in the morning, conduct the tour, and give Ilya visibility and access to the tech team.

It was a complicated exercise that would protect Viking, Chinta and Flame with alibis. Chinta would enter a beauty treatment pod at 7 am for molecular treatment. Ilya taught her how to reprogram the pod to show the treatment taking place and manipulate her security so she could leave disguised as Flame. The Flame glamour was relatively easy for Chinta to create once Ilya showed her how, and she would leave the compound using one of her secret exits. The deception was familiar because she organised many private meetings for Prime for business and pleasure.

Viking would sit in plain sight of his staff, working on new recipes and delivery creations, until Prime summoned him to his mansion. Chinta had organised the invitation, and Viking would meet with staff to discuss menus while Prime watched from a distance. It was all very tame, a test, so Chinta excused herself as her beauty routine was paramount.

Three verifiable alibis and Ilya would hide Chinta's movements as Flame until she met the tech team. He would also create footage of Flame leaving her quarters to arrive at the rendezvous, mesh them together, and the city would see everything run smoothly. There wasn't an anomaly for prying eyes to detect in sight. Chinta's snooping system would alert her if he failed, but Ilya was confident in his planning.

Chinta was enjoying herself as Flame and had done her homework. Schematics ran in her head, so she knew exactly where to go. She prepared a brief on each tour participant, filed it in her memory, and added a deep background check. Flame's mannerisms, voice inflexions, and body cues were all mimicked to perfection, but Chinta supplemented charm with telepathic suggestions.

Flame enchanted the tech team, and she focused on their Team Leader. Touching his arm flirtatiously, she reached into his mind, distracting him while Ilya hitched a ride through her connection. It was going much better than planned. Ilya could ride along with the team, exposing Chinta to less risk. Flame didn't have access to the secure area, and she wouldn't need to venture off-limits. Ilya felt the disappointment of his host as Flame wished them luck and turned to depart.

"Wait, Guide Santander," the Team Leader read off her pass, "could we meet later for a drink?"

Chinta turned back, a smile lighting her face. "That would be lovely, Tech Kazdan. I will send you a secure comm." Why not organise Flame a date, she thought? Chinta could plant the tour, the flirting emotions and perhaps Flame would recover from losing Viking. It amused Chinta to play matchmaker, but her focus didn't waver as she had to return home in haste and stealth.

Jonty Kazdan was brilliant at his work. Ilya was relieved to review the modifications in advance, as they were creative innovations. They were lacing Prime's security system with a series of traps designed to trip, identify and hold any invader unaware of them. While Ilya believed he could navigate them now, he doubted the other EBs could without training.

The system upgrades included telepathic intrusion and mind manipulation detectors. Ilya's disappearance spooked Prime, so he protected himself – but too late. Ilya could see everything through Jonty's eyes, including the system brief with Prime's in-house team, and Ilya stepped inside the design. Once inside the security system, Ilya could merge and manipulate the program to report and do his bidding.

Ilya spotted the problem immediately. Prime tagged his household with an invisible skin-tattoo tracker, which alerted Prime the minute Chinta left the building. Ilya had underestimated Prime, who could see where any of his household members were at any time.

It was pure luck that Prime was watching Viking's interview from his breakfast room. The tracking map and silent alert system resided inside an antique writing desk in Prime's bedroom. Ilya worked furiously, altered the alerts to a 'change in routine' flag for housekeeping, and erased all records of Chinta leaving the mansion. After exploring the system, he found hidden data dumps of Chinta's excursion uploaded into multiple external repositories. Like a cyber bloodhound, Ilya traced them, erased them and overwrote the records. If he missed anything, they were both dead.

"I'm so sorry, Chinta, my oversight almost cost us our lives. What an idiot I am! I need you to go into Prime's bedroom. In the second draw of his desk, you will find a low tech alert device. Messages can only be erased in person manually with buttons. I will screen your entry and exit – go now."

As Chinta tubed into her dressing room behind her shoe rack, he detected a spike of fear before she hid it. She undressed swiftly, grabbed a robe and headed to Prime's bedroom through one of the secret entrances. The desk was locked.

"Ilya, there is no second draw, and nothing will open."

"Show it to me." Chinta rested calmly on the chair at Prime's desk, casually examining her nails as she had many times before while waiting for him, but inside she suppressed a sense of rising panic. *"It's an eighteenth-century mechanical desk. I am finding a blueprint for this design - there it is. Reach under the desk. You will feel a tiny lever on the left-hand side, right at the back. It moves in an 'L' shape so push it back first, then slide it to the right."*

Chinta followed Ilya's instructions and heard a satisfying 'click' as the mechanism activated, and the front panel slid open to reveal a set of draws. The offending device was blinking silently. Chinta saw the tracking console flickering under a garment, but her marker showed she was in her dressing room, so she deleted the multiple alerts about her absence. She exhaled a sigh of relief as she slid the draw and front panels closed.

Prime's door opened.

"What are you doing in here?" Chinta asked. Her eyes narrowed suspiciously.

A startled Xenon covered his surprise with aplomb.

"I was about to ask you the same, Chinta. Aren't you scheduled for your beauty treatment this morning?" he queried with a raised eyebrow.

"I finished early to organise a surprise for Prime. So, what brings you here? The bedroom isn't one of your usual haunts." Her smile was sweet, but her voice was steely.

"Come on, Chinta, you know I am supposed to be making Maya, and therefore Shand, believe I'm a reliable source of information for them. Prime asked me to undertake the task and do whatever I needed. What better way than to provide them with a pilfered but unimportant snippet?" Xenon's smile was warm and conspiratorial.

"Oh, what a good idea. You're too clever for your own good," Chinta giggled. "But shoo, because I need the boudoir for my surprise. I will let you know when it's finished, and we never saw each other." She winked at Xenon, allowing her robe to drape open, revealing how naked she was. Xenon was only too happy to make his exit. Encountering Chinta was careless and unexpected, and he needed her support to retain his position.

"That was close. Can you erase Xenon's visit here, Ilya? I believe we can trust him, and I don't want to deal with a new second Assistant right now."

"Yes, I can. We must take more care. What if I missed something again? If Prime exhibits any unusual behaviour, you have to warn me because it means I have fucked up."

When he shared the information, he betrayed his frustration with himself for failing to keep Chinta safe. What he blocked from her was his mental self-flagellation and the haunting trauma of his error. Had he occupied his body, he may have been unable to contain his nausea – Ilya felt sick. Chinta was alarmed at his archaic cursing, but she knew her fate if she betrayed Prime.

While Ilya was busy with security, Viking was charming Prime's staff. The routine Prime's team instigated was thorough. Even when a new person entered the mansion, they still didn't get face-time with Prime. His minions guarded him jealously because they valued their lives and privileges.

None of the Assistants attended because the chefs, kitchen staff, banquet and entertainment coordinators were assigned the task of Viking's first in-house vetting. Prime observed Viking with intense interest. He wasn't just gorgeous, there was something other-worldly, charismatic about Viking Argos, and Prime found himself straining toward the screen to see better.

Assistant Frankie, who was supposed to be serving Prime breakfast, was transfixed – lips parted, hand at his throat, staring at the holo. The youngsters massaging his legs and feet watched the dull meeting unfold with curiosity, as they had never witnessed screening protocol before. Diagnostics ran with results displayed above the holo, revealing Viking's physiological and psychological readings. His heart rate was slightly elevated, consistent with the nervousness betrayed in his emotional activity centre. He was charming and confident on the surface, but his vitals were consistent with a new entrant to the mansion.

Ilya didn't take any chances. He analysed the data for all Prime's cleared personnel to develop appropriate settings for Viking. The more interesting data to Prime was the reaction of his staff to Viking. Ilya noticed the spike and smoothed the data. Adding in the occasional heart-flutter blip to mask the initial surge and prove Viking was interesting.

"Frankie are you going to serve my breakfast or simply drool on it?" asked Prime tritely.

"I'm sorry, I confess I was distracted by Argos. He is quite dreamy in an unsettling sort of way." Frankie blushed while he poured tea and placed Prime's breakfast on the table. "During the Greek Games, I spoke with him briefly even though he was busy; he is quite charming. Shand's Assistant Maya barged her way in, totally disregarding his attention to his duties. I should have pulled rank and saved him." Frankie sighed to himself as if imagining what might have been.

"He must be fascinating, the way you all carry on. Pass me the fruit bowl." Prime always enjoyed a large breakfast, setting his body up for whatever the day held or whatever he wanted if it wasn't busy.

It was as if Viking Argos held court with Prime's staff. They appeared to be amused by his stories and comments, often witty and delivered in a conspiratorial manner. Viking Argos was younger than Prime expected. He could have been a politician, and he had a presence. Prime experienced a thrill of excitement, intoxicated by Viking's youth and inexperience.

Chinta slunk in, wearing a bright yellow silk robe, with hair piled atop her head, skin still pink from her treatment. It was just after 10 am.

"Shoo, you two, and Frankie, I will clear Prime's breakfast."

There was an unmistakable ring of authority in Chinta's voice, leaving them in no doubt of the pecking order. Frankie looked like he might object but instead cast one last look at the holo before leaving. "Did I miss anything, Prime?" She was young, eager, all ears and seemed about 12 years old again once they were alone.

"Nothing noteworthy other than Frankie salivating on my breakfast and my staff being captivated by a handsome stranger." What a gem of a girl Chinta is, thought Prime.

"And what about you? Does he interest you? He is a little older than you prefer, and I can easily remove him if he isn't to your liking. Perhaps I decided to reel him in based on the response of my genitalia and erotic dreams." She smiled sweetly - a filthy-minded, over-sexed child of Prime's making – or so he thought.

"Not at all. Come over here."

Chinta scooted onto Prime's lap and covered his face in breathy kisses before turning her attention to the holo. Prime stroked her arm while they watched their quarry together until the excitement became too much. As Viking Argos left the mansion, Chinta and Prime lay sprawled, sated, but quivering with anticipation. They knew how to play a long game.

With his first visit to the mansion over, the security incursion completed successfully, if not smoothly, Viking returned Flame to her quarters hidden in an enormous box of flowers. After the tour, Ilya doctored the surveillance footage, Chinta implanted the memories so he could recalibrate them, and he left Flame napping on her divan.

Viking took the box of rare flowers to his office. He wowed his staff with abundant blooms available for their first catering event at Prime's mansion. They understood the importance of impressing everyone in attendance with new, never-seen-before catering. The excitement was enormous, but so was the pressure. If you failed Prime, you would be second-rate forever in Sanctuary.

After an intense planning session with his staff, Viking left them to practice his new recipes and decided to check on Flame. On a whim, he took her some flowers. Flame was surprised when Viking appeared on her commscreen, seeking clearance to tube to her quarters.

"I was passing by on my way home and thought I might surprise you with a gift." Viking smiled on Flame's screen, and she cleared his access, smoothing her dishevelled hair after her nap.

"How lovely of you to drop by Viking. I wasn't expecting to see you so soon." Flame kissed his cheek in a familiar greeting, and he captured her hand, touching it to his lips.

"I trust you enjoyed our evening as much as I did. You are a wonderful friend, Flame, and I couldn't resist bringing you these gorgeous flowers." Viking presented her with a transparent cylinder of exotic blooms, in myriad shades of orange and red, in homage to her hair. Flame was taken aback by his thoughtful gesture.

"Viking, they are beautiful. Thank you, I don't know what to say." Face flushed with pleasure; he was genuinely pleased she liked them. "Would you like to come in for some tea?"

"No, thank you. I am incredibly busy with the upcoming event at Prime's mansion, and I don't normally impose on people unannounced.

It was a spontaneous decision. I will leave you to get on with your evening, but yesterday we shared more than dinner, and I felt you deserved a gesture of appreciation." He grinned cheekily, teasing her as he returned to the tube.

"You are incorrigible Viking Argos," Flame called after him as he disappeared, "and I think I love you," she whispered to the flowers.

Ilya was plundering the databanks of Prime's private security system. Prime was at the apex of the food chain for a reason. His intelligence gathering network was extensive, and his ability to recognise threats was a highly evolved art. The recent access and review of Ilya's files was testimony to that. There was data on all the Council members, but information banks on Stryker and Montreaux, who Prime identified as the highest-risk internal threats.

There was also information on Ming, her threat-risk level during her life, and the Erase Order. Prime monitored Stryker's entire family. Julia was rated low-risk, as she never visited Sanctuary, started a family, and was occupied in a monitored profession. He could also see the records regarding Chinta and how her profile met Prime's selection criteria and his approval for her acquisition, which led to her abduction. Chinta's physical training and psychological manipulation had been akin to Pavlov's dogs. Fortunately for Chinta as an EB, she exceeded expectations by rising above their crude methods. Her ability to shield herself mentally from whatever task she was engaged in, and have a normal telepathic conversation appropriate for her age, saved her. She also learned to control and manipulate them instead, rising through the ranks and casting herself as Prime's most trusted Assistant and companion.

Prime anticipated and disposed of anyone who posed a threat to him. He eliminated those foolish enough to stand in his way as he rose to power. No wonder he watched Montreaux as she was following in his footsteps. However, Prime had leverage, and he knew everyone's dirty little secrets, while Prime's background was both intriguing and disturbing.

Born Charles Roderick James Martel, he was a gifted child who began studying medicine at 15 in 2010. His father was a French-English aristocrat and business investor in technology, and his mother was a Japanese-American psychiatrist and artist.

At 20, Prime relocated from London to Tokyo to further his studies and boarded with his mother's dearest friends, Patrick and Masako. They had a 10-year-old daughter, Keiko. Although the official records showed, Prime led an everyday life as a doctor completing his hospital training, dated a few girls, and had a couple of relationships, his most private cache of data told a different story. Charles had always been a privileged, spoiled predator and paedophile. Covering up his illegal activities and protecting himself from exposure was necessary from a young age, and he became increasingly adept at it.

Charles' lifestyle was the perfect training regime to acquire the skills required to develop and maintain his position as Prime. Officially he reunited with Keiko when she was seventeen, after a brief separation when he left Tokyo for Paris. Ostensibly, she had moved to Paris to study art at the Sorbonne. Charles and Keiko became engaged when she was 18 and married when she was twenty, all very respectable. Keiko's parents were thrilled to gain a brilliant and charming son-in-law who they knew well. If only they had known the truth. Charles had groomed their beloved daughter into his chosen lifestyle since she was 10. They were a couple and lovers for almost ten years when they married. It didn't last long. By the time Keiko was 25, Charles had long grown bored with her, and she conveniently committed suicide.

Ilya flowed like smoke through a keyhole into Charles' and Prime's most protected data vault, where he stored diaries and treasured mementoes of his conquests. The man was a twisted, perverted monster – he had to go. Keiko hadn't been his first victim. Charles' offending had begun as a child.

When his parent's high society friends brought other children to their country house, he discovered he enjoyed the power of dominating them sexually. He began to look forward to entertaining their visitors in this manner because it satisfied him. Finding Charles' keepsakes and trophies reinforced Ilya's resolve to depose Prime and the Council. However, he needed to tread more cautiously as Prime possessed a dangerously inventive mind.

One of the five per cent, Charles was neglected as a child by hedonistic parents, raised by resentful servants, abused by his parent's friends, but he had survived to wipe them all out. If Ilya had a fault, it was his lack of comprehension of the drivers of ruthless people. The Goodness Algorithm hadn't erred. He needed Chinta more than ever to decode Prime and anticipate his manoeuvres. This incursion would prepare him for the horrors he would encounter in Prime's psyche, but first, Ilya must find a way inside.

They found Flame's body floating in the lagoon naked. A lilac scarf still hung around her neck, the marks in her flesh proclaiming the cause of her death – strangulation. Nobody had committed a crime in Sanctuary for over forty years. Gossip and speculation spread like a contagious disease through Nirvana. Chinta was one of the first people to become aware of the issue and alerted Ilya immediately.

She pounded, which wasn't necessary as Ilya recognised her mind's touch and distress. *I am sorry to be the bearer of bad news, Ilya, but your friend Flame is dead. Delivery workers found her body in the lagoon a few minutes ago. Someone strangled her with a lilac scarf. Wasn't Montreaux wearing lilac the night you met her on the lagoon?*

"Yes, she was. I also declined an invitation from her as you suggested and spent the evening with Flame instead. Do you think it was Montreaux? She is capable of murder. Poor Flame, this is all my fault, Chinta – how can I ever forgive myself? I nearly cost you your life, and now Flame is dead because of me. My rewiring of Montreaux was too powerful."

Chinta was overwhelmed by sadness and guilt as Ilya's grief momentarily escaped him. He had used Flame as an experiment, then as a pawn in their plan, only to find his kindness sentenced her to death. A second mistake, an error of judgment with a fatal result, shook Ilya's confidence, and they could not afford self-doubt. He believed he should have anticipated Montreaux's reaction to rejection.

"Don't be silly, Ilya. Pull yourself together. You can't anticipate psychopathic behaviour from somebody you have only met once. However, I fear you underestimate your appeal, as my own feelings for you are rather turbulent. I feel sorry for the loss of Flame's life, but the jealous monster residing in me isn't so magnanimous – I am ashamed of that. You and I cannot control every thought or reaction of other people and certainly not the Council. We are just beginning to understand them. Where were you this evening? Do you have an alibi? You will be a suspect and should expect an investigator any time soon."

Chinta's words provided the metaphorical slap Ilya needed to focus on the plan, and she was pleased with her distraction.

"I have been with my staff the entire evening. We are still in the kitchen, preparing for Prime's event."

"This is good news Ilya, you have an alibi, and you have no power to organise Erase Orders. The investigators are on their way up. Love you."

Chinta disappeared, just as Ilya had when he told her he loved her. Now they were even, and Ilya could ponder what those words meant to him. She hoped it wouldn't distract him from protecting himself against Montreaux's wrath. It was unlikely Montreaux would admit she eliminated such low-ranked competition, but she was sending Ilya a clear message that she considered him hers.

It was a tricky situation for Viking when Prime felt the same propriety that Montreaux did. It rankled Chinta that Viking, therefore Ilya, was considered fair game for sport. They behaved like spoiled children, fighting over toys with no thought of consequences for anyone else. Ilya was her friend, but she also loved him and wanted him to love her as more than a friend. While they battled to change the world, she must find a way to capture his heart and share her life with him. Not an easy task when the competition was so fierce.

The investigators were indeed at Ilya's door.

"Viking Argos?"

"Yes, I am he."

"My name is Yannik Shaq, and I am an investigator with the PSA, Personal Security Authority. I believe you are acquainted with Flame Santander – is that correct?"

"That is correct. Flame is a friend of mine. We met when I arrived in Nirvana. Has something happened to her?"

"What makes you ask that?"

"The fact you are here from the PSA without an appointment." Viking washed Yannik with his concern for Flame, an entirely authentic emotion.

"Flame Santander was found dead a few minutes ago, floating in the lagoon." Yannik Shaq observed Viking's face to gauge his reaction to the news. His face paled, and he seemed genuinely concerned, but this city was full of actors and liars.

"Where have you been for the last two hours?"

"Right here, in the kitchen with my staff. We are preparing for an event at Prime's mansion tomorrow. Preparation takes meticulous care and attention. Would you like a drink? I'm sorry, but this is a shock, and I need one."

"Yes, thank you. I have heard much talk of your ambrosia, and I may never have an opportunity to try it again."

"Rania, would you be so kind as to fetch two cups of ambrosia, please?" The girl nodded at her boss shyly and returned briskly with the beverages.

It was the truth, he wanted to try ambrosia, but Shaq also wanted to spend more time with Viking Argos. After many years on the job, Shaq trusted his enhanced instincts to notice anything extraordinary. This man was not ordinary. He seemed genuine, shocked, and upset, but although Shaq couldn't put his finger on it, something was jangling. Santander and Argos had been occasional lovers – not unusual in Nirvana.

The rumour mill was whispering Argos had been entertained personally by at least three Council members, even though Prime had tagged him. That was extraordinary and likely to inhibit his investigation, as the Council members were above being questioned. He was certainly attractive, and once one of them wanted you, the rest of the pack joined in the chase.

Shaq suspected someone had killed Flame Santander because of her relationship with this man. In over sixty years as a senior investigator, he had never encountered a death of this nature. Murder no longer existed, only Erase Orders, and only Councillors could issue those – case closed. In this case, the problem was that the death was in a public place, so everyone in Nirvana knew about it. He would discuss it with the Head of the PSA. A night of passion that went awry, something of that ilk would satisfy the public without causing panic. Some dispensable innocent person would be blamed and punished by the Council.

"Forgive me, Officer Shaq, I fear I am neither good company nor helpful. What exactly happened to Flame? I saw her yesterday. Apologies if you aren't permitted to share information with me."

"It is, unfortunately, public knowledge – somebody strangled her, and the coroner confirmed the cause of death at the scene. She had no clone insurance, so she is truly dead." Both men sipped their ambrosia, its deliciousness circumnavigating each tastebud, causing sighs to escape their lips.

"That is better than any description I ever had," said Shaq, closing his eyes to savour a little more. "Did Flame seem upset about anything? Or did she talk about any unusual encounters or occurrences in her life?"

"No, we gossiped, laughed, talked about poetry, fashion, food and – well, we were lovers, no talking necessary. I dropped by yesterday to take her some flowers, and she seemed happy." Viking sipped his drink while he sat deep in thought.

"We were on the scene quickly and have retrieved Flame's memory images, which we hope will assist us with our investigations. Can you think of anyone who wanted to harm Flame?"

"No, no, I can't." Viking looked at the ground when he responded. Shaq sensed he felt guilty and maybe a little scared, unsurprising when one of the Councillors he spent time with was Montreaux.

"She never mentioned a man by the name of Jonty Kazdan?" asked Shaq. Viking shook his head. "They met on a security orientation and were supposed to meet for a drink. Not surprising she didn't mention this to you," said Shaq silkily, watching Viking's face for a reaction. "Allegedly, she never showed up. We are questioning him and checking his movements. If you remember anything, please contact me at the PSA. Thank you for the ambrosia, and good luck with your event."

Yannik Shaq had lived in Nirvana long enough to understand it was wiser to be polite than make enemies. He was authentic in wishing them good luck, as everyone knew disappointing Prime was a one-time experience. Prime had sent people on deep-space missions for less than serving disappointing food.

12

Preparation

Xian kept in close contact with Julia and Alex. He doted on Tamara wistfully whenever he came over, and they bonded in such a sweet way, comforting each other in the absence of their siblings. It was lovely for Tamara to have a big brother to play with and eat treats together. Julia knew they shared EB news and spent time with Chinta and Ilya. Externally they played, but Julia wondered what they discussed. The world's future sat heavily on the slim shoulders of children – how had it come to this, she questioned? She organised a delicious afternoon tea with plenty of treats, benefiting Tamara's tiny frame and high metabolism.

"Would you like juice, milk or tea, Xian?"

"Tea, thank you, Julia – do you have jasmine?" She nodded and made jasmine tea for two but poured Tamara a strawberry protein thick shake. Alex joined them, and they chattered happily, enjoying being four people around their table again.

"I have some news," said Xian, "my parents are considering making a new start on another planet. There are so many memories of Chinta here for us; they feel a change of environment might be beneficial. Close a chapter, if you will. After so many years, we have to go on living," he sighed sadly but looked pointedly at Julia. Xian knew Ilya spoke to her and that Chinta was alive, so Julia deduced there was a purpose behind his musing. Protecting his parents was Xian's job, just as Ilya watched over them.

"Are we going to move to another planet, Daddy? How will I'ya find us if he comes home?" Alex's brow creased in a frown, considering how to answer Tamara's question without hurting Xian's feelings.

"We haven't considered it, Tam. Ilya hasn't been gone as long as Chinta, and I hope he will come back. I do understand why Xian's family are thinking about it, though. Everything here reminds us of Ilya." He ruffled Tamara's hair and smiled at her, his grey eyes bright.

"Alex is right, Xian. We have never thought about it. Have your parents decided where and when you might go?"

"They are looking at prospectus at the moment. Tamara is right, we want Chinta to find us if she ever does come home, so initially, we looked at Mars or Io. My parents don't believe it's likely Chinta will ever return, so they are also considering other star systems."

"How do you feel about that, Xian?" Julia put her hand on his. If she was concerned the conversation might be distressing him, that was what she would do.

"Devastated Julia, I am torn in two. I love my sister, and I'm desperate to believe she is alive. At the same time, my parents aren't coping well. My mother still cries every day and is undergoing grief therapy regularly. My father never speaks of Chinta, but sometimes he sits in her room and looks sad. If they need to move, I must go with them."

"I don't want you to go, Xian!" Tamara's bottom lip trembled, and her eyes filled with tears.

"Oh, Tamara, I don't want to leave you either, but I am now my parents' only child. They will never grant my mother another child permit after the issues with Chinta and her emotional instability – understand?" Tamara nodded but looked glum.

"Come, Tamara, I didn't come here to make you feel bad. Why don't we play a game? You can choose whatever you like?" The offer perked

Tamara up, and she raced to her room, Dash yapping behind as she decided what to play. "Hope that is okay, Julia?"

"Of course, it is Xian. She looks forward to your visits because she misses Ilya. You are very kind, thank you." Julia hugged Xian affectionately. He was a terrific kid and a talented EB. Ilya would fill her in at some stage because Xian's news caught them by surprise. That was undoubtedly the point, to create a genuine reaction. They were planning something together, and she needed to play along.

"Alex, do you think we need to move on? I will never give up, hoping Ilya will return and we are lucky to have Tamara, but our lives have – changed, diminished. We can't replace the space Ilya left." Julia ran her fingers through her hair.

"I – I can't move on, Julia. Ilya was my best friend – if I ever gave up on hope, I think I would die. You and Tamara are all that keep me going, but I find it difficult. Maybe we could try relocating to another city if you believe it will help us, but I don't want to leave without knowing what happened to our boy." Alex's face crumpled with distress, so Julia moved to his side and drew him to her.

"We don't have to do anything you don't want to, Alex. Who can say if that's a solution for us or not? You know me; I am a logic girl, so let's not rule anything in or out – keep all options open. What do you say?" Alex rubbed the tears from his face against her and nodded, his pain palpable. Nobody could fake those emotions.

The following day, Julia worked in her office on the EB data when Ilya arrived.

"It pains me to hurt Dad this way, and I wouldn't do it unless it were necessary. His pain is quantifiable. It excludes him from suspicion and allows me to provide you with similar data. The weakest chinks in our EB armour are our humanity, kindness, and love for our families. Before we

embark on our plan, we need to get our families to safety. There will be an enormous drive to colonise new cities, other planets and systems because we need to get the people we love out of reach, or the authorities may use you as leverage against us. You are one of the few people who understands the Council, perhaps the only human who recognises them for what they are. That is a dangerous position. Our evacuation plan has been underway for two years, and most EBs have relatives in secure locations. Xian and I can't afford to draw more attention, but you must be safe as we enter the final stages. Granny was assigned to explore the depths of Jupiter's moon oceans last year, and Grandpa Dmitry has been offered several promotions and will accept one when you all move. Grandpa Leo will volunteer to be with you, and Tamara will implant ideas to smooth the transition."

"But Ilya, how can you expect us to leave you behind? You can implant all you like, I'm your mother and researcher, and I forbid you to mess with my reasoning. What if you need me?" Julia conveyed her exasperation well telepathically, which amused Ilya.

"Funnily enough, I anticipated your reaction, so relax. You aren't actually leaving. Your shuttle will malfunction, and my whole family, all Stryker's off-Sanctuary relatives, will die. You need to trust me and have faith in me. When the time comes, I will tell you what to do, and you must follow my instructions without deviation. Can you do that for me - please?"

There was a ring of authority in Ilya's voice as he outlined the plan, but the tone of his 'please' reminded Julia of him asking for movies and popcorn. She missed those days on the couch with Alex and Ilya.

"Ah, so you admit you need your long-suffering mother! That's more like it. Ilya, I will follow you to the end of the universe, and I trust you implicitly. I promise to follow your instructions precisely because my instincts tell me that our lives may depend on them. So you promise me

that your plan is solid, well thought out, logical and that you will succeed. We cannot lose you again."

"You are a taskmaster Mummy," he laughed. *"I swear I will do everything you ask. And I still need your expertise, so stay on that research."*

"I finished working on our data concerning Grandma's death Ilya. There were no dramatic changes to you or me. Tamara, however, exhibits major development in her flight-fight region. I don't know what the change means for a young child, but I monitor her. I love you."

The familiar ache of separation filled Julia as Ilya departed to his physical life. She was grateful for the contact and the knowledge that Ilya lived, but it wasn't easy letting him go. At least she had communication, unlike poor Alex, who tossed and turned last night. After Alex left, Tamara reassured her that Daddy would be okay, and Julia just needed to organise a nice dinner. Then magically, her Dad commed to ask if Tamara could have a sleepover at his place. Now there were two children taking control of their lives. The thought brought a smile, so she opened her work portals and dived in.

Julia was analysing the social relationships of the Council, the pecking order. There was a lot to digest. From what she could ascertain, Stryker ranked second, probably driving him mad. Shand was third, as she maintained a staunch affiliation with Prime, voting with him and supporting his recommendations. There were two long-serving Councillors, Cassini and Xao, who predated Prime. Both were capable, intelligent politicians and maintained status above the rest of the pack until recently.

Montreaux was rising in rank. She muscled her way into the halls of power, taking control of anything on offer that nobody else wanted to do. Her command of technology bordered on genius, and nothing phased her. Everything was a game. Anything was a weapon to her

- beauty, sex, gossip she could use as leverage, to the appeal of her many Assistants. She enjoyed manipulating other Councillors into the position she wanted, using bribery, blackmail, or any other form of influence that would work. Montreaux was climbing to the top of the pack with no loyalty, morals, or scruples to keep her in check.

The most aware, or perhaps the most threatened Councillor, was Shand - hence their fierce rivalry. Prime kept an extensive dossier on Montreaux, so he monitored her, but Julia wondered if he or Stryker considered her a serious threat.

One dynamic that never changed in the Council was its leadership by men. Prime and Vice Deputy were male-dominated positions, female representation was only thirty per cent, and Shand had achieved the highest status since the Council's inception. The social interplay between the Council members was complex, with constant vying for importance, relevance and significance. Prime ruled over them, but their obsession with 'sport' was an extension of the competitive environment.

Julia wanted to share this information with Ilya because it could be helpful to him. He had left so abruptly that she didn't get a chance to share her findings, but she had an idea.

"Tamara honey, want to come to my office and we can comm Grandpa Leo? He wants you to visit for a sleepover tonight – what a surprise, huh!" Tamara grinned, looking pleased with herself and skipped into Julia's office. Julia secured her official files but left her unofficial report on an old tablet Tamara used for play. While Julia was chatting to her Dad, Tamara scanned the information and shared it with Ilya before turning it upside down.

"Will we have ice cream if I come and visit?" Tamara's love of ice cream was legendary, but she never put on any weight because of her brain driven energy burn.

"What kind of Grandpa would I be if I didn't get my best girl ice cream? And I have cartoons and anime. I can pick you up in two hours. Does that give you enough time to decide what flavour ice cream you want?"

"You know I always pick strawberry, Grandpa. You are sooooo silly. I'll be ready. See you soon." Tamara jumped off her chair and went back to her developmental game.

"Thanks, Dad. She is always so excited to spend time with you. I really appreciate it."

"No problem, Juli, I love her to bits, same as you. See you soon."

"I have it, Mummy. Good thinking with Tamara. The information is fascinating. Thank you, and is there anything else? I forgot to ask last time." Julia let Ilya know she would have more research in a few days but would wait for his contact unless it was urgent.

Face to Face

The big moment was upon them. Viking Argos and his team were catering for the most powerful man in the land, Prime. Activity had been frenetic, nerves taut, stress levels high, but Viking breezed through it all. He praised, cajoled, tasted, laughed and clapped his hands, applauding the enormous effort they made. The catering team dressed as magicians, witches, wizards, magi, fortune tellers, genies, for they would be creating magic.

The event concept created by Chinta was brilliant, and Xenon organised entertainment. A cavernous banquet hall now masqueraded as an enchanted forest, with a tinkling waterfall and stream. Life-like virtual birds and beasts roamed in the woods while nymphs played music, wending through floating tables. Prime would be seated on a throne, placed on a dais, dressed as the forest king.

Six Council members had private tables. They never attended entertainment events together, as it was too risky. Since Montreaux refined the security on Sanctuary, they were comfortable attending soirees but took turns at events. Prime's events were lavish and infrequent. Nobody wanted to miss out, but the computer excluded Stryker and Montreaux from the randomly selected invitations.

Shand was beside herself, as she loathed them both and would be the highest-ranking Councillor next to Prime. Accordingly, she attended as

Queen of the enchanted forest with a large entourage. Chinta shared details of the event with Ilya to aid Viking in making an impression. Guests arrived at the event early as the screening was meticulous. Once everyone invited or those participating was inside, security would seal the venue until Prime retired.

Viking waited in the catering glade until everyone was in before unleashing his witches and warlocks to conjure drinks for their guests. They waited for Prime to make his grand entrance. And grand it was. Prime arrived atop a bejewelled elephant, flanked by Xenon with tigers on leashes, Chinta with spotted leopards and a troupe of gorgeous forest fairies descending from above on vines.

"Welcome to the enchanted forest. Let the festivities begin," boomed Prime.

The lights dimmed, the trees lit with festoons of fairy lights, and it was suddenly an enchanted night forest, which matched the costumes of Prime's staff. Chinta was stunning, scantily clad in animal skin and strategically placed leaves, while a butterfly wing cloak floated around her. Xenon gleamed like polished wood adorned with leather and flowers.

Viking was momentarily distracted by the show, eyes snagging on Chinta, affected by her allure like everyone else in the room – she was powerful. Snapping back to his duties, Viking launched his catering show.

A genie coaxed an ambrosia fountain from the floor to great fanfare while the witches and warlocks whisked it away in leaf-shaped dishes to waiting tables. Giant butterflies flew in bearing edible trays laden with canapes shaped like bugs, each an artfully crafted bite, bursting with flavour. Fluorescent mushrooms grew from the floor next to the tables. Their crowns opened to reveal lobster disguised as mushrooms and truffled potato dressed as a lobster. The chocolate mousse was pate, jelly that was salted spinach, and apples were cheese encased with toffee crackling. Viking created Daliesque eggs from chicken with saffron mayonnaise, melting artistically, and so the magic went on. Robot peacocks circulated with cocktails laced with natural aphrodisiacs while a parade of delicacies flowed past on bamboo rafts floating on the stream.

The guests were stunned by the show and seduced by the delicate tastes stroking their palettes. They had thought Viking talented before, but now they believed him a genius, and Prime was impressed. Xenon's entertainment commenced allowing the guests time to recover while Viking and his team prepared the dessert.

Erotic fairies twirled on vines provocatively or hung from swings on the trees. Snakeskin clad dancers entwined their bodies to music before teasing the guests by involving them in the dance. Animals performed tricks or danced with the musicians, bringing much laughter to the merry banquet. Finally, it was time for dessert.

Magicians marched on each table and conjured fruit from their hats, sleeves, and thin air. The caterers did not simply produce fruit but had made the watermelon from candy lime skin, vanilla cream white, and raspberry flavoured flesh with chocolate seeds. The oranges were peach and pear, lemons banana flavoured, and the strawberries made from pomegranate and mint. Nothing was as it seemed, and the guests clapped their hands in appreciation. Chinta fed Prime grapes that were plum and guava jelly sweets and saw his eyes sparkle with the novelty of surprise – he was enjoying himself. She noticed Prime dart furtive glances at Viking, who was too busy to see anyone - a magnet to a man used to commanding attention. Smiling sweetly, Chinta whispered in Prime's ear.

"I saw you undressing him with your eyes. He is so delicious that I could devour him like this strawberry." She crushed the pomegranate flavoured fruit between her teeth, allowing the juice to trickle from her mouth onto her breasts. Prime licked the liquid off, making Chinta squeal, "it tickles!" They both erupted in peals of laughter.

The finale of the dessert was spectacular. From the centre of each table, a tree began to grow. It was a chocolate tree adorned with hand-crafted leaves, each one a dessert of a different flavour – crème Brulee, pavlova, Sacha torte, crème caramel, truffle mousse – they were exquisite. If that wasn't enough, it began to snow delicate creamy flakes of white chocolate and sparkling golden honeycomb, which eddied to coat each tree with another layer of beauty.

Guests clapped and stamped their feet in appreciation, passions fuelled by the accompanying dessert drinks. Viking Argos summoned his team to his side, where they took a bow together. The diners showered them with the exotic flowers they had used to decorate the tables and chairs. Glowing with pride, Viking was radiant as the head magician. He wore a bronze mask over his eyes, tight breeches in deepest green, long boots in soft fawn suede, but he was naked from his bronze belt up. Magical runes and symbols chased across his bare skin below a gold snake torque. Golden, perfectly painted lips smiled as Viking waved his staff in the air, struck a rock, and released a flow of his latest creation – nectar of the Gods. The banquet dining came to a triumphant close to more rapturous applause.

Chinta materialised at Viking's side. "Prime would like to thank you. Please follow me." Viking signalled his Second to oversee the dispensation of beverages and followed Chinta towards the dais. Heads turned as Chinta passed. She was the most famous Assistant in the land, Prime's favourite, young, fashionable and alluring. Even Shand envied her and her relationship with Prime. She forgot Chinta had been abducted as a child and grew up in servitude in the mansion, hardly a perfect upbringing. After Chinta passed they found themselves gawking at Viking Argos – they were both beautiful, and Prime would have both! Xenon cued the entertainers.

"I present to you, your banquet dining organiser, Viking Argos." Chinta stepped to the side, ushering Viking into the limelight to be examined by Prime.

"Well, Argos, I enjoyed the fare this evening. Extremely creative." Prime's grin appeared predatory.

"It was an honour to work in your banquet hall. I thank you for the opportunity to conduct my food experiments upon such illustrious guinea pigs," said Viking cheekily, eyes twinkling, as he executed an elaborate bow. Prime clapped his hands laughing. The boy was a natural entertainer and hadn't uttered the usual banal, polite pleasantries. He was more than a pretty face with a fine body.

"Chinta, Xenon is busy. Perhaps Argos can join us to entertain us for a while. Maybe you should pour him a drink- what do you say?"

"I say that is a splendid idea, but I was going to propose he sat in my lap," she pouted prettily, already pouring and eliciting more laughter from Prime.

"I'm sorry, Argos. Chinta has no shame. That is why she is my favourite."

"No need to apologise. I can see many reasons why Assistant Chinta would be anybody's favourite." Viking and Prime chuckled, enjoying the flirtation, and felt the pull towards each other.

For the rest of the evening, the three engrossed each other. Conversation sparkled as the trio discreetly made fun of many people, discussed the entertainers candidly, sometimes crudely, laughed until their faces hurt, and sparks flew. Chinta and Viking implanted subtle thoughts for Prime, and Viking radiated attraction, pushing all the buttons Chinta had shared with him. Ilya was weaving a net of magnetism around Prime with pheromones, mind bonding, physical body cues, internal stimulation of hormones and chemicals.

"Time for me to retire from the banquet. Come, Viking, join us." It wasn't an invitation, or a command, but an assumption. People didn't refuse Prime. "Chinta, you too. I hate to break up our merry trio, we've had tremendous fun, and the night is young." Chinta smirked, but she hoped Prime would entertain Viking alone as they had planned.

Everyone in the hall paused and rose to their feet as Prime exited, signalling an end to the banquet. Each had plans for the night of sport ahead. Shand watched the departing figures disappear, and she was disappointed she didn't receive an invitation to join Prime. She was Prime's most loyal supporter, and Viking Argos had been hers first. With a frown, Shand whispered instructions in Maya's ear. She didn't care for the sleight and all was fair in love and sport.

Chinta walked ahead to the exit tunnel, while Prime took Viking's arm with a proprietary air, leading them to a private lounge area in the mansion. It was one of Prime's favourite rooms in the house, less cavernous, more comfortable and intimate. A vast circular bed occupied one end, scattered chairs and divans with low tables, muted lighting, and a rotating entertainment stage. If Prime wanted to be alone, he could get rid of any act with a wave of his hand. The décor was art deco, a high-class bordello. Out of the public eye, Chinta poured Prime a glass of 100-year-old scotch whiskey, his favourite post-event indulgence.

"May I offer you a drink, Viking?" Chinta was a consummate hostess.

"As Prime has chosen a historical beverage, I will do the same. How about a Gin Fizz?" He grinned a challenge at Chinta. She surprised him by smugly serving the perfectly mixed classic cocktail in a period cut-crystal glass. Prime hooted with laughter as Viking took a sip before inclining his head to appreciate Chinta's skill. It was quite a feat to impress a caterer of Viking's calibre, but Prime frequently called upon Chinta to create refreshments for the fussiest people. "How did you find the perfect woman, Prime?" Viking drawled lazily between sips as Chinta moved to the other side of the room.

"Chinta was trained in this house, to create the perfect companion, entertainer and hostess. Impressive, isn't she? Whip-smart, politically savvy, stunning in a sea of never-ending beauty, and filthier than an avalanche of mud." Prime chuckled to himself. "Chinta knows more tricks than all those entertainers at the banquet put together and anticipates my desires."

He brought his face within millimetres of Viking's and swam in his unusual eyes before pulling away to help himself to a plump stuffed olive. Prime, like Chinta, was intoxicated by the self-denial and anticipation of the chase. It was almost unbearable and made him feel so alive. A band started to play. All youths dressed in 1920s costumes played jazz while Chinta, now attired as a cabaret diva, crooned classics. Her voice was husky, dripping with sex appeal and smoky with unfulfilled lust. It provided the perfect backdrop for Viking to enthral Prime and Ilya to make his first foray.

Chinta reached her familiar presence into Prime's mind, and Ilya flowed in on her connection. Viking was engaging Prime's senses on many levels. Chinta rotated the stage to exit the room and replaced the band with a troupe of erotically cavorting nymphs. She was out. Chinta had no desire to share Ilya with Prime, even as Viking. He meant too much to her, and she wanted to monitor Ilya's progress and help him if she could. Prime was a subject she knew well, and Ilya would link if he needed her.

Ilya could see Prime's brain areas alight with Viking's stimulation and the superhighway of neural connectivity. Stealthily, he eavesdropped on Prime's thoughts and emotions, making himself tiny and invisible. Unlike Montreaux, Prime experienced emotion, but his feelings were disciplined through years of regimented control.

EB, Chinta, had wormed her way past his defences – using her abilities over a sustained period, leaving a minuscule chink in his armour. The entry point appeared before Ilya. He approached the inner workings of Prime's mind cautiously, knowing he had blundered once already. Intuition signaled a warning to Prime, but Ilya drowned him in a flood of sexual desire for Viking while he calmed the intuitive area with rapid rewiring. Ilya slithered past Prime's defences through the chink, and beheld the inner sanctum of his mind. It was disturbing.

The warning of Prime's intuition was fortuitous if ineffective because his private data was exposed. Over a century of foul deeds, his own and other people's brutality, depravity, scheming, genocide, and the extermination of entire nations like ant colonies were all filed inside Prime's head.

The Council had positioned itself as the saviour of the human race. This handful of people had controlled a disproportionate percentage of the planet's wealth. They were the cause of many of the woes that afflicted the earth. In their greedy quest for more wealth, they had overthrown governments, started wars, hoarded resources to drive profits, eventually banding together to take control. The Black Years began. The elite designed them to achieve calculated objectives and create a utopian vision. They wrote history that was a collection of lies, casting themselves as the saviours of the human race.

A tiny beacon shone alone in that dark place, a speck of goodness. It was the essence of Chinta who dwelt in Prime's mind. In all these horrors, Chinta's kindness and inner beauty remained authentic and untouched. Chinta looked after Prime with unstinting care whether he was her abductor or not.

Prime was considering keeping Chinta as his permanent companion; he had already halted her physical development to keep her from ageing – that was why he'd indulged her request for breasts. Ilya didn't dare share the information with Chinta, as nobody should see something so distressing without warning. He enhanced Prime's sex drive to give himself more time to absorb information. Prime would have a sustained evening of pleasure with his latest conquest while Ilya searched for anything to help their cause.

There it was - Prime's desire for continuity drove his ability to identify threats and neutralise them. Prime was constantly identifying, hunting, and training like a prize-fighter seeking to retain his position at the top. The next threat would come from Stryker or Montreaux. He wasn't sure which one would move against him first. That posed a dilemma. Conflict with one would leave him vulnerable to the other. He would assume the position of the aggressor. Dispose of one of his enemies first, but he had to decide which one to eliminate.

The wily old fox searched for Ilya, and he had executed the Erase Order. Ilya sensed the shift in brain activity driving Prime's body and knew it was time to leave. Again he took extraordinary care, slipping out secretly, rewiring behind him as he went, marking the path for his return.

Chinta preceived Ilya's walls going up. She assumed Prime's mind was even uglier than Montreaux's, and Ilya tried to shield her. Considering she was Prime's play-thing for years, lived in his mansion, she wondered what was so horrible Ilya needed to hide it. Prime displayed unusual self-restraint and stamina this evening. As she watched the holo box, Chinta thought it a pity Viking was wasted on such an old man. But Prime was her old man and benefactor for the moment, she thought with an exasperated sigh. Just as the entertainment reached a climax, Chinta reconnected with Ilya in a surge of energy.

"How was it? Did you get in? What did you find?"

"That's a lot of questions at once, Chinta. I need to gather my thoughts, such a lot of information, and I want to focus on building Prime's need for Viking. I can imitate his feelings for you. There, that's better. Gosh, I thought Montreaux was ugly. She is out-classed by Prime, it's like comparing a piranha with a shark. I did get in, thanks to you, Chinta. You have wheedled your way into his affections, and Prime is considering you as a permanent companion."

"Yay for me – slayer of perverted old men's hearts," she said, devoid of enthusiasm.

"It's important, Chinta, because you created a chink in his armour, giving me access to his fortress. I don't want to share the horrors with you yet. We have a job to do, you still live here, and have a part to play. However, I will show you what I found out about his plans for Stryker and Montreaux." Ilya shared Prime's plan and the dossiers from the security data bank with Chinta. She immediately grasped the opportunity presented to them.

"Are we ready, Ilya?"

"Almost Chinta. I need to implement a strategy and mobilise the EB network. Is it conceivable for Prime to remove me from my catering duties?"

"Yes, of course, he can do anything he wants. You need more time and access. We can achieve this quickly between us – I have to go, Ilya, Prime likes to shower after...I'll be in touch."

It was helpful Chinta was returning to Prime. Ilya linked with Xian, who connected with Paul, an EB in Greenland who activated the underground telepathic network. They always cloaked Ilya and relayed his messages through different EB activation points for unpredictability and security of the group.

Thousands, hundreds of thousands of EBs joined their minds to listen to Ilya. A call to action was coming. One person would relay the plan and each person's part in that plan individually—EBs with single-cell tasks to avoid compromise or failure. Ilya was formulating a daring strategy with fail-safe protocols and workarounds, so they could execute if authorities discovered any person or their piece of the puzzle. Ilya would undertake most of the frontline work with Chinta and the EBs located in Nirvana, whose minds were authorised by Ilya. Not all were trustworthy, so Ilya walled the risks out of the operational team but left them socialising with trusted friends who fed them the information Ilya wanted circulating.

Viking left Prime's mansion in the early hours of the morning. He needed REM sleep. Before he tubed to his quarters, Maya grabbed his arm, kissed him and pushed an object into his hand.

"Watch it under your sheets." Then she turned and left.

He put the device in his cloak pocket to examine in his apartment. When he entered the apartment, the lighting was soft, and music came from his bedroom. On his bed, draped in a black negligee, was Montreaux.

"Poor baby, I didn't think the old man had it in him to entertain you for so long. I waited here, impatiently, for you to come home. Don't worry; the security won't show us here. They are diverted into a loop from a boring night. Be a good boy and take your clothes off, as we need that footage," she purred.

"You flatter me, Darling. Can we speak freely?"

"Yes. The audio security is activated. So, how was your night?"

"A triumph of catering, a spectacular event. I pleased Prime, have been rogered silly by the boss and a troupe of erotic nymphs, and now I'm jolly tired," he replied in a stuffy British accent. Montreaux laughed at his comical response, then pouted.

"Not too tired for a visit from me, I hope? I was sorry to hear about your friend. Perhaps Shand was jealous."

Viking remained composed, although Ilya was seething inside at how callously she tried to transfer the blame for Flame's death to her rival. Moments like this tested the boundaries of Ilya's self-restraint. Chinta's abuse, Ming's death, and now Flame's murder were stoking his anger. He knew he must not lose control.

"I am never too tired for you, Darling, although I regret you may find me used, abused and a trifle disappointing. Yes, I was sorry to hear about Flame. A nasty business but I hardly knew her. We enjoyed a bit of sport - still, thank you for your condolences. Do you think Shand was involved, Darling?"

"Entirely plausible. Shand's claws were in you first and she may consider you her property - I would. She isn't a nice woman. Powerful, yes, but for all her wealth and power, she still resembles a mouse." Montreaux's wide-eyed innocence and sweet tone didn't quite mask her hatred of Shand.

"Can you believe it? I am hungry. A whole banquet served by Viking Argos, catering extraordinaire, and no time to eat any of it. Will you join me for a late supper? I just need to shower."

"Your cupboards and cool store are laden with food. Why don't I pour us a drink while you shower?" Tempted as Montreaux was to join him, her artful dressing took so long that she didn't feel like getting wet. "Leave the doors open. I want to admire what I haven't sampled."

She smiled wickedly, licking her lips as she sashayed to the bar. Filling two cups with ambrosia, she dropped a ball of sex stimulants in Viking's drink. As much as she enjoyed the sexual tension and game-playing, Montreaux hated missing out, so he wouldn't be sleeping for some time.

But he surprised her. After showering, Viking strutted out in his towel and, to her pleasure, tore off her negligee and ravished her. Being dominated was a new experience for Montreaux, and she thoroughly enjoyed it. Viking placed food strategically on her body for the second round and satisfied all his appetites. Montreaux decided she simply had to have him – Prime or no Prime. She left secretively, just before sunrise with her body sated, aching sensuously and satisfied. Ilya indulged in further exploring her mind, rewiring emotions, and implanting ideas and concepts to boost her attachment to Viking.

Chinta tipped him off that Shand was seeking another meeting, and Montreaux's Assistant had acquired a sex stimulant. Her advice was to trust his instincts, probe their minds, and give Montreaux whatever she wanted. It was bitter advice for Chinta to dispense, as she was falling in love with Ilya, but the mission came first. Montreaux wouldn't suffer another rejection, so it was also the safest path.

Finally, alone, Ilya was grateful for a rare day off. The Nirvanans were insatiable, and his body craved rest. The evening left him feeling tired, dirty, and he threw up the contents of his stomach before crawling into bed exhausted. He fell asleep before he was horizontal.

It was late afternoon before Ilya's eyes fluttered open. He showered again, unable to cleanse his body of the vile taint of Montreaux or his self-disgust. To replenish his strength, he consumed an energy shake before stretching tight and tired muscles. The sleep worked wonders, and after a workout and meditation, Ilya felt better. His young body thrived on the energetic lifestyle and release of sexual feel-good hormones. However, Ilya believed the casual sex was callous, he recognised sexual abuse for what it was and longed for something more meaningful. On impulse, he reached for Chinta.

"Good morning, enchantress of the enchanted forest. How do you do it?"

"Do what? Organise the entertainments?"

"No, live with this constant round of sex and parties? Last night I was accosted by Maya, then found Montreaux in my quarters on my bed after a night of carousing with Prime and a troupe of horny nymphs. I was exhausted, felt unclean, and I've never been so tired in my life."

"Oh, diddums! That will teach you for showing off. It is the reward for being the hottest sport in Nirvana," she teased.

"I have never admired you as much I do this morning. Your dedication to your role is admirable, Chinta. My arrival is so recent-"

"You forget Ilya, that I have never had a choice. If I wanted to survive here, I had to adapt, find coping mechanisms to be permitted to live." Her response was sharp – a rebuke.

Chinta's walls slammed up, but not before he detected her pain and humiliation.

"My education, food intake, exercise regime, beauty, medical care and the ability to spy depended on achieving a position with status. Our survival instincts are as strong as theirs. I would like to be kind, good, make sound emotional and environmental decisions, but the privilege of choice doesn't exist here. I am flawed and a – a Nirvanan." The share was more gentle and controlled.

"But you are good, kind, everything you should be, Chinta, and more. I believe I see you more clearly than you see yourself. Who else could create light in the darkness of Prime's inner sanctum? You are amazing. Already I long for more than physical gymnastics, pleasure and pain. Your relationship with Prime does at least have some intellectual depth. To Montreaux and Shand, I am a piece of flesh to fight over."

"What you feel is completely normal, Ilya. I too long for more than this. A charade of unending decadence and worthless folly. We all want to love and be loved, Ilya. It is a human affliction, whether we seek it or not, or whether the object of our affections can be attained or not. What do you long for, Ilya?"

"I don't know, Chinta, but I would rather converse with you and your beautiful mind than cavort naked and be ripped to shreds by monsters dressed in attractive shells."

"My Ilya, please don't ply me with too much flattery! My beautiful mind may no longer fit in my swollen head." Chinta bristled with sarcastic indignation.

"Oh, I'm sorry, Chinta. I'm not very good at this personal stuff. Viking is a wonderful creation, and perhaps I should send Argos to you."

"Mmmm, maybe you should, as he is rather dreamy." She deliberately projected images of Viking naked to embarrass him. *"Of course, I know that your 'nice' persona resides inside him."* She selected the word nice because it was so insipid and to repay him for implying only her mind was beautiful. *"What I dream of is love, Ilya. A grand passion. Share my body, mind, soul and life with another being as partners, lovers and equals. Existing in a state of bliss, where we almost merge into one."* Chinta sighed dramatically. *"I know, I'm a dreamer, but I have to hold on to hope, Ilya. At times hope kept me alive. Hope and my conversations with you. You probably think I'm crazy."*

"No! Not at all. You describe love with such pure emotion. It is what I want too. I was unable to articulate it that way."

"Where will I find such a person to love Ilya? Perhaps when I can connect with the EB network, when our mission is over, someone perfect will be waiting for me."

Ilya was about to agree with Chinta but paused to consider how that would change their friendship. He didn't want their relationship to change. They had always shared a bond, sense of humour and fun. If she found a partner, or rather when she selected someone, she was gorgeous inside and out – would he still be part of her life? Suddenly Ilya felt confused, disturbed, upset, not anything he was used to feeling.

"I need to go, Chinta."

Chinta was left alone in her dressing room, brushing her hair. She wondered if her ploy to have Ilya consider living without her was working or if some overzealous admirer had arrived at his quarters. If she wanted to win his affection, she couldn't spook him, and needed to be patient. She regretted snapping at him because nobody would ever understand what her childhood entailed or the cost of becoming Prime's Assistant.

Part of her believed that the favourite consort of the most powerful man on the planet should be able to capture the heart of an inexperienced boy. Ilya, however, was always a fast learner. Amongst the EBs, he was their champion, the saviour, revered, and everyone loved him.

How could she make her love stand out when he was drenched in adoration every day? Even the cold, self-centred Council members fought for a piece of him. Chinta pondered how she could compete and win Ilya's love.

14 |

Departure

It was fortunate that the family remained in the larger apartment. With Ilya's disappearance unresolved, there was a chance he would return, so the protocol to downgrade the apartment was unfulfilled. Julia and Alex organised a morning tea get together with Dmitry, Claire, Leo, and Monica would connect via interplanetary comm. Tamara was ecstatic to have her fan club in one place. They exchanged pleasantries until everyone was seated with a drink. An expectant hush fell.

"As we mentioned in our comms, we have an important announcement, and we wanted to have you all here," said Alex with a nervous smile. "Julia and I have been considering making a new start somewhere else." The grandparents all began to speak at the same time.

"I know this is a shock, but the truth is everything here reminds us of Ilya. We haven't given up on him. One day he will come home. We have to believe that, or we won't cope. Tamara misses Ilya – don't you, darling?" Tamara nodded sadly, snuggling into Grandpa Leo's legs. "She deserves more than parents who throw themselves into work to survive. We honestly thought they would find Ilya and that we wouldn't still be wallowing in sadness every time we do or see something that we did together," said Julia pausing, eyes closed to try and regain control. Alex came to her rescue.

"Tamara has a bond with Ilya's friend Xian, who lost his sister unexpectedly. Xian's parents are in a similar situation, only for longer. Julia and I spoke with them after Xian told us they were leaving to make a new life on another planet. At first, their decision seemed extreme, but the more we discussed and thought about it, the more it made sense." Alex gave everyone time to digest the bomb he threw in their laps.

"There is no question that when Ilya returns, we will reunite as a family. Until then, we must go on and raise Tamara to achieve her full potential." Tamara implanted ideas, manipulating the thoughts of her grandparents. She radiated what a good idea this was, rapidly followed by a notion that they must leave with Tamara. While she sat playing with her toys in apparent innocence and ignorance of what was happening, Tamara diligently carried out Ilya's instructions.

"Where are you thinking of relocating to?" Dmitry was the first to recover his composure. Alex and Julia were grateful they progressed to questions, especially Julia, as Alex had staunchly resisted the idea of leaving. Ilya said Tamara went back to him several times for instructions. They tried to be subtle, but altering Alex's stubborn refusal to leave without Ilya required constant effort.

"Well, we don't want to be too far away, so we think Io. It's in our solar system, so when they find Ilya, we can return to Earth, or he can come to us easily. It also means we aren't taking risks with Tamara. Deep space travel is much improved, but there is still the occasional incident." Alex paused again, waiting for further questions.

"The last thing we want to do is divide our family, and we hope you will come with us," said Julia. Her eyes pleaded with her father. Tamara looked right at him and smiled.

"Oh, what the heck! I can't live without her or you, Juli – I'm in. There is nothing here for me without you, and Alex is the only son I have." Just like that, Leo was on board.

"What about you and Claire, Dad? I know your department constantly offers you promotions. Would you at least think about it?"

"Alex, like Leo, I can't imagine my life without you. Claire and I have no other children. We will discuss it and consider our options. When are you planning to leave?"

"There is a transport next month. I can transfer, Julia can work from anywhere, and the colony is in a lather over the prospect of having her there. We want to book passage on that ship," said Alex. "Mom, what about you? We would be a lot closer to you on Neptune?"

"Selfishly, I believe it's a wonderful idea because you would be close enough for the holidays. I want what is best for Tam, and I cannot fault your logic. There is also a possibility Ilya won't return. As a scientist, I acknowledge all probabilities and possibilities. As your mother, Alex, I want what is best for you, Julia and Tamara, and Io is a brave but wise choice. It's beautiful there, a well-established colony with many facilities and opportunities, and they have an Education Department that may surpass what we have on Earth. I'm in." Monica blinked from the screen as if surprised that the decision was so easy. Tamara beamed one of her angelic smiles at Nana Monica.

"I want you to come on holiday, Nana. Please come too, Grandpa Dmitry, we are going to have so much fun. Come with us into space. We can look for Twinkle Star." Dmitry read with Tamara a lot, and when she was little, Twinkle Star's Adventures was her favourite story.

"Grandpa can't imagine life without his favourite girl. I have people to talk to," he squeezed Claire's hand, "and some loose ends to tidy up." Dmitry didn't want to commit to anything before discussing the idea with Claire, but he didn't want to live apart from Tamara or Alex and Julia. They looked at the holo brochures together as a family and spent time talking about Io and what plans they needed to make. Through it all, Tamara worked her magic, calming everyone into a state of acceptance. They were moving to Io, and everyone was excited about it.

It was several hours before the family parted ways. Julia and Alex were tired but satisfied with the outcome.

"That went better than I thought it would," said Alex rubbing his neck.

"Yes, it did. I thought Dad would join us because he has nothing to hold him here. The change will be good for him. If he is somewhere else, who knows, he may pair again eventually. I would like that for him.

Your Dad is lovely. He didn't want to put pressure on Claire in front of everyone. I admire his thoughtfulness – it reminds me of someone." She put her arms around Alex's neck and grinned at him.

"It was considerate of him. I know my father, and he has already made up his mind to come. Claire has family in Good Hope, and she may not leave. They will have to decide if their relationship is strong enough to keep them together."

"Oh, I hadn't thought of that. I feel guilty tearing your Dad's relationship apart."

"I wouldn't, Julia. Remember, Dad is on his fourth pairing. Four or five years is his limit since my mother left him. He loves me but has dedicated his life to Tamara and Ilya. Dad will return to Earth to look for Ilya regularly, and I suspect he has set up a network here to continue the search."

"That gives me comfort. I must thank Dmitry. Thank goodness that conversation is over. Fancy relieving some tension while Tamara is with my Dad?"

"Let me just check my calendar, and I might be able to squeeze you in-" Julia's open hand connected with his buttocks before she tickled his armpits in retaliation. Alex crushed her to him to get her to stop, claiming her mouth. He picked her up, threw her over his shoulder, and headed to the bedroom while she squealed with laughter. It had been a while since they indulged in any fun.

They made travel arrangements smoothly. With so few personal possessions, work and education accessible from anywhere, there wasn't a great deal to do when moving. Julia would retain control of her team remotely, the city didn't want to lose her, and the work they produced was so acclaimed nobody disrupted them. Alex was a first-class engineer, and with his experience, his superiors promoted him to a senior position on Io. Leo was in the same situation, and Tamara was excited about making new friends.

Alex was right, Claire wasn't keen to move, but Dmitry was. They parted ways as friends, and Dmitry was hopeful he might find his soulmate on Io. Time flew by, and before they knew it, Julia, Alex and Tamara were spending their last night in the apartment. It was now devoid of any personal touches. They had farewelled their favourite haunts while waiting to depart and were ready to go. Tomorrow they would meet Leo and Dmitry at the private shuttle depot. Ilya insisted that they take a private shuttle, a specific transport, at a specified time. When Leo suggested the idea and Dmitry agreed it would be a family adventure for Tamara, nobody else protested. Julia assumed her children were responsible for this turn of events. Alex and Julia lay snuggled together before she propped herself on one elbow and stroked his hair.

"I love you, Alex. Promise you will always trust me."

"Well, Julia, that depends on what you propose," Alex teased.

"Especially tomorrow," she whispered in his ear, then kissed him so he couldn't ask any questions. They locked eyes and lips, and Alex got Julia's message – he must trust her tomorrow, no questions asked. Life was never dull with Julia.

Tamara awakened early and crawled into her parents' bed, wide awake and full of chatter. They abandoned sleep, washed, dressed, and ate breakfast at their table for the last time. Each person carried a travel pack because the shuttle company stowed their voyage luggage on the interplanetary transport. Alex let the Grandpa's know they were leaving and would rendezvous on time. They hugged before tubing out of their former life, excitement beginning to claw as they embarked on an adventure. Leo was there when they arrived, but Dmitry was uncharacteristically late. By the time he was five minutes late, Alex was worried.

"Dad is never late."

"Mummy, I need you to walk down the corridor to your left and take the third exit on your right. Ask the others to follow you. Tamara is helping, and I am looking after Grandpa Dmitry – he has a problem," announced Ilya.

"Right, we need to go this way. Dmitry will meet us there, trust me," said Julia firmly while looking at her commscreen as if she had received a message. Tamara grabbed her hand, and they marched off, Alex and Leo trailing behind.

"When you get to the shuttle boarding gangway, go to the end. Activate your travel chip and ID scan, but take one step back from the gate, don't go through. Get everyone else to do the same. When everyone is identified and has stepped back, turn around and walk back down the gangway. I will be masking any speech so you can tell Grandpa and Dad what to do if you need to. The security will show you all boarded the shuttle. Before you get to the end of the gangway, I will give you instructions," said Ilya.

"There are instructions for our shuttle. We need to approach the ID gateway one at a time, present our travel chip but step back from the gate. Follow my lead. Tamara will go after me, then Alex and you last, Dad." Julia looked pointedly at Alex, who nodded. Julia followed Ilya's instructions, and so did Tamara, Alex and Leo. Julia signalled they should follow, turned around and walked back. Tamara went through the same protocol as her mother. Alex followed their lead, so Leo shrugged and did the same.

"I need you to trust me blindly. Open the maintenance door on the left and step out. Don't look down, don't pause and don't think. Do it now." There was command in Ilya's voice.

Julia opened the maintenance door and stepped out. Tamara was right behind her, grabbed Alex's hand, and pushed him through before claiming Leo's hand to pull him behind her. The shuttle launch tower was 1000 metres high. Julia stepped into the black of nothing – freefalling in the maintenance shaft. She closed her eyes.

"Everyone is in the shaft. I have you all."

A whoosh of air was draughting upwards, slowing their fall until they hovered. Gently they touched down on the maintenance platform, fifty metres below ground level. The family checked on each other silently, understanding that Julia was somehow receiving instructions.

"Open the door and step into the transport unit, and Tamara will need to sit on one of you. Strap yourselves in tightly. Your shuttle will explode after take-off."

Julia settled Tamara on her lap and strapped them in with an air-cushioned harness. Air pressure would hold them firmly in a fixed position, adjusting automatically to avoid pressure on skin or organs. Leo and Alex followed suit. They didn't know what was happening, but they trusted Julia implicitly and knew she would never endanger Tamara. The transport launched, gaining speed rapidly as they exited the maintenance tunnel. An explosion bloomed behind them; they saw through the transparent roof. It was strong enough to buffet the transport vehicle, even from a distance. The fuel core consumed their shuttle, leaving nothing but particle dust vacuumed by eco-robots from the atmosphere.

"There is a communication blocker shielding the transport so that you can brief the family. I am taking you to a safe place, where I hid when I left Good Hope. Your passage doesn't exist; I am erasing all records. Everyone believes you died on that shuttle. Grandpa Dmitry continued the investigation into Grandma Ming's death covertly, and unfortunately, his persistence yielded evidence but created a security breach alert. I found his Erase Order in Montreaux's mind, so I intervened to try and save him. The world will assume he died on the shuttle, as I activated his travel chip remotely. Whether he will live or not, I cannot say. Montreaux believes you were collateral damage of the Erasure – which pleases Prime but will enrage Stryker. There will be a change of transport when the shuttle stops. When the doors open, you will see an air-hovercraft L65. I modified it myself and will fly you to pre-programmed coordinates. I will brief you when you arrive."

Tamara was relaxed on Julia's lap because she knew the plan. Alex and Leo were silent, solemn, trusting and clueless.

"Ilya is alive. He organised all of this. We are in a comm-blocked space so that I can speak, and we will fly to where he hid when he left." Julia begged Alex's forgiveness with her eyes. She wasn't sure if he saw her because his eyes filled with tears. Leo threw his arm around Alex, wiping tears away and running a hand through his hair.

"Isn't it neat! I miss Ilya." Tamara was bright as a button, making them all laugh at once.

"I am sorry. There were so many times I wanted to tell you both, especially you, Alex, when I could see your raw pain. It was safest for everyone not to know and the best guarantee of Ilya's safety. He found a way to talk to me telepathically. Please forgive me?" Julia choked back tears of remorse. Tamara patted her hair to calm her.

"You know I would do anything to protect our boy Julia, I understand." Alex smiled through his tears, and Leo reached out to stroke Julia's hand.

"Do you know where we are going?" Leo raised his brows to emphasise his question and distract Julia.

"No, I don't. There is a craft waiting for us when the shuttle stops. We board, and it will fly us to pre-programmed coordinates, Ilya said."

"I know where we are going, underneath an old government building. In the 20th century, it was called the Beehive, where the government built two bunkers. One was official, but the second was a state secret, a bolt-hole for the Prime Minister during dangerous times. A natural disaster destroyed the old capital Wellington with an earthquake and tsunami in 2038. Nobody made it into the bunkers, and the casualties were tragic. It was abandoned, reclaimed by the forest, and buried under layers of rubble. There was a secret tunnel entrance and exit, and Ilya found the only copy of the design in classified historical files. No one had ever broken the cypher to open the schematic until Ilya did. Nobody else alive even knows it exists."

"Gosh, Tam, your speaking has advanced in the last few minutes," joked Leo.

"I don't have to pretend I'm clueless anymore," Tamara grinned at her Grandpa, "but I still love ice cream. Do you think Ilya will have some?" The adults all chuckled. Her speech was advanced, but her tastebuds still ruled her head.

At last, the transport came to a halt, the exit opened, and they stepped out under a thick canopy of trees. Leo spotted the camouflaged

L65 craft immediately. Although Ilya was screening them, they proceeded cautiously, silently, boarded, and secured themselves in the passenger pods.

Stealth mode retracted from the transport and glade to wrap tightly around the L65. Engines kicked into life quietly, and the controls adjusted themselves, locking in the familiar route. Hovering for a moment, the L65 accelerated so fast it simply disappeared. The passengers relaxed because they had complete faith in Ilya's programming abilities and followed in his footsteps.

Strange that they were dead to everyone. Friends and colleagues would mourn their loss, Monica and Claire distraught, but they couldn't help it. The deaths needed to be authentic. None of them had any idea what the future held – but that excited them. The system controlled their lives from the moment of creation, so the freedom felt heady. They were in uncharted territory, having an adventure. The craft tilted, flying vertically through a crack in a concrete wall, into a tunnel. Moving back into a horizontal position, they touched down inside the Earth.

15

Competition

Feeling the object in his pocket, Ilya removed the mini-comm from Maya. It was only last night but seemed a lifetime ago. He activated it with the password Maya had whispered – ShanÐ*wants¥ou. Shand had also wanted entertainment. Viking was in the unenviable position of having stood up the third most senior Councillor. Unless he cloned himself another body, he would never satisfy everyone. Ilya decided Viking should comm Maya on her secure channel and explain himself, hoping she would read between the lines. Fortunately, she was available. Having earned the ire of her mistress by failing to produce Viking, Shand dismissed Maya for the day. Maya was now peeved but needed Viking, so she took his comm. He looked as gorgeous and fresh as ever, youthful without trying; she really wanted to lure him into their games again.

"Maya, how beautiful you look, as always. Thank you for taking my comm, especially after I was detained last night and unable to communicate with you. I barely made it inside before an uninvited guest hijacked my evening! And I was so exhausted afterwards that I slept for hours. So my apologies, I only got the message this morning and now feel incredibly rude." Ilya looked straight at Maya.

She was astute and figured out exactly what had happened. Maya even surmised it was probably Montreaux. Shand would forgive her and direct all her anger at her rival, so it was good news for Maya. Poor

Viking was a mouse hunted by two cats while owned by the top dog, and Maya didn't envy his position. He would likely be erased or shipped out once his popularity waned with influential people. One less rival for Shand's affections wouldn't hurt.

"Thank you for contacting me, Viking. I must say, Shand wasn't pleased to be ignored by a Catering Manager. She is busy, but I will relay your apologies and convey your regret, and perhaps she will forgive you. Of course, I understand how difficult juggling competing interests can be," Maya smiled prettily, showing off her perfect teeth. "It was lovely to see you." She terminated the comm abruptly, dismissing him. Maya couldn't wait to share the gossip with Shand and get back in her good books. Shand took her morning coffee in a cabana where attendants massaged her feet and dressed her hair.

"Leave us," said Maya. Shand raised eyebrows at Maya. She was still annoyed with her.

"Viking just contacted me. He was 'hijacked' last night when he got home and apologises for being rude. My understanding from our conversation is that he had no choice. Allegedly he was exhausted after the evening with Prime, then the intruder. He just viewed our comm. I took the liberty of checking my intelligence. Montreaux was unaccounted for last night and only arrived in her chamber this morning. She also had retainers acquire a sex stimulant, and they remained in the vicinity of Viking's quarters until this morning."

Shand was incandescent with rage. Nothing aggravated her more than Montreaux. She held the higher position in the Council and had been on the Council longer than Montreaux, but the upstart dared to thwart her at every opportunity. Shand screamed her frustration, flinging a hairbrush at a pitcher of water. It exploded in a shower of tinkling glass, drenching a plate of fruit that had the misfortune of occupying the same table.

"That bitch will pay for her insolence. Come, Maya, we have work to do." Maya trailed after her stalking mistress, pleased to be back in favour.

Ilya hoped Maya would convince Shand to forgive Viking. Maya would figure out it was Montreaux, so he sowed seeds of division within the Council. Ilya shared information with Chinta to add to her intelligence reporting for Prime. Chinta hurried to Prime's breakfast room when he awakened.

"Out, everybody out." She swept any staff attending to Prime swiftly out the door. "Sorry to invade your dining pleasure in such an agitated state Prime, but I have news for your ears only." Chinta activated the privacy shield, poured some tea and sat across from Prime. "You won't believe what happened last night after Viking left us." She paused, leaning closer to Prime in a conspiratorial manner. "It is preposterous that people choose to ignore your claim. Before Viking arrived home, he was accosted by Shand's Assistant Maya, seeking an assignation. He didn't respond to this request because Montreaux was inside his quarters. You know she doesn't accept refusal. Your poor boy Viking was exhausted, but her Assistants acquired potent stimulants. Montreaux spent the night with your new toy, and Shand has the audacity to be furious with her." Chinta choked out a scoff of indignation at this last piece of information.

"Poor boy indeed, he's in a tug-of-war between at least three Councillors. I'm not particularly fond of sharing unless I choose to. How do you propose we most enjoy the sport, my dear?" Prime knew Chinta would have ideas. She was craftier than the other Assistants, thinking several moves ahead, precisely the same way she played chess.

"I believe you should stamp your ownership on Viking. Appoint him as your Personal Caterer, and move him into quarters in the mansion. We could put him in one of the cottages on the grounds, but they aren't as secure as the house. If he's going to be fun, he needs to stop working tirelessly and providing sport for everyone. Perhaps you should ensure his safety. Montreaux could easily Erase him if she feels he favours Shand or becomes bored. Flaunt Viking mercilessly in their faces and feed them crumbs of favour. Grant them time in his presence at events, or invite them to watch entertainment. I say we torture them with what they can't have." She clapped her hands, a wicked grin, ghosting girlish lips. "You can use Viking to manipulate them while they jump through hoops and tear each other to shreds." Prime chuckled as he brought Chinta's hands to his lips, the gesture Viking made fashionable.

"You are the most beautiful, wicked child who ever lived." While Prime strove to keep the Council in accord, Chinta had provided him with an idea to solve a problem. He strode to his dressing chamber and returned bearing a velvet box. "I have a gift for you because you please me." He planted a fatherly kiss on Chinta's head. Her eyes were bright with excitement, like the children from Christmas commercials when he was young. Chinta opened the box and gasped, hands covering her mouth, unable to suppress her reverence for what was inside.

"It is the Marie Antoinette necklace. It was made by De Beers, in the 18th Century, for the Austrian Princess who became the notoriously frivolous Queen of France. The pink diamond at the top reminds me of your girlish youth, the yellow diamond in the centre – what a rare example of femininity you are, and the last - the delights beneath it. Do you like it?"

"Are you crazy! I love, love, love it!" Chinta was dancing around the room, caressing the jewels, clutching them to her throat in joy. "Thank you, Prime. It's the most glamorous necklace I've ever seen. I want to put in on – just a moment." She tore into the nearest grooming salon and fastened the necklace around her throat, admiring it in the flat mirror. Eager to please Prime, she stripped and donned a filmy pink baby-doll nightie, pinched flushed cheeks, and pursed her lips until they were plump with blood.

When she peeped around the corner, she called, "close your eyes," in his favourite breathy little girl voice. She exuded waves of charm at Prime before making her grand entrance. Prime applauded her poses and pirouettes enthusiastically, satisfied she adored his gift. As Chinta snuggled onto his lap and fed him the remainder of his breakfast between kisses, he marvelled that he wanted her so badly. Although she loved the pretty necklace, Chinta was celebrating the execution of her plans.

Ilya was packing his belongings to move into Prime's mansion and checking in with Xian.

"My family are safe, Xian. How are your plans going?"

"Well, Ilya, they awoke from Cryogenic Suspension early, just as you programmed. They took the stealth transport and have settled into the deserted moon-base you found inside Phoebe. Thanks for hiding them on Saturn's moons, where they can return home easily. The instruction implant with my voice worked brilliantly, and I can see they accessed all information. It's good to know they are aware Chinta is safe and that we will be a family again."

"Chinta is brilliant, Xian. She's had me recalled to Prime's mansion, so I can contribute to the next phase. Viking will also be physically safer there, at least from external threats, and any division in the Council benefits us. The clever part of Chinta's plan is that Prime is ridiculously pleased with her. He even presented her with a gift. She elevates her influence with Prime and creates opportunities for our cause. Chinta is Prime's Achilles heel. One of the few flaws I have found to exploit in Prime besides his superior arrogance."

"How is she, Ilya? She left here my little sister, but Prime raised her in a house of monsters. Will she recover?" The emotional distress for Xian was evident to his friend.

"I believe she will, Xian. Chinta is resilient and positive, highly intelligent, beautiful beyond words – she will have a bright future." Ilya's admiration for Chinta was evident to Xian. *"Once we free ourselves, Chinta will take her rightful place amongst us, I am sure of it."*

"You aren't falling for my sister, are you, Ilya?" Xian teased Ilya, but it was a legitimate question.

"She is beyond my reach Xian. The most powerful human in the universe eats out of her tiny hand. I can't let myself be distracted by her charms, and that isn't easy, to be completely honest." Ilya shrugged mentally. Ilya had admitted he was attracted to or maybe a little in love with Chinta to Xian. Xian decided he would be pleased if his friend and sister became a couple. Ilya didn't acknowledge his position as the most

powerful influencer of the future when he undoubtedly was, which amused Xian.

"The network is fully deployed globally and universally, Ilya. There are EBs in every Councillor's house, in each department with critical access. We are in a position to disable the world as everyone knows it. We are poised to create a better world for everyone Ilya if only we can bring our plans to fruition. The greatest risk is that someone will betray us. As you asked, I have trusted EBs monitoring everyone in the network in Nirvana, and influence has been necessary. Nirvanans have a higher rate of addictive behaviour than anyone else on the planet, unsurprising with the lifestyle they lead. Substance or behavioural dependence makes them susceptible to external influences. It is encouraging to know that you read their thoughts easily, but we are many now, and you require more assistance. Your entry into Prime's sheltered environment is a relief to us. When you are amongst so many wolves, almost alone, your flock quails."

"Oh Xian, you are becoming quite poetic," laughed Ilya, a boy again. *"How I miss you. Imagine when we are all together again. We will eat burgers with our Dads, Tamara can have ice cream, and Chinta can eat chocolate truffles till she pukes - do you remember that time? - Julia can have macaroons and your Mum mooncakes. I cannot wait, my friend."* Ilya shared his vision with Xian, which filled them with hope.

Ilya had thought Viking's quarters luxurious when he arrived in Nirvana, but they seemed like a transport shed compared with Prime's sprawling mansion. The décor was ornate, reminiscent of an Italian palazzo, dripping with chandeliers and covered in frescoes. Art was everywhere, sculpture, paintings, artefacts, while Romanesque baths and banqueting facilities abounded.

Viking's suite of rooms was situated on the third floor, overlooking tropical gardens and the ocean lapping on a private beach beyond. It was the sort of building Ilya studied in texts but never expected to live in. Coming in, and going out of the compound, wouldn't be easy with strict security protocols, but Viking wouldn't need to leave often. He was given an extensive tour by the housekeeper, who he had met before.

There were exercise buildings, a cinema, a library, research facilities, laboratories, an observatory, an enormous kitchen, gardens, vegetable beds, orchards, swimming pools, cabanas, gaming, entertainment, sitting and ballrooms.

The compound was vast. No reason to leave unless you were attending entertainment elsewhere. For Ilya, it was perfect. An air of serenity reigned in Prime's mansion, confident in its role as the centre of power. Prime and Chinta watched Viking arrive, enjoyed his approval during the tour, and schemed about what they would do next. They opted to pamper him and let him rest.

"He needs to be in peak condition, Prime. As mouth-watering as he is, imagine if he was rested, free of stimulants, and scrubbed clean of the others. We could massage him, oil him, feed him food cooked by someone else, have his hair seen to, and body manicured-"

"What's wrong with his hair Chinta?" inquired Prime with amusement.

"It is beautiful hair but unfashionably short. We could also provide Viking with some new clothes, although I do like his sense of style. Why don't we invite him to dine with you this evening? A civilised evening of conversation in your private dining room and an early night with no demands on him."

"That sounds refreshing. Why don't you join us? Wear something gorgeous to show off your new jewels privately." He smiled, remembering the gift he received in return.

"As you wish. But remember, unlike you, I haven't yet sampled your merchandise. If I retire early, I do so to relieve the tension of my self-restraint." As insatiable as she was unpredictable, Prime couldn't envisage his life without Chinta. He would commence proceedings to rid himself of his last companion, as he hadn't seen her for years, and install Chinta in her place, at his side.

Viking was served a light lunch in his quarters, advised to dress formally for dinner with Prime, and left to his own devices. The quiet was more luxurious than anything Ilya had experienced so far in Nirvana. He took an actual book, History of the Pacific Islands, from the library and retired to the cushioned window seat in his room.

"You have time, Ilya. Tonight is supper and conversation only. Prime agreed to pamper you and retire early. The preparation won't start until a couple of hours before dinner, so you have six hours to yourself to work. I will try to buy you more time and access to Prime. Just guide me on what you need."

"Thank you, Chinta. The EB network is ready for action, and I need as much work time as possible. What do I wear this evening?"

"I am having clothes sent to your room, 18th Century garments, for fun. Au revoir mon amour!"

Ilya opened the book but connected to the internal security system. There were loops, low and high tech booby traps for intruders, spy-holes, mirrors you could sit behind to observe people, secret doors and tunnels – he checked everything. Prime was wary, constantly evolving his security, and Ilya would have to check for upgrades regularly. As Prime was with Chinta, he slipped inside Prime's mind again. Ilya quickly isolated two newly weaponised security features and Prime's plans for Shand and Montreaux. He rewired swiftly, ensuring Chinta was secure in Prime's affections, before diminishing the intuition centre, dulling his caution and increasing his already-high confidence. An adversary with reduced defence mechanisms would be advantageous.

Viking curled up on his bed for a nap. Ilya linked to the EB network with the assistance of Shaya in Ecology City, in old Papua New Guinea. The EBs were emitting collective nervous energy, excitement, fear, and hope as the time for change approached. They received the brief from Ilya, their leader, eagerly. He was risking his life to save the world and them.

They showered him with love, adoration, thanks and good wishes, feeding his psyche with positive energy, filling him with empowerment, promising faithfully to do their part. Ilya radiated throughout the network, connecting them more intensely and feeding them in return with confidence, reassurance and pure love. *"How can we fail?"* they asked, confidence surging.

"For each good, there is an equivalent evil and vice versa. We can't underestimate the cunning or intelligence of the apex predators who rule us. At the moment, evil has ascendancy. They have dominated humankind for thousands of years. It is time for good to triumph. For a better world, are you with me?"

The response rolled in silent waves of joy, rippling hope through the universe. They were ready.

Rejuvenated by his connection with the network, Ilya turned his mind to weakening the Council. Shand was obsessed with gaining an advantage over Montreaux. She and Maya spent the morning ordering so many garments from Montreaux's favourite fashion house that they would be unable to take new orders for a month. They also purchased all available ambrosia, her favourite drink, and next week's harvest of oysters, her favourite food. Shand's tech team created many disruptions in the security service, including some nasty new viruses, Montreaux's area of responsibility. Maya booked Shand and Montreaux's favourite entertainers for the next three months.

What her mistress desired most was to have Viking before Montreaux did – that was the sport. The entire city was abuzz with the news that Viking had moved into Prime's mansion. Shand intended to utilise her unswerving loyalty to Prime to her advantage and taunt her rival. Ilya and Chinta were planting ideas and fuelling the competition. With Chinta's assistance, Viking sent an intimate gift to Shand with a cryptic apology note which referenced their night together. It was a signal that Viking remembered her fondly, even though he had spent a night with Montreaux. As Shand loathed Montreaux, she blamed her for the missed opportunity.

Ilya didn't spare Montreaux, flooding her thoughts with sexual images of herself and Viking. She found herself watching security footage alone and marvelled at the ease of their conversation. Was Viking the mate she craved, she mused? The more connections Ilya made, the more neurons fired in her emotional centre, and she became obsessed with Viking.

All Montreaux's Assistants focused on obtaining an invitation to Prime's mansion. Not an easy task when their mistress had ignored his claim – but that was sport. Chinta was dedicated, incorruptible and guarded Prime's social calendar jealously, making access difficult. Montreaux's staff cowered before their mistress' wrath, dodging hurled words and objects. As a rule, Montreaux got what she wanted. Ilya pitied her servants.

The network couldn't afford to ignore Stryker, but Ilya was nervous about exploring his Grandfather's mind. Chinta had met Stryker on several occasions, and as he always admired her breasts, she was confident she could link Ilya to him. She scheduled a gambling night, and it was Stryker's turn to grace the guest list, so Chinta could assist Ilya.

She chose a moment alone with Prime to lay a foundation.

"I have a cunning plan to help you fleece Stryker of all his gambling chips," announced Chinta over lunch. Prime raised his eyes from reports, his interest piqued. "Stryker loves breasts, and he can never keep his eyes off mine. I intend to distract him so badly that he can't concentrate because I am yours, and he desires whatever you have. The entertainment and staff will be spectacular," she clapped her hands, "and our corsets will display more assets than they hide." She pushed her bosom up playfully to show Prime the effect she was planning, her nipples peeking out invitingly. Prime laughed as Chinta pouted, turned left to right, then bent over front-on, giggling at her reflection. "I hope it will amuse you – it's a bit vulgar, I know, but indulge me, and your purse will bulge with gold. You will probably have to save me. That man is a predator!"

"Chinta, you are so dramatic, my darling. There is nothing to worry about with Stryker, and I won't let him lay his sadistic mitts on you. He wouldn't dare." Prime's grin was wolfish, almost wishing Stryker would try. "Now I must finish reading these dull reports, be a good girl and fetch me some juice."

With the matter settled, Chinta jumped to pour Prime's fresh watermelon juice. She had thought long and researched carefully to isolate the most effective distraction tactic for Stryker. Prime generally left entertainment to the Assistants, especially Chinta. This time, she wanted his approval as it wasn't a typical event for him.

To ensure Prime's pleasure, she would cheat mercilessly by reading Stryker's thoughts and suggesting Prime's moves. It would infuriate and distract Stryker further while Ilya did his work. Montreaux was on the guest list to attend the gambling soiree as well. Prime didn't revoke her invitation, but to show his displeasure with her behaviour, Viking wouldn't be attending at all. She and her entourage would be seated in the worst position, as far away from Prime as possible, announcing her disfavour to everyone in attendance. Viking would be waiting for Prime when he grew bored, so Ilya would be free to concentrate on his exploration while the soiree played out. Chinta was satisfied that she created the best possible environment for Ilya. After lunch, she excused herself, already absorbed in planning.

"This isn't like you, Chinta, to develop such a tawdry concept. What's your plan?" Xenon was no fool. Chinta gleefully shared her idea with him, and he applauded her. When Prime was content, their lives were easier.

"I suppose you will cheat to ensure our master wins all Stryker's chips?"

"Au contraire! We work for the smartest man in the world. He doesn't need help from his underlings," she said, eyes gleaming mischief. "Please keep an eye on Montreaux. Prime is punishing her, which will make her angry. She is overly ambitious, dangerous even, a threat to us." Chinta's eyes were serious and old beyond her years.

Xenon had tried to attain the position as Prime's Head Assistant for years, but Prime's affection for Chinta was always a barrier, and she was damnably clever. Now he was too old. He would be twenty in a few months, so content to hold his position as second to Chinta. They worked well together, and when you worked for Prime, it was a lifetime position. Younger children were already replacing them as companions to Prime, but they were both extraordinarily gifted at their jobs.

The chefs were in a lather when Prime brought Viking into the mansion, but they realised the kind of food he produced would require all of their services. At the moment, Viking was a companion only, he hadn't even visited the kitchens, and Xenon pondered what that might mean for him. Maya was plying him for an invitation to the mansion. It wouldn't hurt to have influential people who owed him favours. It might allow him to hold his position longer.

The saloon burlesque show Chinta organised was an enormous hit with almost everyone. When Montreaux arrived and found her party was nearly seated outside, she wasn't amused. The bejewelled cowboy outfit Montreaux wore glittered with gold and cost a fortune. She had dedicated the whole afternoon to readying herself to persuade Prime to indulge her and lure Viking into her games. Her staff circulated on the prowl for Viking, but he wasn't there yet. As the evening wore on, Montreaux became annoyed she couldn't see the show.

Prime was displeased with her and had no intention of sharing Viking Argos. Nothing Montreaux's minions did, pleased her. She rejected food, left drinks untouched, ridiculed their jokes, despised the circulating entertainers and slapped Erik for speaking to her. As her rage built, she called the wardrobe manager to her and whispered instructions.

"I'm not going to stay here and put up with that shrivelled old man insulting me, Erik," mumbled Montreaux before throwing her gambling chips on the table, kicking over her chair and stalking out the door.

A bevy of buxom beauties constantly surrounded Stryker, and Chinta flirted outrageously before darting back to Prime, only to direct smouldering looks at him. He was completely distracted, and Ilya trickled into his mind. Telepathic detection sentinels implanted in Stryker's brain were less sophisticated than Prime's. They were easily avoided, and he disabled them by sending a permanent signal that there was nothing to detect from the alert centre. Ilya blocked their relationship from his thoughts as he delved into Stryker's past. Like Prime, his past was chequered and ugly.

The son of a wealthy mining magnate, Stryker had always lived a privileged existence. He was ruthless as he rose to power within his father's business organisation. Third world countries were exploited mercilessly, with a few well-placed bribes. Indigenous populations were steam-rolled with endless legal loopholes, creating civil unrest or war, while Stryker filled the family coffers. His father died, ostensibly of natural causes, but he was denied life-saving therapies by the family doctors, leaving Stryker to assume control of the business.

Stryker strong-armed family members and shareholders out of the boardroom through extortion, causing financial collapse, entrapment, physical threats or whatever he needed to do. He even married the young widow of a significant shareholder, Ming's mother. The Earth wasn't enough for Stryker, and he expanded his business into space, continuing to exploit new territories. They left toxic waste, destruction, and space junk wherever his company went.

Meanwhile, they cleaned up their image on Earth by promoting a clean, green planet. The discovery of new minerals and compounds in space made Stryker the wealthiest man on Earth. Stryker first proposed the 'Cull' to the board as the world spun out of control. The wealthiest people on the planet had banded together hundreds of years before. They manipulated events to build empires and crumble civilisations throughout history to serve themselves. They introduced slavery, caused the Great Depression, and more recently influenced currencies, market values, and real estate prices before reigniting space exploration. Ilya dreaded exposing Stryker's habits because Prime's history had sickened him.

He was relieved to find his Grandfather was merely a misogynist and sadist. At least not another paedophile, simply a ruthless man who took what he wanted. Who would ever have believed a psychological profile like Stryker's wouldn't be the most shocking he would uncover. Like Prime, Stryker had accumulated extensive files on Ilya. At first, they were the files of an interested grandparent, but once Ilya's Goodness Algorithm results were available, he commissioned scientific analysis in secret. Stryker sought to utilise Ilya as a weapon in his struggle for supremacy with Prime. He was disappointed when Ilya's growth trajectory flattened but still had an acquisition team searching for him.

Chinta had read him well. Wet nurses breastfed Stryker until he was four, and he had never outgrown his obsession. Ilya could see the frustration being number two caused Stryker. Although he was aggressive, ideally suited to being a dictator, he lacked Prime's influencing skills and political acumen. Ilya found it interesting that Stryker was attracted to Montreaux and intended to propose they get rid of Prime and rule as a couple. He knew the success of a union between them for long was unlikely, as both were ambitious. But, Stryker believed Montreaux would be easier for him to overcome than Prime. He had learned Prime would punish Montreaux tonight and intended to take advantage of her anger. Ilya sorted through his security arrangements, appointments, habits, and projects, looking for anything useful that could drive a wedge of division between the Councillors.

While Chinta was serving Stryker a drink, Ilya flowed back into his body. On the way through Chinta's mind, he glimpsed data from the PD. She had copied the mate-compatibility algorithm. Ilya didn't probe as he couldn't violate the privacy of his friend and their most important spy. However, once he was back in Viking's resting body, he began to wish he had investigated.

Had Chinta already profiled and identified potential matches? The possibility bothered him, unfocused his attention from the analysis he was conducting. He felt protective of Chinta, and after all, Xian was his best friend. Then it hit him, as Ilya was honest with himself. His feelings for Chinta weren't platonic, and the thought of her being out of reach was torturing him.

It was the most inconvenient time to develop a crush, obsession, desire, love – whatever it was. Or was it? They were fighting for their freedom, to remodel society and for the ability to love without fear. Ilya remembered Chinta had told him she loved him, just as he had told her he loved her. Possibly his feelings had been developing for some time, but he chose not to acknowledge what was unfamiliar. Chinta was also the most beautiful person he ever knew. At the moment they were friends. Did he dare to risk that friendship and the pain if she rejected him? He would never compromise her mind or feelings, so rejection was probable. Ilya pushed his emotional dilemma to the side to finish his work.

Prime annihilated Stryker in a final game of poker after winnings moved back and forth all night. Outwardly magnanimous, Prime was smug regarding his dominance. He retired to the mansion for the evening, leaving a stony-faced Stryker fuming. Viking awaited him in his private quarters and poured Prime his favourite whiskey. They were laughing animatedly and chatting when Chinta joined them.

"Excuse me for interrupting Prime, but I have something urgent to show you." Chinta took Prime's hand and led him into another room, where she activated a screen.

"Look closely. That is Stryker's security personnel hidden behind a screen, deep in conversation with Montreaux's wardrobe manager earlier this evening. Stryker and Montreaux departed in different directions. Both have used a circuitous route and taken complex security precautions, but they are now at the same location. I noticed the earlier meeting in my interest alerts, but there was also a tip-off from Shand's household. They have been spying on Montreaux for days and courting Xenon for an invitation from you. Why would they be sneaking around if they didn't have anything to hide?"

"An astute question Chinta, why indeed. Another question is why isn't my head of security in here briefing me instead of you? Tell Viking to get a good night's sleep, call my secretary, fetch Xenon and meet me in my Council office." Prime was already out of the room, stalking down the corridor, eyes cold, brain analysing options. He was right about Montreaux and Stryker, but they were too late.

Maya awoke Shand gently from her deep-sleep beauty cycle. It was a regenerative treatment that usually took hours, but Prime's secretary was insistent, and Shand was desperate to get into his mansion.

"I'm sorry to wake you, but Prime wants you at his mansion. A code 535, and you are required to use protocol AA13. Your garments are ready, and we await your instructions." Maya wasn't privy to the code or protocol information, and only a Council member would understand. Messages delivered this way typically indicated the Council required a quorum for an urgent decision. Maya knew better than to pry. Shand was meticulous with security when it came to Council business.

"Thank you, Maya. I don't need you for the rest of the evening." Maya departed curious but no wiser.

Shand was in a good mood. She wanted an invitation from Prime, and here it was. He needed her for something. The AA13 protocol was a stealth entrance gated and guarded with similar systems to the Council chambers. If Prime was grateful enough, she might win some time with Viking. The thought of rubbing Montreaux's perfect nose in a loss at their favourite competitive sport made her smile.

Xenon met her, kissing Shand's hand solicitously, and he ushered her through the exquisite interior of Prime's private quarters. Shand had never been here in all their years of acquaintance, but neither had anyone else. Chinta greeted her in a grand foyer, its vaulted ceilings decorated with frescoes. A beautiful girl Chinta, perhaps if Prime was indebted enough, he would grant access to her too, mused Shand. Sanctuary's rumour mongers whispered that Chinta was astonishingly creative. And she must be to have enthralled Prime for so long.

"Welcome, Councillor Shand. Prime awaits you in his interior private office. You enter through this doorway. Once you are on the other side, I will activate our in-house security protocol, and once I exit, only Prime will be able to deactivate it. Your AA13 clearance will take you halfway through the corridor. For the other half, you will need this."

Chinta handed Shand a small device with an electronic screen. "Prime will send you encrypted clearance codes in real-time, so you, and only you will be permitted access. Prime asked me to reassure you that the conversation you are about to have is private and confidential." Shand nodded at Chinta.

Shand's curiosity ran rampant, but there was no point in questioning Chinta. As an Assistant, she wouldn't be privy to anything more than Maya. Security was tight, and Shand needed to concentrate as Prime's unique authentication was complex. While Prime was unusually paranoid, there had to be something critical driving this meeting. Finally, a scanner identified Shand's face, sampled her DNA and completed a full-body scan before the heavy anti-blast door slid open. Prime's interior office looked like the command centre of a spacecraft. He sat at a table laid with refreshments and one vacant chair.

"Councillor Shand, thank you for coming quickly. May I offer you tea or juice? A thirsty business clearing security, but an unfortunate necessity in light of what we are about to discuss." He paused and indicated for Shand to take the other chair.

"Indeed, you have intrigued me, Prime. I will have tea, thank you." Prime poured the tea himself before sitting back and taking a sip with a sigh.

"I asked you here tonight for two reasons. You are number three and have always supported my decisions. Montreaux is planning an attempt to oust me, assassination or murder, I presume, and I know you detest her. The Council has existed in its current form for over 35 years. I attribute this stability in part to my leadership but also the strength of our working relationship. Calm heads in concert settle more volatile members. We make decisions in accord, and our society thrives. Not only is Montreaux a traitor, but she has approached Stryker." He showed Shand the security footage Chinta brought to his attention and further information he had since uncovered. "Montreaux exploits her position as head of security and has personnel placed within our household staff. My Chief of Security became Montreaux's man a year ago. He believes himself in love with her and supports her ambition to rule. Fortunately, I utilise a variety of external consultants outside of the in-house loop. If it weren't for one very observant Assistant, I would have retired for the evening, unaware of this meeting." Prime paused to give Shand time to digest, react, and plan.

"The nerve of that woman," whispered Shand, voice quivering with barely controlled anger. "She could plunge us into war. Destroy everything we have built. We have to stop her. What do you propose?" Shand immediately processed the potential consequences and assumed her enemy would also kill her.

"We don't know yet how Stryker will react. As a founding member of the Council, he may turn Montreaux from her path. Our relationship as Prime and Deputy, however, has always been fractious. Stryker believes he should have been Prime from the inception of the Council, and his ambition drives him to discredit me. The immediate threat is Montreaux, but I would rather have you as my second Shand if I am honest. I propose you deal with Montreaux, and I will take care of the Stryker situation to make way for you. To avoid any instability, we must remain above reproach. We won't replace them on the Council, our influence will increase, and the world will thrive. Do you agree?"

"A sound plan, and yes, I agree. I need access to Viking Argos to execute my plan. He fascinates us all, but especially Montreaux. She defied you to pursue him and murdered an innocent citizen for being his occasional lover. The woman is a dangerous survivor, and I need bait." Shand sipped her tea, trying to pretend indifference when Prime had delivered her wildest dreams to her on a pretty plate – wrapped up in a Viking bow. "I suppose the vigilant Assistant was Chinta? She is intelligent, loyal to you, gorgeous and rumoured to be exceptionally imaginative."

Cheekily negotiating now, Shand saw no harm in acquiring any personal rewards on offer. Prime glimpsed carnal desire in Shand's face when she spoke of Chinta. He needed to enforce some parameters now Shand was in his confidence. It would also be prudent to elevate

Chinta's status - she wasn't something he would barter because Chinta was his. Unlike Montreaux, Shand was popular. Shand treated people well, rewarded effort, possessed a cheerful temperament, and was considerate, so consequently, people wanted to work for her. Chinta was loyal to Prime alone, and he liked it that way.

"I agree, using Argos against Montreaux is a smart idea. The competitive tension between the two of you will cloud her judgement. We will work independently, but Maya knows how to contact Xenon for anything you need."

Prime made Shand aware he knew about her overtures to his Assistant and wouldn't discuss Chinta. With the urgent business concluded, Prime made the necessary deactivations so Shand could exit. She understood that if she hadn't agreed, she wouldn't have left the building alive.

16

Divide & Conquer

It was relatively easy for Ilya to merge with Shand. She spent enough time with Viking for him to structure a neural pathway and had no telepathic defences. The meeting with Prime was enlightening, and it was satisfying to see the power base at the top split. The rest of the Council would divide. Cracks were already defined; three would try to remain neutral, so there were three separate camps for Prime and Shand, Stryker and Montreaux supporters, the neutral fence-sitters.

Cells of EBs influenced Council members. They permeated their lives, homes and routines. The network fed all information to Ilya, who synthesised it into coherent reports to disseminate back throughout the web in tiny pieces. Xian had visibility of everything, and two friends, Chrysalis and Tombo, had half the data each in case the Council assassinated Ilya and Xian. The most challenging aspect of executing the plan was preventing Prime, Shand, Stryker and Montreaux from changing tactics and striking each other before the EB's project was initiated.

While it would be convenient to allow the Councillors to murder each other, that was a well-beaten path to failure. Unless they wanted to replace them, the EBs couldn't remove the current regime violently. Prime had already executed an Erase Order for Montreaux to be initiated by Shand. Grounds for the Erase Order, Code 535 – treason. Shand's staff compiled evidence and filed a complaint with strict adherence to Council procedures. It would be up to the Council to determine

Stryker's level of involvement, and they would investigate and question him. By removing Montreaux and implicating Stryker, Prime would eliminate two significant threats to his authority. On balance, Prime was pleased with Montreaux's actions, as she provided him with an opportunity while conceding the moral high ground.

"Chinta, Prime and Shand intend to Erase Montreaux. Only they and we possess this information."

"Our plan is coming to fruition, Ilya. I am scared but excited for the future. The price of failure is our lives, but the chance of obtaining freedom is worth the risk. Imagine Ilya, how the world could be."

"The vision of it consumes me. A world filled with kindness, balance, tolerance, love, and learning - where children don't have to conform to a narrowly defined concept of perfection. We are ready for this, Chinta, the EBs. My only concern is the migration of the general population, but the most primitive human population resides here - ironic, isn't it."

"What do you want for yourself, Ilya, when our revolution is over?"

"I want to see my family and find somebody as crazy as my mother to share a life with."

"So you will be searching for love when this is over?" Chinta executed the telepathic equivalent of holding her breath.

"Yes, I will be. And what about you? Already found some lucky, highly-evolved male?" Ilya asked wistfully. *"There will be many admirers to choose from for someone as beautiful as you."*

"Thank you, Ilya, that was a lovely compliment. I'm not so sure my unfortunate role here will make me the most desirable partner. I need to find someone who can see past my position as the kinky, infamous mistress of the enemy – and everything that entails." Ilya perceived her self-disgust and uncertainty.

"You will also be a heroine. The most famous spy who risked her life for everyone else. Anyone would be lucky to have you, Chinta, and you are well – amazing." Ilya struggled to find words that wouldn't betray his feelings. He didn't want Chinta to be uncomfortable or laugh at him and break his heart.

"I don't want anyone, Ilya. I want someone. Someone who understands me treats me kindly, shares my dreams, knows me for who and what I am and loves me anyway. I want a friend as well as a lover. Do you think I ask for too much?"

"Not at all, Chinta, isn't that what we all want – for someone to love us for who we are? Have you found your someone already?" He couldn't stop the thought in time.

"Yes, I have, but I honestly don't know how he feels about me."

Xian was knocking on the walls of Ilya's conscience to enter, so Ilya let him in. It was a timely interruption as he could feel himself becoming upset that Chinta had found someone already. He needed to stay focused because their lives depended on it. On the other hand, Ilya didn't want to lose Chinta without ever telling her that he loved her. Usually, he would talk to his best friend, Xian. Xian needed to stay focused and not be distracted by Ilya's infatuation with his sister.

"Shand has mobilised her Erase contractor, but Montreaux recruited an admirer to move on Shand. As you didn't engage, the network rerouted intelligence to me. The situation is evolving rapidly, and I wanted to ensure you are in the loop."

"Thanks, Xian. Chinta and I were just discussing someone and the future. Apologies, I was distracted for a moment."

"It was my fault Xian. I have become rather self-obsessed since I moved to Sanctuary. It takes two to have a conversation. We might have to keep our private planning time to a minimum, Ilya. I will leave you and Xian to business, and let me know if you need anything. Love you both."

"Did I just interrupt your spying activities? I feel a bit awkward - like I intruded at a bad time."

"No, Xian, it's fine. The future, freedom, excites us, but first, we must get past executing our plan perfectly. We are both scared and hopeful at the same time. Thanks for your rapid action. I am tapping into Montreaux's thoughts to see how much time we have, and then I will do the same with Shand. Goodness, there's no need to go in with Montreaux; Shand's death consumes her thoughts so that any embryo EB could comprehend her

intent. We have three days until Fabien, one of Shand's security detail, will act for the woman he adores - Montreaux. She laid plans well in advance, then moved them forward because Montreaux's instincts are tingling, and she longs to eliminate her rival. Let's have a look at Shand. The Erase contractor is the best available professional and makes extensive preparations. However, they also planned for this day and were awaiting the Erase Order. This contract will activate when an optimal opportunity arises, which is problematic. It could happen any time from tomorrow. Shand desires the contract to be fulfilled within five days, with no loose ends. We need 24-hour thought surveillance on the assassins, and I need to monitor the four vying Councillors. I need assistance to remain awake for the next five days, Xian."

"That's a long time to be conscious, Ilya. It will impair your judgement and abilities. Are there any alternatives?"

"I can link strongly through Chinta. She could sustain surveillance while my body rests and Chinta's adept at separating her thoughts from her functioning body. Whenever I sleep, I am vulnerable. So calculating the minimum rest, I need to maintain proper functionality for five days – two hours, 43 minutes, 25 seconds per day. Can you convey this to Chinta Xian? I need to speak to my mother urgently?"

"Of course, Ilya, I'll tell Chinta to await your contact. Now go."

The emergency bunker provided everything Ilya's family needed and more. The accommodation was spacious, comfortable and large. There were several self-contained apartments with washing and cooking facilities. They didn't know how to cook, but Ilya had prepared tutorials and left recipes for their supplies. Julia had a state of the art laboratory with a few of Ilya's inventions to analyse her data.

For Alex and Leo, there was plenty of work to keep them busy, maintenance of the bunker, vehicles, defence and cloaking systems. Ilya left detailed diagrams, 3D schematics, instructions, and holo briefs on sensitive tasks, meaning Alex and Leo were like children obsessing over the dessert menu.

There was a uniquely equipped medical unit with modifications of Ilya's design. Dmitry was the sole patient. Moments from death, when Ilya rescued him, he was suspended in a cryogenic pod. With Dmitry's body functioning at a low temperature, Ilya's repair nanobots gained valuable time to attempt the reboot of a failing nervous system. Ilya was giving his Grandfather a slim chance of survival, but he could respond or slip into death. The family checked on him several times a day, but they could do little. Ilya had automated everything to an optimal level.

Tamara thrived. For the first time, she was free to be her – a super-intelligent EB who shared Ilya's knowledge but thought for herself. Her personality was quirky, with an offbeat sense of humour. It was a revelation for her family to realise how mature Tamara was once she didn't have to pretend to be her age. She was never bored and devoured information enthusiastically. Tamara assisted her Dad and Grandpa with maintenance work, checked Dmitry's data progress, and enjoyed helping Julia in her lab.

Julia experienced a pang of loss for her baby, who had grown up in a few hours. Positively, she gained the best lab researcher she ever had. Tamara helped herself to Julia's knowledge and experience to leap ahead in designing new queries, investigations, data sets, and she formed intuitive conclusions that astounded her mother.

It was Tamara who proposed the antidote to the Dominance Quotient. The formula was incredibly complex. They tested trillions of hypothetical variables. They applied Tamara's equations to hormone levels, neural pathways, chemicals in the brain, organs, bloodstream, then overlaid them against paleontological and environmental knowledge, learning, and behaviour. The query structure was genius. Each Councillor's unique data yielded a tailor-made countermeasure, the UADQ (Unique Antidote - Dominance Quotient). Neural rerouting would be necessary, and Ilya could do this. Tamara was confident she could also execute the necessary brain modifications if required. Julia was proud of her daughter and protégé.

"You have found it. I knew you would be able to complete this with Tamara's help," said Ilya

"Thanks for your confidence Ilya. It was Tamara who found the solution. She is brilliant. She can't hear us can she?" asked Julia.

"No, she can't, so we can praise her all we like without overinflating her ego." Ilya's humour flavoured his thoughts.

"Oh good, because I might as well retire or become her junior lab assistant. In all seriousness, are you planning on utilising the UADQ?"

"Yes, but the less you know, the better. What you have achieved is outstanding. Thank you. Mummy, can I ask you for some personal advice?"

"Of course, Ilya. That's what mothers are for, and clearly, I need another job, so please ask me anything you like," she joked wryly.

"Well – this is awkward. I know I need advice, but I feel embarrassed. It's about Chinta. We are busy trying to execute a quantum leap for humankind, and we need to stay focused, but I have developed feelings for her. Gosh, that sounds lame coming from an EB. I'm an evolved being in many ways, but a dithering idiot around Chinta. She told me she's found 'someone' which upsets me. Do I tell her how I feel? I don't want to lose the girl of my dreams without even trying to win her affection, but I'm afraid she'll reject me. It is distracting me at the worst possible time, and I can't stop thinking about her."

"Oh baby, that's what love is like, unfortunately. All logic and reasoning desert you. It's magical, wonderful, confusing, scary, and all rolled into a roiling ball in your stomach. You are in love for the first time Ilya. It may not be the last time, but the first time is intense. Has she expressed an interest in you? Told you how she feels? Have you picked up on her emotions?"

"We work together a lot, she's fantastic company, and we are friends. She has told me that she loves me, and I have told her, but in conversation when saying goodbye, so I don't understand what it means. Chinta's emotions and thoughts are off-limits to me, as I don't want to invade the privacy of a friend. When she told me there was 'someone she cared about' – I was jealous and felt terrible. What should I do?"

"Sounds to me like the two of you have an excellent relationship Ilya. Has she ever told you, you are just a friend? Is there a possibility that someone could be you? If she rejected you, would that be worse than never knowing how she feels about you?"

"No, she hasn't said we are just friends. I suppose, in theory, the someone could be me. Chinta did say she wanted a friend as well as – a lover. You are right. Not telling her and losing her is the worst possible scenario. Do I tell her now or wait until after completing our plans?"

"Honestly, I believe you should tell her as soon as possible. The distraction and emotional stress this is causing will yield sub-optimal mental capabilities, and you need to focus on your tasks. Listen to your mother, trust me, and tell her now."

"Thanks, I love you."

People were evolving, but love remained a mysterious beast. Julia smiled to herself. Ilya was walking a familiar, often rocky path to his first relationship - she hoped. He was still her boy, and the realisation pleased her because his confusion was so typical. If Chinta didn't have feelings for Ilya, Julia would wrap her arms around him, let him cry and comfort him.

"Ilya didn't talk to me. He is busy, but I miss him." Tamara pouted and let out a sigh. Also, a predictable action from a disappointed child and, therefore, a comfort to Julia. Her children might be abnormally brilliant, Evolved Beings, but they were human and fallible.

"Ilya was impressed with your work Tamara. It will make a difference. He thinks you are brilliant, and so do I. Want some ice cream? I think I'm getting better at making it."

"Um, no thanks. I'm not feeling hungry right now." Tamara smiled sweetly at Julia.

"So I'm not getting better at making ice cream? You are breaking my heart Tamara, so I will have to tickle you!" Julia chased a shrieking Tamara through the bunker, grateful for her family and the joy freedom gave them. It wasn't that they weren't happy before, but now there was another life to compare.

The majority of decision making in Good Hope revolved around work and the rigid structure of society. Now they realised how controlled they were. While they had shelter, adequate food, education, family and community, they never had freedom. For the first time, the family were experiencing spontaneity, being creative, determining their schedules, and they all felt different—drivers of their destiny.

The conversation with his mother settled Ilya. She was right, and her logic was sound, so he took her advice and connected with Chinta.

"Hi Ilya, Xian said you wanted to discuss our plans for managing the next five days," said Chinta.

"Yes, I do." Ilya took a deep breath. *"Before we start planning, Chinta, there is something important I want to tell you. Please listen carefully, and don't interrupt. Can you do that for me?"*

"Of course. You have me intrigued, Ilya. My ears are yours."

"We have known each other a long time, and I consider you one of my best friends. I have always cared for you, but my feelings have changed lately. It doesn't matter how you feel about me or if you have found someone else. I want you to know that - that I love you. If you don't feel the same way, I respect your choice, and I don't want to lose your friendship. The truth is, I think about you all the time. Sorry to tell you now, when we are about to embark on the next phase of our mission, but I can't risk distraction – I could place us all in danger. Thanks for listening and not laughing at me. I feel much better." Ilya could sense Chinta was masking her emotions from him. His heart was thumping in his chest. He imagined he could hear it beating, roaring in his ears. What if Chinta was so embarrassed that she didn't know what to say?

"Oh, Ilya, I can't believe it. I have loved you my whole life. Just you, never anyone else. First, I was your best friend's baby sister, then Prime's plaything, and I am damaged. I hoped if you came to know me better, you might reciprocate my feelings. I love you, I love you, I love you – I'm so happy."

Lying on a divan feigning sleep, Chinta buried her head in a pillow to absorb the flowing tears. She let Ilya feel the truth of her words by sharing her emotions with him. Ilya enveloped Chinta in his love. The emotional exchange was intense, as they entwined on a level that transcended the physical, baring their souls to each other.

"We have so much to win, Chinta. Our future together, my whole life, just came into focus. Let's plan. I want us to live in a better world."

Ilya and Chinta were lit from within by their love for one another. Their senses heightened. They felt invincible, overflowing with purpose and a desire to carve out their future. The declaration of love strengthened their resolve – there was so much to live for, failure wasn't an option.

17

Revolt

Montreaux paced like a caged lioness as her hatred for Shand consumed her, and the pent-up aggression allowed Ilya to slip into her mind. If there was anyone likely to go off plan, it was Montreaux. There was the consuming thought occupying her prefrontal cortex, parietal lobe, and angular gyrus. If she initiated a kill order now, not waiting for an opportune moment, what were the odds of success? If she lost her best-placed field asset, could she enable others and give them a high success ratio percentile without unnecessarily squandering pawns? She sieved all options, brain whirring, calculating the odds.

Ilya activated neural connections, building on his groundwork. Gently he nursed her brain through an advanced set of mathematical calculations, odds, and variables, leading her to conclude that irrational action would dramatically reduce her chance of success. Ilya directed her thought patterns away from the hatred and rerouted her pathways to add an emotional dimension to her brain. The usual emotional highway was the equivalent of an abandoned wasteland.

A Councillor's child conceived on Sanctuary, Montreaux would have been terminated by the QCB as a flawed embryo anywhere else. Ironic that she rose to power so spectacularly. Ilya soothed her, calmed her raging aggression, and filled her thoughts with bathing, eating and sleeping. Montreaux bathed, ate a meal, and curled up like a kitten to nap. Once Ilya completed his tasks, he filled her head with wholesome dreams of spending time with Viking. He tip-toed from her thoughts, leaving an improved person behind him.

Chinta was accompanying him on his Shand excursion. They merged with a sigh of completion. The change in their relationship was exhilarating, and they were powerful together. Ilya was mindful of proceeding without detection and coached Chinta through shielding her presence, looking for telepathic sentinels and detecting traps. She was a superb student, absorbing thoughts and knowledge he shared like a sponge. He kept a lid on his pride in her, lest it glowed.

They ventured into Shand's memory vaults, so Ilya could show Chinta how to search and sort. On the surface, Shand seemed a more benign Councillor than Stryker and Montreaux, but she was vain, greedy, corrupt and self-centred with the obligatory blood-soaked past. Her family made a large chunk of their fortune in blood diamonds, precious gems mined by children, and the exploitation of mineral wealth, especially gold, silver, copper, and lithium. The Shands bent the technology sector to their will. If companies wanted resources, the Shand Corporation demanded shares, board positions, and eventually, the Corporation swallowed them whole. A lifetime of manipulation, mergers and acquisition, callous disregard of consequences to others equipped Shand with the perfect skill set for the Council. Her mind was structured. She was sticking to her Erase Order plan, confident the contractor would execute. Happiness lit Shand's brain with positive emotions, from Prime's confidence in her and the impending demise of Montreaux. She daydreamed of assignations with Viking – sex, love, and more sex. Viking was already occupying Shand's thoughts, and Chinta naughtily planted entertaining ideas.

Together, Chinta and Ilya went through disconnecting and reconfiguring neural pathways to create the map Julia and Tamara created for Shand. After filling Shand's head with thoughts of massage, erotic play and sleep, they slipped back into their minds. As they peeled away from the mind-merge, Ilya and Chinta experienced a vacuum, a feeling of loss.

"That was intense, Ilya. Different from sharing. I feel sort of – empty without you."

"It's the same for me. I haven't done that before, and I'm glad it was with you. The merging is beautiful and intimate, a completion of myself. It may be because of the love we share. I can't imagine it would be the same merging with Xian, for example," he laughed. *"You are an excellent student, Chinta. I'm confident that if I build a bridge with the key Councillors, you can monitor while I rest. The most complex defence system belongs to Prime. I have disabled it, but it reports as if it is functioning. You are a familiar ghost in his hallways. The influence you have exerted subtly over a long time means you are familiar. You need to take care. Prime is the leader for many reasons, and we must never underestimate him. We will test the bridge later today. We mustn't deviate from routine, so time to return to the fray."*

"I understand, Ilya. I love you."

Chinta hadn't deviated from her routine. Her ability to separate her mind from a functioning body was an art form developed by a child in survival mode. After her nap, she showered, dressed carefully, and did her hair while rifling through Shand's memories with Ilya.

She smiled as she planned a game for Prime's entertainment, determined to keep her status as favourite.

"Viking will have to be second," she giggled in the holo mirror, admiring her perfect teeth and playing her part as a vain pawn to perfection. Her happiness, the joy of being in love and loved in return, was shining like light escaping through a cracked door. Better mask it, Chinta, she told herself. Working on cloaking, Chinta wrapped and contained the tell-tale love until only she would know it was there. Maybe Ilya was clever enough to find it because he knew, but Chinta was no stranger to keeping secrets.

The staff primped the mansion for entertainment, but no Council guest was invited, just the household and contracted entertainers. Tonight an Egyptian throne room was the setting. Xenon and Chinta worked together to arrange plays, poetry, dances, story-telling, and music as Prime enjoyed culture. He would attend as Pharaoh, and they would treat him like one.

An army of Assistants researched diligently to find interesting facts and history that Prime didn't know. Prime enjoyed the stimulation of the mind as much as his body. A trait Chinta appreciated as it allowed her to command his attention. She plundered the library, film archives, and old computer-based files, committing volumes of text to memory on a vast array of subjects. Whether Prime wanted to discuss politics, customs, history, literature or physics, Chinta could listen attentively and ask pertinent questions. Although she could have given him lessons at times, she never did. An Assistant or Companion knew their place.

Viking was stunning as ever, attired as an Egyptian Prince, hunting falcon perched on his arm. Chinta chose Cleopatra as her inspiration and Xenon, High Priest Amenhotep from a film. The pomp and pageantry of dressing up created interest and alleviated Prime's boredom. While many problems occupied them, it seemed ridiculous that Councillors suffered from boredom—the plague of a privileged few.

During the performance of a dramatic play, Ilya linked with Prime. Chinta crossed the telepathic bridge as planned, making herself as undetectable as possible, and ghosted through Prime's mind with Ilya to the monitoring centres he frequented. Ilya invested time and risked frequent visits to dull Prime's formidable intuition. Prime's brain developed new neural pathways when existing ones were compromised. Primaeval survival instincts evolved over thousands of years, protected Prime, and Ilya was cautious. If there was a choice available, he would not involve Chinta.

Chinta slipped in. They halted—alert, watchful, poised on the edge of Prime's mind. The brain activated. It wasn't an alarm but an awareness. Ilya raced to circumvent the activity, sharing with Chinta what he was doing before strengthening Prime's interest in the play as a distraction. Ilya showed Chinta the traps, the sentinels, and how to check they were still reporting what Ilya wanted them to. There was a safe zone, almost a guardhouse, created by Ilya to monitor Prime's lateral frontal pole – the planning and decision zone. Once Chinta was familiar with where she needed to go and what to do, she returned via the link alone. Her progress was monitored closely by Ilya.

It was a test of her cloaking skills. Ilya wasn't sure if Prime's familiarity with Chinta would be a hindrance, boon, or of no consequence. Prime's awareness of her wasn't necessarily an unusual reaction, but Ilya didn't want to take risks. Once Chinta was safely in herself again, Ilya returned to Viking.

Ilya and Chinta shared their observations. Prime was satisfied with the advanced surveillance in place on Montreaux, Stryker and Shand. His plan was running smoothly, with little involvement from him. All he needed to do, was protect Shand long enough for her to execute the Erase Order, leaving him free to participate in the investigation. Protection assassins were in place, ostensibly organised by councillor Wei, subtle circumstantial evidence placed, and rumours circulated regarding Stryker. A master of deception, Prime was two steps ahead of the rest.

Over twenty-four hours, Chinta made familiarisation excursions with Ilya to all the Councillors. She needed to be familiar with their differences, the routes, and the more experience she accumulated, the better. The brain maps of the top four Councillors were outstanding against the others—another example of evolution in a hostile survival landscape that triggered skill development. Prime was an evolved being in his own way – more ruthless and clever than the others. It was why he led the pack of evolved predators. Chinta was confident in her abilities, and so was Ilya. The EBs laid out the puzzle pieces and made plans as they waited, poised for action. Tomorrow they would fight for freedom on their terms.

"We are ready, Xian, as ready as we will ever be. Please activate the network – and good luck."

"Same to you and Chinta, Ilya. Link when you can. We will be streaming you complete updates continuously unless people become compromised. For a better world Ilya."

"Chinta, Xian is activated. Are you ready?"

"Yes, all preparations are made."

"Start the timer for relief of monitoring. I love you, Chinta. For a better world."

The people of Sanctuary went about their business, unaware that the next few hours would determine the future of humankind. EBs monitored security staff, Councillor Assistants, house servants, and the thousands of people identified as potential intermediaries between Councillors and assassins. Decision-makers were influenced, gently at first, but more persistently to ensure arms were discarded, then secured where Ilya could control them.

A broadcast began in the real world, where most humans lived, on far-flung colonies and spacecraft in transit. It was a documentary, played through all comm mediums on a repeated cycle. The history of the Earth. A true story of the Black Years and the Council, complete with footage of life on Sanctuary in Nirvana.

The role of the EBs was to moderate the response. Stimulate thought, dampen anger and adverse reaction to irrefutable facts. Ilya severed Sanctuary's communication links from the world, so they were the only place in the colonised universe unaware of the broadcast. In the cities of Earth, Department Heads met to discuss the information. They were unused to making decisions or thinking for themselves without the Council to guide them.

A realisation was dawning for them, as it had for the EBs. The Council controlled their lives with a strict, structured set of rules. Thought leadership was bred out of them, while compliant obedience took its place.

The second broadcast explored the question of how could life be? The EBs presented people with the choices available to humanity. It didn't tear down the world they knew because that would scare people. Instead, they highlighted the positive gains and potential improvements. Questions were posed to the general population, provoking thought and input and empowering them to consider a positive change. It was challenging for the EB population, but their numbers and increasing telepathic powers served them well.

Many people were troubled, especially the parents of terminated children who had harboured doubts for a long time. The balm for them was the possibility to have another child in the future. During Ilya's exile, the EBs worked through every possible scenario. The armed forces warranted particular consideration. They studied senior personnel, attempting to identify anyone who might decide to launch an armed offensive in place of instruction from the Council. Happily, the Council had genetically engineered the population for moderation. Military personnel were as horrified by the lavish lifestyle in Nirvana as everyone else. Ilya changed codes for arms strikes from land, sea, or space, but without direct orders from the Council, any action was unlikely. The EBs released a plan, the Path to a Better World. It made sense to the logically minded population, and they were ready for change. The only unanswered question was what happened to the Council?

On Sanctuary, events turned differently. In a fit of rage, Montreaux authorised her asset to assassinate Shand. Ilya knew when and where the attempt would occur and moved an EB into position. They must avoid bloodshed.

Shand was going about her daily business, unaware she was in danger. Trusted security guards flanked her party as they walked through a corridor.

"Move my massage to later in the day, Maya, I must speak with Councillor Wei. There were bugs on my roses this morning, so retire the gardener with a generous pension of course – I no longer find him attractive or competent. You can also read the dull accounts from the moon and give me the highlights, I am too-"

Guard Fabien held out his hand to direct her. The EB on lookout stunned Fabien, who dropped like a stone to the floor. It was a simple plan with a deadly weapon. In Fabien's outstretched hand was a tiny EMP needle. Once embedded, it armed and released an electromagnetic pulse that would destroy the heart, brain and decimate all major organs of the body. It was a horrible weapon outlawed for over seventy years, and most people didn't even know it had existed.

Shand was horrified. She knew who ordered the attempt on her life but finding proof would be difficult. The guard, however, was unharmed, merely stunned. Her Assistants clustered around Shand. Maya ordered the Head of Security to defend Shand as they made for the nearest exit. Shand activated a saferoom lockdown protocol, and only Maya was permitted to stay with her. The incident shocked Shand. She was seething at the security breach and the bold audacity of the attack. It was a hallmark Montreaux initiative. Shand sent an encrypted message to the Erase Contractor that the enemy had made a pre-emptive strike.

"Maya, who saved me? I want a commendation for the security officer who was observant enough to react decisively. Perhaps I need a new Head of Security, one who can maintain a watch on their minions." Her voice steadied, calm now and cold.

"It all happened so fast. I didn't see who it was. My primary concern was your safety, but I will look at it now." Maya accessed surveillance of the corridor and played back the incident. They examined and viewed the footage repeatedly but couldn't isolate which guard acted against the assassin. "I will have to ask Zylo unless you have any other ideas."

"Go ahead, ask him while he still has a head to respond with," said Shand calmly. Maya commed Zylo, the Head of Security for now, and ensured he was secure. She hoped Zylo wouldn't lose his life over this incident. He was young and until today, brilliant at his job with a flawless record. Violence was unexpected, but moving Shand about in secrecy wasn't easy when everyone watched each other.

"What happened, Zylo?" Maya cut to the chase and hoped, for his sake, he could provide a good answer. They were also occasional lovers. She liked him and thought about him far too often.

"I saw an unscripted movement from Fabien and activated a kill switch. It is a failsafe mechanism I install in all the guards when they receive their tracing bots. Normally I can see where everyone is all the time to monitor their contacts. Someone has overridden Fabien's bots and replaced his movements with false data. Whoever did this carried it out so well that it is undetectable. I only know it occurred because his movements placed him in the mansion yesterday when I checked. One of the other guards Toko, saw him returning through a covert entrance as he was leaving last night. Please let Shand know I will resign over the breach. We vetted Fabien thoroughly. Under memory interrogation, I discovered he is in love with and has been sleeping with the enemy – Montreaux." Maya flicked her eyes to Shand, who heard the exchange.

"I will brief Shand. Please proceed and secure all necessary evidence to bring an investigation against Montreaux, and any other conspirators, before the Council. You know she will attempt to terminate Fabien. He may be dying as we speak, so keep us updated." She broke the link, not trusting their security measures.

"I can't very well take the life of the person who saved me. Zylo's only crime was being out-teched by Montreaux, a Councillor and the Head of Cyber Security. I argued vehemently against Montreaux's appointment to the portfolio, but to no avail. The Council can see for themselves how right I was. Maya, make sure Zylo places any evidence in multiple, offline, secure locations. Montreaux's people will try to cover her tracks. It was good work from Zylo to extract information before she eliminated Fabien. Montreaux wasn't aware of the failure, but that won't last; she probably knows now. Let's file our report with the Council immediately and move to suspend her from duties while they investigate my murder attempt. While you prepare that, I will brief Prime."

Zylo hadn't used a kill switch. He was an EB, following Ilya's instructions, and he disabled the guard after reading his thoughts. Fabien was in a cryopod, having Montreaux's termination bots extracted. There was no need for him to die. His crime was loving the wrong person. A person who was manipulative or prescient enough to convince him Shand would kill her if she didn't strike first. They had effectively diffused the first threat to the EBs plan.

Ilya made a decision. The Erase Contractors employed by Shand were so covert that he could place them in an induced coma until the Council was deposed. They didn't associate with anybody else when they were scoping work unless they were under-cover. Ilya would make their reports to Shand. The best course of action was to allow the Council to convene. It reduced the time he and Chinta had to complete their UADQ work but diminished Chinta's solo monitoring time. Montreaux's rush of blood and rash behaviour worked in their favour. Ilya contacted Xian with the updated strategy. An evolving plan was more difficult to detect, so they made slight modifications to the resources affected. Only five people would know of the tweak – Ilya, Xian, Chinta, Chrysalis and Tombo.

Prime chuckled to himself once the comm link with Shand disconnected. The outcome was better than he had ever imagined. Shand had caught Montreaux red-handed in the assassination plot and shared irrefutable proof with him for safekeeping. Stryker was unlikely to wriggle his way out of the trap Prime had laid, not when there was legitimate evidence of him conspiring with Montreaux. Chinta appeared right on cue.

"Time for a celebration Chinta. Me, you and Viking. Champagne, ambrosia, caviar, oysters, foie gras – all my favourite treats. Send Argos to the kitchen to prepare it. Now come here and kiss me. There is something I want to discuss with you." Chinta scooted onto Prime's lap, kissed him, and snuggled into his shoulder, sucking her thumb. Prime laughed.

"Now, don't give me that. I will become too distracted for our serious discussion."

"Have I been naughty?" asked Chinta, hanging her head to one side. "Not sure I like serious talk."

"It is nice serious. I would like you to become my permanent companion Chinta. Being my Assistant is nice, but I want you by my side. You have earned the right to a higher status." Chinta's eyes were wide, and she brought a delicate hand to cup Prime's face.

"I can't believe you would do that for me, Dada." Prime adored her calling him Dada in private. "That is....wonderful." Chinta threw her arms around him, choking back tears and squirming in his lap as he liked her to do.

"No time for play now, Chinta. Run along and organise our dinner with Viking. Tonight will be a night to remember." Her smile was a chandelier, lighting the room with brilliance. The night would be memorable, thought Chinta, but maybe not in the way Prime thought.

Ilya rested for a few minutes with a power nap to restore his energy to optimal levels. He and Chinta must focus on their tasks for the next few hours. As Chinta had provided a brief respite for Viking, Ilya would conduct the majority of neural modification to the Council.

Chinta's few minutes of solo monitoring were uneventful. Xian linked with her frequently, not wanting his sister to shoulder too heavy a burden until she shared with him that he was distracting her. Chinta and Ilya worked well together. They followed Julia and Tamara's neural maps meticulously. It would take just one tiny connection to activate the new pathways in the Councillors' brains. Another section of the plan was complete.

The Council assembled for the emergency meeting. Prime disabled Montreaux's security clearance. He contacted her to notify her of the investigation, suspended Montreaux, and guards escorted her to the holding chamber adjacent to the meeting. Montreaux considered all options but elected to plead self-defence. While she wasn't a hundred per cent certain Prime and Shand had issued an Erase Order; her security alerted her two days ago. They believed a professional organisation was in play. She dressed carefully, topped up her pheromones, rehearsed her defence in her head, and armed herself with stealth weapons. Montreaux projected an air of worried contrition, but she was confident in her cunning and martial skills. While the rest of the human race eschewed violence, she embraced it. Ilya perceived her thoughts and shuddered.

Montreaux's unpredictable nature made her a natural first selection for Ilya to activate. Her early isolation was a bonus. They could test the rewiring and chemical reboot on her first.

The holding chamber was secure, but Ilya could go wherever he wanted. Micro-nanobots designed by Julia, and Tamara, then built by the EBs in Nirvana, deployed through the atmosphere refresh system. Silent, invisible, and too minuscule to detect, they propelled themselves into Montreaux's body through eyes, nose, ears and mouth. Each micro-nanobot carried a chemical payload, destined for a precise location in the body – the antidote to her Dominance Quotient. Ilya flipped the switch on Montreaux's neural circuitry. The connections flowed. Once a void, Montreaux's emotional centre lit with activity. Her eyes rolled back in her head for a few moments as the chemical hit rebalanced her hormones, pheromones, amino acids, and proteins.

Within minutes, for the first time in her life, Montreaux felt as a human should. Holding her hands in front of her eyes, she turned them over in admiration. A smile lit her face, and love surged within her. Ilya finally observed her beauty as the reboot banished the ugliness inside her.

"It worked, Ilya. I see it too, and the change is magnificent."

"It's a wonder, Chinta. Now we know our plan will work. The connectivity is simple. We need to be swift with Prime, Stryker and Shand."

"Any amendments to the schedule, Ilya?"

"No, we will proceed in the order we planned. I will hitch a ride to the meeting with Prime and you take up your position with Stryker. Shand is distracted but we can't give the dominant Councillors any time."

18

Reboot

"Thank you for coming at short notice. It is an emergency meeting. Montreaux is suspended from the Council and is currently in the holding chamber. Shand alleges Montreaux attempted to have her assassinated earlier today. Shand's Assistant filed a 10:85XX report, which is all in order. There is a substantial body of evidence for our consideration, including the memory of the unauthorised assassin. Please activate your commscreen to view."The councillors did as Prime asked. They should have been shocked, but Shand accused Montreaux, so they weren't. There was a long history of antagonism between Shand and Montreaux. It was only surprising that Montreaux failed and left evidence for Shand. She had most likely killed Flame Santander, but investigators found no proof.

The Councillors wondered how Montreaux would talk her way out of the situation. It was unlikely the most beautiful woman in Nirvana would be punished by the Council as a commoner would. Nobody wanted to make powerful enemies either, so they watched commscreens in silence, waiting for Prime to voice his opinion.

"Councillor Shand, you filed the report, so please stand down from IP (Investigation Panel) selection. Fellow Councillors, we will nominate a chair and four others to deliberate, ask questions and examine the evidence. Under Council Article 1345Bj, the IP must decide if they uphold the report and recommend action."

The Councillors nodded in agreement, although none were keen to be chosen for the IP. Prime was the sole nominee for Chair, and his appointment was almost unanimous. Only Stryker abstained. The other nominations were logic-based, utilising Council operating procedures honed over decades. They selected four Councillors with the most negligible bias, vested interest, and loyalty to Montreaux, to the IP. Although unexcited by their appointment, they were relieved to have Prime in the driving seat. He would protect them from any reprisal over decisions made – they hoped.

"I understand it's not easy to sit in judgment of a peer. However, we must maintain our standards and ensure the safety and continuity of our rule. Does anyone have questions for Councillor Shand regarding the report while full Council is convened?"

The report was thorough, evidence sound, and many were surprised Shand still lived. Each Councillor thought of the security upgrade they might need and whether their Head of Security would have saved them. Sanctuary was once a secure, carefree environment, but the Councillors were nervous. Murder, attempted murder, Erase Orders, and assassins had no place in Nirvana.

The alert systems in the Council Chamber reported no unusual activity, but micro-nanobots streamed in unchecked. The Council, in their arrogance, never imagined the security of the indestructible Council Chamber could be breached. Ilya and Chinta poised, in position – Ilya in Prime's mind and Chinta in Stryker's.

"Activate now," Ilya signalled.

They flipped the circuits in synchronicity, moving from one mind to the next before connection entirely lit the neurons. It was a race. Distraction waves radiated throughout the chamber to inhibit the Councillor's focus. Shand was blinking her eyes furiously, and Prime was shaking his head. Stryker pushed his palms against his temples as Councillors lost their train of thought. Prime voice-activated security. Safe-air masks wrapped each Councillor in preparation for a toxic gas release to disable intruders. The gas wasn't released, as Ilya was in control. If it had permeated the chamber, it wouldn't have affected Ilya or Chinta.

The chemical cocktails for each Councillor were deployed internally by the micro-nanobots that delivered the prescribed payload to precise areas. Expressions softened as suppressed emotions took their rightful place in the brain, and Ilya brought them to a state of calm. Stryker attempted to alert his security team with a panic button, but Chinta disabled it as he succumbed.

Prime's face was ruddy – he fought it. He managed to activate the island destruct sequence. Ilya allowed him to do so, having already disabled it. Shand's blink sequence released 50 lethal seeker bots. The Council armed the killer bots with a synthesised concentrate of box-jellyfish venom, which paralysed the nervous system instantaneously. They were programmed to seek unrecognised people in the chamber. The bots conducted three sweeps of the room before returning harmlessly to base. Telepathic invasion provided the bots with no targets— every action consumed time. Time the micro-nanobots needed to do their work.

Desperately, Prime tried to disconnect the neural flow and reroute it through his preferred channels. The chemicals were sapping his will, but he clung to his task with single-minded determination. If Prime broke through, Chinta was poised in the first safety zone, ready to move in and rebuild the emotional flow. On the incoming rush of love, Prime perceived Chinta. He grabbed her. Prime slammed her inside his inner walls. Abandoning his brain and body changes, Prime bent his draining willpower to lock himself and Chinta in a mind trap.

Ilya's concentration broke when Chinta disconnected. His brain worked up all possible causes in a heartbeat. Prime had Chinta in a mind trap. Ilya knew he must trust her abilities and continue executing the plan. It was the only way. Against Ilya's love and protective instincts for Chinta, he abandoned her, willing her to conquer her foe.

The bots altered Prime's brain. He was human again, in every physical cell – normal. The essence of Prime, Council leader, was enshrined in a trap within his brain. Chinta chastised herself. Ilya warned her not to underestimate Prime, but he easily ripped her from the safety zone. Two beings locked in a mind trap together.

What to do, Chinta pondered until Ilya freed her? Calmly she cycled through available options with EB logic. Prime was naked, exposed, frightened. He perceived Chinta because he loved her. She wrapped herself around him and let him feel loved. Chinta channelled good memories they shared into a blanket of comfort, and in doing so, she became the first person in Prime's long life to nurture him. Their relationship shifted. Vulnerable, Prime clung to Chinta – the mother he craved but never had. Letting her maternal instincts flow, Chinta soothed him with the tenderness a wounded child needed. While he perceived her, he couldn't communicate with her, but Chinta knew his thoughts.

Compassion welled inside her. Circumstances had programmed Prime's relationship behaviour long ago. Scars in his mind - indelibly carved incidents, which he survived, were no longer hidden. They were hideous. Prime believed he was about to die. Chinta placed an image of them drinking whiskey and discussing art in his favourite room. She casually sorted through Prime's memories while he was distracted. It was an ugly and disturbing place, but Chinta distanced herself from the horrors, soothing Prime with care. Even when she found the files on herself, she didn't falter and flicked past them quickly.

While Primed trembled, uncertain for the first time in his adult life, his thoughts turned to regain control. Chinta found the information she sought, grasped the key, and sprang the mind trap. Ilya sighed in relief as he sensed Chinta's presence once more. She cradled Prime, coaxing him to return to his new self.

"Prime believes we will kill him, Ilya."

"He models our actions upon his behaviour. Death is what he would choose for us. You comfort him in his darkness, Chinta. I have never been more proud or in love with you than I am now. Your spirit is breathtaking. I must go-"

Ilya broke the link with Chinta. He needed to work, to focus, and she was like looking into the sun. Marshalling his emotions, Ilya returned to the task of assimilating the Council members to their new reality.

The Councillors stared at each other. Gingerly, they touched fingers to faces. Looking at themselves in a new light, they marvelled at the flood of feelings. A black and white world was suddenly filling with vibrant colours. Long suppressed feelings emerged. Some of the Council members sobbed as tears trailed down perfect cheeks. They recalled parents, partners, children, and lovers through a new lens. It was overwhelming. Ilya circulated amongst them, reading their thoughts, emotions and providing them with whatever they needed to stabilise.

As Ilya observed Stryker, his Grandfather raised confused eyes. Here was a man born into a dynasty that controlled other people - someone who existed in the lap of luxury and, until today, lacked empathy for others. To be gifted an array of feelings was foreign. His body tried to reject the transplant, but Tamara's emotional map, and Julia's chemicals, made that impossible. Ilya ghosted through Stryker's mind, painting a mental picture of the leader he could be. This man wasn't the Grandfather who plundered the universe. The man in front of him was a Grandfather who could contribute to society. Gentle, kind and skilled, Stryker had much to offer. The EBs imbued the Council with a purpose and a genuine desire to serve their people because they were capable of caring.

Chinta emerged with Prime, settling him into his new self, and he clung to her, the last bastion of the Prime who entered the chamber. Ilya and Chinta merged for a moment to cement Prime's commitment to good. Ilya scanned Prime's body for deviations from the desired blueprint, repairing anomalies. The EBs tasked Tamara with monitoring Prime's physiology, as his resistance to change was unusually robust. Ilya was satisfied he had subdued Prime for the moment. However, he noticed that Prime was less remorseful and not as committed to the purpose for good as the others. In short, he persisted in resisting. Nothing registered in any chemical or physical measurements, but Ilya's intuition sensed it. Prime was still a dangerous man. Ilya instructed a bot to take a tissue sample and send the data to Julia.

"Tamara, I have sent data on Prime. The UADQ isn't working as effectively on him. Our priority is to identify why."

It was a thought, no more, all Ilya had time for but could be critical in containing Prime. The EBs remade the Council. Time to give them work, let them redeem themselves and serve their people. The EB central network linked supporting Ilya and surrounding the Councillors. Montreaux didn't join them. Having never experienced many emotions, she wanted to immerse herself in the flower garden, poetry, and art - everything moved her. She needed time. Her new self was like gifting a person born blind with sight on a sunny day.

The large holo screen came to life. A pre-recorded message from Ilya, but the figure in the holo was Julia, in a white hooded robe. The messenger was a representative of the people – all people. Nobody wanted to create a world leader, or an image, so the messenger was faceless. The voice was moderated, unthreatening, androgenous and musical to the ear.

"Councillors, we have an opportunity to create a better world. Humanity must retain the values which define us as beings. Love, compassion, and care for each other, our planet, and the universe are not characteristics that deserve scorn. We must strive to restore the balance of the natural world. During the dark years, the Council took dramatic actions to ensure the survival of a few. Now, I stand before you and remember alongside you that we are all equally human. Over generations, you systematically deprived yourself of the higher human traits. Unwittingly you created lesser beings, driven by greed, self-interest and primitive human drivers. Outside Sanctuary, people evolved, while you became the most genetically defective people on the face of the Earth. Today you have been upgraded. Your future starts now. It is time to restore the balance of power.

The Council will play an essential role in supporting democratically elected leaders. Your knowledge of logistics, commerce, interplanetary colonisation, cybersecurity, and law is valuable to your people. There is a portfolio for each of you on your commscreen. To aid each Councillor, we will assign a highly skilled People Manager (PM). Your PM will organise travel arrangements to your new locations, as Sanctuary will be evacuated and redesigned as a holiday resort. The work you do will be critical. Should you win the goodwill of the people through hard work and deeds, they may elect you. The ability to vote is the right of every human."

The Councillors watched the screen intently, digesting information as the EB network allayed fears and provided answers they wanted. Like most humans, they didn't like the unknown, so the EBs showed them images of their new homes. Brain maps lit in an enthusiastic response. These people were hopeful and excited about the future. EBs suppressed the Councillors' feelings of self-disgust by muting memories of depraved pasts. Everyone needed to remain future-focused. If they could not achieve this, bloody retribution would propel the world into another age of violence.

Julia then addressed the general population as herself. In laymen's terms, she outlined the 'upgrade' of the Council, how and why the degeneration occurred, and what the future held. Her perspective was unique and allowed her to reach out to other families who had experienced loss.

"The Council that exists now aren't the same people who assassinated my mother, terminated my baby brother, or caused my son to disappear from Good Hope. I must forgive them. I will look forward to the future and not dwell on the past. We have evolved too far as a race to slide back into the darkness. All our thoughts and efforts must refocus on building a better world. A remade Council will support the transition into governance by a democratically elected group. Chrysalis Entika will explain in detail how this will work. Direct all questions through your commscreen as the information package ends. We will broadcast your questions and answers and deliver a data package to every citizen. The former Council will be live after that to address the people."

A familiar face worldwide, Julia's factual briefing was assuring to many. The data package was extensive and answered every question the EBs thought of over the two years it took to build. The population was so controlled and identified that elections were relatively simple. Candidates, however, needed time to prepare. Changes for the general population were slower than for the citizens of Sanctuary. They led simple lives. The general population were good, kind-hearted, hard-working people who were used to being told what to do. The careful logic and planning in the data package didn't cause alarm.

A broadcast from the Council would endorse the change, and the people would accept it. Controls would be rolled back by each Department, allowing more freedom and creativity. Goodness Algorithm testing terminations would cease immediately, replaced by a research program, while lawyers updated the parenting license system and the QCB. Changes would be ushered in strategically, with the well-being of everyone and everything taken into account.

There were no kneejerk reactions, no popularity contests, no vote-buying. The EBs based the election process on logically allocated scores of critical measures cast by every citizen. The lazy, intimidating or self-interested, who did not exist outside of Sanctuary, had no chance of being elected. True leaders would emerge through a new algorithm—the thought-leaders who would propel the world in a new direction. The age of the Dominance Quotient ended, replaced by the Electoral Leadership Algorithm (ELA).

As Chrysalis replaced Julia on-screen, Tamara skipped to Julia's side.

"You were right. I've found what you were searching for." They hurried back to the lab, and Tamara revealed the data on her screen. "It wasn't easy to find. Prime possesses a gene that causes perpetual mutation. The gene is so oriented toward survival that it can hide its mutant ability from external detection. It exhibits the behaviours of a virus and repairs like a nanobot. The mutations boost Prime's intuition and survival. As soon as his neural pathways deviated, the mutating gene repaired or enhanced another area. Have you ever seen anything like this?"

"No, never, in all my years of study. It could be another evolutionary leap. The more we tamper, the speedier the changes. Or it may be a cleverly engineered, illegal genetic enhancement. How did you find it?"

"I was searching the gene segment you isolated earlier, and I sensed it, then saw the mutation in the nanoscope. It's the reason I am continuously busy with Prime's physiology."

"Ilya is right. Prime is still a dangerous man. His body and brain have unique abilities. Any ideas on how to contain this Tam?"

"We can find a trigger to switch off the gene mutation or utilise gene edit therapy which I will need to run risk models on; it's complicated. I need to focus on Prime for a bit. He's in survival mode and learning. The more often I repair and reroute, the faster his reaction rate becomes. I don't want the EBs to encounter any surprises." Tamara closed her eyes to concentrate on her task. With eyes shut, Tam returned to being Julia's child instead of her lab colleague. Julia sighed before turning her efforts to finding an off-switch for Prime's gene that wouldn't place his life in danger.

"I am not an EB because the safe genetic off-switch isn't exciting me. If he accidentally dies, I won't shed any tears," Julia mumbled. She had taken to muttering to herself while she worked. Being without surveillance had benefits. Talking things out verbally to herself hastened her work progress.

"Find it yet?" asked Tamara, opening her eyes a short time later.

"You are an impatient little person sometimes, but yes. It needs refining, but what do you think of this protein composition? Change the way the gene expresses itself. Can you run the risks and come up with modifications? Ilya wants it to be safe, and this is quick, dirty, and my heart's not in it. Forgive your Mama for being a less evolved person, sweetheart. My sympathy for Prime has left the building. Perhaps I'm more of Stryker's grandchild than I thought."

Julia smiled at Tamara to soften her words, but their truth was evident to the child. Tamara empathised with Julia. After monitoring Dmitry struggling for life in his cryopod, Tamara noted she had no feelings for Prime. If he died, he deserved his fate. Ilya, however, wanted him alive, so she went straight to work.

The Council presented a united front on commscreens, in holo-cast, on Earth, and throughout the colonised universe. Tamara hadn't just repaired Prime this time; she had saturated him with neural influence. The initial address must come from him, and nothing could go awry.

"Greetings citizens, fellow humans. We enter a dawning age of self-improvement and peace for humankind. The life we, the Council, have led on Sanctuary is unsustainable. In creating Nirvana, our citizens fell behind the evolutionary curve. Please forgive us. We intend to utilise our skills to support the democratically elected officials. All Council members will be relocating to wherever we can best fulfil our tasks."

Prime paused, then turned to Stryker, relinquishing his dominant speaker position. Stryker spoke passionately of his desire to serve and allow creativity to flourish. Shand espoused the value of freedom and self-expression in the future, so it went with all the Councillors. Therefore, the Council gave reassurance and support to the democratic process and the population. Within hours the EBs remade the Council, reset the path for the future and ushered in a new age without spilling one drop of blood.

Tamara turned to Julia, wearing a smug grin. It announced the successful completion of her task. Julia mused that if she recruited someone like Tamara earlier, she could have retired five years ago. Who knew her baby daughter would be so creative or competent. Petite fingers tapped out equations while her brain whirred with formulas, queries and algorithms – it was quite a sight to behold.

"I have made some refining adjustments to the protein, run the models, and the risk is acceptably low. The nanobots are loaded, and we should deliver them as soon as possible. The mutant gene is highly active. Do you want to check it?" Tamara raised her brows at her mother.

"No, we don't have time. Deploy Tamara."

Produced by the Nirvana EBs, the synthesised suppressant for the mutant gene left an air shaft on Sanctuary in a nanobot and entered Prime. Once the suppressant was delivered, the gene ceased to express itself through mutation. Tamara removed the last hurdle to Prime's evolution into humanity. His entire face softened. Finally, he was able to embrace his emotions and advanced thought processes. It was a testament to his indomitable will that he had learned to love. Then again, Chinta was unique. Her subtle influence had played an essential role in Prime's brain function. Prime dominated Chinta's life from the moment her profile matched his ideal Assistant requirements when she was eight years old, but in the end, it was she who overthrew him.

19

Reunion

The EB network sang. Surging positive thoughts suffused the environment, and the population, in consort with the network. The EBs hailed Ilya as a saviour, congratulated Xian and showered Chinta with adoration for her selfless sacrifice. Their humble nature meant the trio were embarrassed by the attention. Ilya wanted to curb the enthusiasm, as his colleagues must not put him on a pedestal. Humankind needed to return to a more natural evolutionary path and choose leaders who could steer them into a better future. He was an anomaly – an artificially accelerated genetic leap.

"My friends, we have accomplished an astounding feat together – a revolution without bloodshed. All of us share the credit for the outcome. Without unity, we wouldn't be where we are today. I share your admiration for Chinta's bravery. She has lived in the viper's den to provide us with intelligence, but I repeat - we did this together. I salute you, for we have created the opportunity to choose the leaders of the future."

"But Ilya – you are our leader!" The chorus of thoughts resounded throughout the EB network.

"No, my friends, I'm not your leader and never should be. My genes have been tampered with, and I am Stryker's grandson, a product of a future time. It's time to cease accelerated evolution, an unwelcome by-product of the Goodness Algorithm. The human race must have more time to adapt to the changes in our genetic make-up. We must use our increased

brain capacity to restore ecological harmony to the universe. Eventually, humans will return to our natural reproductive selection. The random combinations provide a balance to society that has been skewing rapidly for sixty years. This change that we have made is more than enough influence from me. Do you understand?"

They were EBs, so they comprehended the far-reaching projections of Ilya's thoughts. Ilya experienced their disappointment and approval. The offspring of the Councillors in Sanctuary were analysed and rebalanced where required. However, there was a unanimous decision by the EBs that Ilya should remain as he was. His propensity for good, capacity for love and care, was inspirational – they refused to change him, Tamara or Julia.

Ilya acquiesced to their wishes but mourned a lost opportunity to have children. The risk of reproducing another advanced being was high, with no guarantee they would possess a propensity for good. Another Stryker, with superior brain capacity, wasn't a desirable outcome. He could ask Julia to screen any child, but that would be hypocritical when advocating for the shift to natural reproduction. Ilya spent the rest of the merge allocating tasks, debriefing, problem-solving, and moving to the next phase. As the plan architect, Ilya ensured he, Chinta and Xian played a lesser role in the post-coup stages. The EBs must identify natural leaders within their network. Once they completed the work, Ilya sought out Chinta and Xian.

"I think it's only fair that we, and our families, should celebrate. The last few years have been taxing, to say the least."

"What do you suggest, Ilya? Chinta, you were the entertainment queen of Sanctuary. Do you have any ideas?" asked Xian.

"I doubt my Sanctuary qualifications would be suitable for parents Xian," scolded Chinta, tongue-in-cheek, to embarrass her brother. *"We do have a world-famous chef in our midst, you know. What do you say, Viking Argos? How about whipping us up a humble family feast?"*

"Chinta, you are full of outstanding ideas for creating work for others," teased Ilya. *"Your parents should be back in earth's orbit tomorrow*

so we could have dinner at the Beehive Bunker. That will give me time to prepare."

"Sounds great, Ilya. I can't wait to see you both in person-" Xian's emotional relief, pent up fears, and worry slipped tightly constrained bonds. *"I am sorry. It has been difficult to be separated from you both while you took all the risks. Love you both."*

Xian broke his connection to recover his composure. A kind person with a good heart. For Xian, the daily prospect of losing his sister again and possibly his best friend had been daunting. Ilya and Chinta remained merged. They basked in their togetherness.

"Physically, we are both in the same building in Sanctuary Ilya. Can I join you in Viking's apartment? There are too many horrible memories for me in Prime's Mansion. I want to escape."

"Why don't we meet at the gate, Chinta. Close the door behind us and never look back. I have a better idea than Viking's apartment, which holds memories I would rather forget. There are untouched islands near here, and I can pilot us there in no time. Pack your things and meet me in ten minutes."

Ilya was nervous. He was no longer the urbane Viking Argos, simply an inexperienced young man going to meet the girl he loved. There wasn't much for him to pack. He secured a fully supplied light-transport craft with sleeping quarters, one of the Councillor's toys. It was luxurious and perfectly romantic. Ilya did take time dressing. Chinta was effortlessly stylish, and he wanted to look good and like himself. He chose a simple white T-shirt, a fitted pair of faded blue jeans, and a soft leather jacket. They would need to decide together if they would keep or remove the enhancements. Ilya suspected neither of them would care. The merging of their minds set their pulses racing, so he wondered what it would be like if they merged physically as well, and he shivered with anticipation. He reassured himself that they would take it slowly, be patient, and give each other time.

Upstairs, packing her belongings, Chinta was faring no better. While she reigned as the most envied mistress in Sanctuary for years and organised the most popular soirees, she was a bundle of nerves. It was easy to be calm and cavalier when you didn't care. Ilya was the boy she loved. Even as a child, she was besotted with him. Chinta had fantasised they would be matched, have a family and spend their lives together.

The situation was unfamiliar and shaky ground for her. She was anxious and changed outfits several times while packing and repacking her bag. While she didn't want to reprise her role as a mistress, she did want to seduce him. Settling on a pale pink activity suit with a charming neckline, she skipped cosmetics, unbound her hair and looked like a carefree teenager. However, she crammed sexy lingerie, swimsuits, and stylish, practical clothes in her valise.

"Get a grip, Chinta. You are already late," she chastised herself. When Ilya turned at her approaching footsteps, she knew the effort was worth it. His mouth hung open appreciatively, which made Chinta giggle. They could have been any teenage couple going on their first date. Ilya wolf-whistled at Chinta, and she blushed with pleasure at the compliment, heart racing, feeling uncharacteristically flustered.

"You look like a pilot from an old movie," said Chinta. "Very handsome."

"And you look like my leading lady. Ready to fly?" Chinta nodded enthusiastically. After arriving in Sanctuary, she had never set foot outside Nirvana. Once her training was complete, Prime became attached to her quickly. He rarely let her out of his sight or risked any danger to her. The heady freedom of leaving her luxurious prison only added to her heightened state of excitement. She hadn't felt this free since she was a child, still living in Good Hope with her parents. It was a volatile cocktail – all made possible by Ilya. Chinta's gratitude, desire, and irrepressible sense of fun affected him. It astounded Ilya that after everything she experienced in Sanctuary, Chinta's personality remained so untouched.

They tubed to the private launch station, stowed their bags and strapped in for take-off. Ilya enjoyed flying, and the day was rapidly turning into the best day of his life. Chinta squealed with pleasure as he manoeuvred the compact craft into a low-fly altitude where there would be no other traffic. It would also afford them close-up views of the ocean, a dazzling mirror of turquoise below them. Their faces hurt from smiling as happiness galloped untethered and irrepressible. They sang, told terrible jokes from their childhood, and admired the sea and its creatures like children.

In many ways, Ilya and Chinta were children. Lives relinquished to responsibility were reclaimed with glee. Although Ilya flew slowly to prolong their enjoyment, they soon arrived at their destination. He set the craft down carefully in the middle of an uninhabited atoll north of Sanctuary. Ilya maintained shields to ensure no sand made its way into the vessel, and they could exit through the atmosphere-scrub airlock. The island was even more untouched than the surveillance images indicated. A white sandy beach encircled the island. The water was clear, almost iridescent, and teeming with tiny colourful fish.

"Ilya, it's so beautiful. Are we the only people here?"

"Yes, nobody else exists today except you and me. I believe we deserve a day off after the last few years of work. What do you think?"

"Sounds great to me. I haven't even done my hair today – sacre bleu!"

They dissolved in giggles again, changed into their swimming clothes, and crammed into the airlock together. Their faces were almost touching. Breath stirred the air between them, heavy and electric with sexual tension. The external doors slid open a few seconds too soon for them both.

"Race you to the beach!" Ilya yelled out loud. Chinta bolted out the door, shoving Ilya back into the craft with a laugh to gain a head start. He shook his head in disbelief that she employed similar tactics to Julia before jumping from the ship in hot pursuit of the fleeing Chinta. She reached the water first. In the middle of her victory dance, Ilya arrived at a dead run, scooped her up and dumped her in deeper water. Chinta surfaced laughing again, water streaming from her hair, choking her with salt. They swam, chasing fish around the island's warm waters until thirst and hunger drove them ashore.

Ilya laid out a picnic blanket, put up a shade, and laid a low portable table with a post-swim feast while Chinta showered. She emerged wearing a filmy white cotton dress over a bikini. Ilya swallowed self-consciously. He couldn't keep his eyes off her, and Chinta's eyes twinkled with knowing mischief.

"Ilya, you remembered all my favourite foods," Chinta clapped her hands in delight. She always chose egg, mayonnaise, and watercress sandwiches when they were children, so Ilya had made them. There was also a sumptuous selection of seafood, salads, and Chinta's favourite dessert – chocolate mousse. They guzzled water to rehydrate, sipped on fruity mocktails and talked about the fish they saw, the coral, and the island's magic as they ate. They continued to eat long after they were satisfied for once in their lives. It was to enjoy the sensation of taste, the camaraderie of relaxed eating, the lack of schedule, stimulating conversation, and being with someone they loved. They were drunk on each other.

"I should shower too, but I have another treat for you while I clean up."

Ilya strung a double hammock between two palm trees. Set out a table with cool drinks, books and games for Chinta. He looked about 12 years old, so pleased with himself. Chinta lay a hand tenderly on his cheek.

"Don't take too long, Ilya. I might just fall asleep after stuffing myself with so much food."

Ilya grinned and bolted off with the picnic dishes, making her laugh. The day was fading, but they had all night – together. She quivered, aching to be with Ilya but taut with nerves. Her experience meant nothing. This relationship was the one she wanted desperately. Insecurity and sexual self-consciousness were new emotions for her, and she wondered if she should make the first move or wait for Ilya? Was he ready, or did he want a physical relationship with her? As she pondered her questions, Chinta realised she wasn't sure how EBs interacted with each other physically. She calmed herself with a cool drink and tried to immerse herself in Persian poetry. There was no sense in worrying incessantly about things she couldn't control. The lack of structure, and form in their day, was blissful.

Ilya emerged with tousled hair, but he didn't fool Chinta's practised eye. It was artfully tousled hair, and his garments were casual but chic. His intense blue t-shirt moulded to his muscular body and intensified the colour of his eyes, while his white shorts highlighted golden skin. Even the soft leather footwear was chic. Chinta admired his appearance from behind her sun visor. The physical chemistry was a bonus, but the intensity of their mind merge was something else entirely. She pondered whether he felt as awkward as she did.

"You look good enough to eat, Ilya. I'm not the only good student."

"You are making me blush, Chinta! It must be due to the fashionista who once dressed me and helped me design my glamour."

"Ilya, do you feel awkward around me sometimes? A little flustered? I am experiencing bursts of intense happiness, followed by insecurity, which I'm not used to."

"Oh, good. I thought it was just my lack of experience. When we are together like this, I.... I don't know how to describe what I'm feeling. It's intense. Feels so good that I don't want it to stop. It's how I imagine people who are addicted to euphoric substances feel. Do you think it's love, Chinta?" Ilya arrived at the hammock and climbed in beside Chinta as she shrieked at him not to tip her out. Finally, they lay side by side, holding hands, faces touching.

"I believe it's love, Ilya. I have been captivated by you since you first arrived at our home. But this feeling is different. As soon as we are apart, I want to be with you again. Honestly, I could spend my entire life with you, and it might not be enough."

Chinta's openness released a surge of love from Ilya. They held each other, basking in their bond. Lips joined in their first kiss. Blood sang in their veins, and they clung tight physically lest they drown in the torrent of released feelings for one another. Both were emotionally naked to each other. When they finally pulled away, they had lowered all the walls between them. Wide-eyed, they acknowledged the depth of their love—

soul-mates, friends who yearned to be lovers. Ilya lifted Chinta from the hammock, eyes alight with need, and carried her to the picnic blanket. Chinta cupped his face with her hands, every cell in her body straining towards him. She realised how hollow the sport of Nirvana was. There was no artifice or arrangement involved, just unadulterated passion between two people in love. Their union was magnificent. Natural, instinctive and shook them to the core of their being. The addiction to each other was complete and they slept soundly, content.

"Ilya, it's Grandpa Dmitry. Mummy wants to talk." Tamara slipped the thought into Ilya's mind before he awoke. His eyes snapped open. He cuddled Chinta's naked body to his and linked with Julia.

"How is he?"

"The cryopod alerted me a few minutes ago that repairs were ninety-three per cent complete but to awaken him because his body was shutting down. I'm sorry, Ilya. I know how much you loved him, but the stress was too much – he's gone. I wanted to let you know, and his last words were to tell you how proud of you he is. Dad and Tamara are distraught." Ilya felt Julia's despair and noticed Tamara had shut him out. They needed to go home as soon as possible, and he suppressed his sadness to protect his mother.

"I will be there as soon as I can. We did our best to save Grandpa Dmitry Mummy, and it just wasn't meant to be. Is Tamara Ok?"

"I don't know, Ilya. First, Grandma Ming and now Grandpa Dmitry. She is experiencing high levels of trauma at such a young age. The sooner you come home, the better. Bye for now," said Julia.

"Thanks, Tamara. Ilya knows. He must be super-busy with all that's happened."

"Yeah, he is busy, alright," moaned Tamara. Their bond meant she wasn't immune to feeling the intensity of Ilya's happiness. She was aware he was falling in love with Chinta before he was. Tamara was glad for them. After years of effort, they deserved to be happy.

It was handy that she was used to blocking out Ilya because Tamara was angry. Angrier than she had ever been in her life. Grandpa Dmitry was gone, and it hurt so much that Tamara didn't want to share her feelings. She hated the Councillors, and she wanted them to die too. Why do they deserve to live, Tamara lamented? As an EB, Tamara recognised her feelings were wrong, and she had always been kind, compassionate, and thoughtful to others. But now, her rage was overriding her logical mind. Dmitry's death left Tamara trembling with emotion and triggered another trauma transformation, evolving to cerebral maturity early.

"Stop it, Tamara! You can't do this and turn into one of them," she shouted at herself.

As her EB mind sought positive comfort for her, Tamara mapped out the far-reaching possibilities and realised Ilya and Chinta might make her an Aunt one day. That made her smile. Only Ilya didn't want to reproduce. Letting her brain loose, Tamara came up with many solutions to achieve her desired status. She hummed to herself as she played chess alone, thinking about what excellent grandparents Julia and Alex would be one day. The brain engagement calmed her, distanced hers from the pain of loss and shifted her mood into a safe zone.

The EBs cleansed Nirvana. People were rebalanced and re-deployed to lead satisfying lives, utilising their skills. A team of EBs monitored the Councillors' behaviour on an ongoing basis. The rest of the population was abuzz with the upcoming elections. While there wasn't much immediate impact on their daily lives, they began to feel empowered. They were going to choose their leaders. People studied profiles, listened to holo-casts, conducted background checks or researched nominees. Families discussed candidates during meals and debated policies and visions for the future. Children took to the new process with enthusiasm, cognisant that they would soon be the custodians of the planet.

Parents listened intently to the innovative ideas of their offspring. When had their children become so astute, they wondered? It was the EBs who influenced the political leanings of their parents. A paradigm shift from elections of the preceding centuries. The EB network hummed with hope and excitement as many became candidates.

Ilya joined Chinta and Xian to meet their parent's transport because it was too soon for the young lovers to be apart. It was a tearful reunion, especially with Chinta, whose family thought she was gone forever. Chinta's parents couldn't stop touching and hugging her. Seeing their daughter alive and well was a dream come true. Witnessing the reunion made Ilya long for his own family, and he pushed the transport into high velocity.

Years had passed since Ilya had spoken with Alex, shared affection, and he missed him sorely. His contact with Julia and Tamara was frequent but not as good as seeing them, and Grandpa Leo would be there. Ilya hoped his return would help assuage the grief of losing Grandpa Dmitry for his family. It was a blow to them all, especially Tamara. Alex had Julia, and he had Chinta, but his little sister had lost two grandparents to violence in her short life, and Ilya was acutely aware of the impact that could have.

The reunion of the families was an emotional, chaotic mess. Ilya bolted into his father's arms, tears shimmering in their eyes before they were bear-hugged by Grandpa Leo. Tamara wriggled into the tangle of limbs while Julia wrapped her arms around the family scrum. Xian and Chinta's family hugged like idiots, having just gone through the reunion process, empathising with the pain of loss and joy of reconnecting.

Eventually, the scrum broke up, and they greeted one another. Julia showed the Katone family to their apartment and guided them through the Beehive bunker. After the dark years of separation, they were fearful of waking to find it was a dream.

"Tamara, please let me in. Why are you shutting me out?"

"Because you are too happy for me, Ilya. I am sad – and I'm angry. So angry I'm ashamed of myself - because I hate them, Ilya, and I want them to die."

The strength of Tamara's distress, anger, hate, and self-loathing pounded Ilya. He knew she would be devastated, but nothing prepared him for the onslaught of her feelings. She had changed. Julia was right about the trauma, and he could see Tamara's neural connections had transformed. Tamara had grown up as an EB in many ways. Ilya knew how she felt because he went through a similar process when Prime's men abducted Chinta, and then he evolved again during the Goodness Algorithm testing. His sister lost Grandma Ming, and now her second evolutionary transformation was losing Grandpa Dmitry.

"Listen to me, Tam. When Prime abducted Chinta, I was angry too. My thoughts were often dark with revenge because I didn't understand how anyone could be so cruel. The Council were brutal. They were flawed, damaged, and perhaps they didn't deserve another chance. But, if we kill them, we become them. You, my brilliant sister, aided us in rising above them. Will you let me help you? I am asking you to allow me to settle your emotional turmoil so you can cope. We will bury Grandpa Dmitry in the ground tomorrow as he wanted, and we need to grieve. Tomorrow we cry together, but then we need to be strong for Dad."

Tamara nodded as tears trailed down her face.

"Make it go away, Ilya. I don't want to hurt this much. It makes me feel bad."

With Tamara's permission, Ilya soothed her with his love, flooded her recollections with the best memories of Grandpa Dmitry, and he diffused her anger. He dulled the pain, but he knew it would be better for Tamara to go through a grieving process with the rest of the family. He also implanted a task for Tamara – 'Dad needs you more than ever.'

Ilya and Chinta couldn't contain their affection for one another, and their families exchanged knowing looks indulgently. They loved the children, and if Ilya and Chinta were happy together, they were glad. There was so much to discuss. Julia made drinks and set out food in a comfy lounge area to hear details of each other's stories.

Strategically Julia placed tissues around the room. They would shed many tears for Chinta and what she endured to win this peace because hers was the greatest sacrifice. Although Ilya told his mother of Chinta's survival strategy, Julia knew Ilya would have rescued Chinta if she chose to leave. Instead, she stayed and helped overthrow the Council. Chinta was brave and selfless. Tamara looked up to Chinta, and Julia was grateful she had helped Ilya through the pivotal moments of the coup. Julia knew love when she saw it, and their family would welcome Chinta with gentle, open arms.

The EBs' evolution included a predisposition to identify appropriate mates for themselves, and they were disinclined to enter into frivolous relationships. Julia wondered if this meant they would mate for life as some creatures did. There might be no need for a Partnership Department in the future.

The telling was painful. Ilya told Grandpa Dmitry's tale first. Contrary to instructions, Dmitry couldn't leave the loose ends of Ming's death alone. He came from a long line of military investigative officers, and circumstances were off, which jangled his instincts. Dmitry followed the trail and found evidence that couldn't be ignored - like a bloodhound with a scent. Dmitry's skills unearthed the organisation that erased Ming, but the assassin's warning system alerted them that Dmitry hunted them. They planned an unauthorised hit to protect their identity when they became aware of him. Only Ilya's intervention prevented Dmitry's death at the time.

Ilya shared his story too. His life in exile. He made plans with the EB network and designed a new identity for himself. Ilya apologised profusely to Alex and his Grandpa for his deception, explaining it was the only guaranteed way of protecting them. Julia coloured as he told of their collaboration and how she learned to communicate telepathically.

Finally, it was Chinta's turn. Tamara and Ilya soothed the Katones, but inevitably they shed tears for Chinta. No matter how cheerful Chinta was, how much she tried to gloss over the horrors she endured with tales of the exotic life in Nirvana – they knew the price she paid. They were most comforted by the love blossoming between Chinta and Ilya. The pair ended the story session by recounting their vacation on the deserted island and their declaration of love for one another. They didn't want Chinta's former life to be the last story for their parents.

"Right, that's enough looking back for now," announced Ilya, "tonight we party! We celebrate Grandma Ming and Grandpa Dmitry's life and how they triumphed over evil. I will astound you, wow you, and send your tastebuds to heaven. To become Viking Argos, chef and caterer to the wealthy and spoiled, I learned to cook like no other. Chinta, Xian, Tamara, you will be my assistants for the evening. Please serve our guests the Viking Argos ambrosia cocktails while I whip up the first course." Ilya turned to the family. "Ladies and gentlemen, let the fiesta begin."

Xian queued some festive Latino music, and he and Chinta danced while they served drinks. Their behaviour delighted their parents. It was a long time since their children were merely kids having a good time. It was an evening of laughter, healing, and a fun-filled family wake party to celebrate being together, alive and with hope. They overate, drank too much, told boisterous stories and terrible childhood jokes. Freedom of self-expression had taken up residence in their lives.

"Ilya, I want us to have a large family. What do you say?"

"Oh, Chinta, I would love that, but it isn't safe for me to reproduce. Now we have worked together; I'm not sure it's safe for you either. We could spawn a superior monster."

"You are so hard on yourself, Ilya. Go and speak to your mother. There are ways we can realise our dreams."

"I don't-"

"Just speak to Julia, ok? She is a smart woman, and your sister is similar to you. I was hoping you could discuss our future with them. Please, do it for me?"

Ilya couldn't deny Chinta anything. He agreed although he was sure he must decline the screening process. Julia was in her lab, so he knocked on the door. She glanced up and smiled, beckoning him to come in. There was no point in securing her work from her children. They shared a long hug. It felt good to be physically together.

"Chinta asked, well ordered me actually, to speak with you about our future. She wants a large family, but I won't risk reproducing our advanced genetic profile, Mummy."

"Oh honey, I know you feel you are a threat to the world, but your sister wants to be an Aunt, I want to be a grandmother, and Chinta wants a family. You have no chance. Just hear us out. We all agree you are correct regarding the danger. I know you don't want to utilise screening, but there is an alternative. It is a little unusual. However, there would be an opportunity for a more natural reproductive choice. Tamara suggested taking sperm from your father or grandfather, and I agree. A frozen egg from Chinta's mother or a grandmother could be utilised from the bank and be implanted or fertilised. While the child won't be yours biologically exactly, it would carry similar genes. There will be enough genetic similarity for the child to be yours. We know that environment, nurturing, and home life plays a pivotal role in forming human beings. If you and Chinta raised children as your own – they would be your children. They won't have the capabilities of an EB when they are born. Their development is up to them and you. Will you give it some thought?"

"I, I will. It seems a logical proposal. I am surprised I didn't think of it myself. Then again, I closed the door on my dream of a family, so I didn't dwell on it. Making Chinta happy is important, but not at the risk of losing everything we have gained. Give me some time."

"You are young, and there is no rush Ilya. Just don't wait until I'm too old to babysit," Julia teased. She rumpled his hair like he was five years old, even though she had to tip-toe to reach. Ilya, her baby, was the catalyst and architect of a new era.

He needed to be alone to analyse Julia's suggestion. Ilya exited the bunker and found a log to sit on in the bush. Birds called around him. It was peaceful here. The dilemma was whether he could trust himself to be objective. Making Chinta and his family happy and fulfilling his dream of being a father influenced his logic. He needed to detach from his internal personal drivers, which was proving a challenge. How do you know you aren't giving in to your desires, Ilya wondered – fooling yourself. It was one of the occasions where telepathy was no help whatsoever. Everyone around him, who he trusted, had a personal interest.

The EB network was inclined to treat him and Chinta with kindness. He sighed and closed his eyes in concentration. There was a detached part of him already, Viking Argos. Viking needed to weigh up the pros and cons of parenthood.

"What are you afraid of, Ilya? The logic of Julia and Tamara is sound. You overcomplicate matters. Do you fear achieving everything you desire and becoming too content?" Viking laughed, mocking him gently. *"What is the worst outcome you can think of?"*

Ilya frowned, thinking intently. *"That Chinta, and I, will unwittingly teach our children at an accelerated rate by example. Our telepathy could stimulate the development of abilities they may not have had otherwise."*

"But Ilya, EBs already exist. Your concerns are illogical. Are you afraid you and Chinta will teach them to be kind, self-sacrificing, humble and fun? Dig deeper, as these are not valid reasons."

"Good grief Viking, arguing with myself is a nightmare! I guess I'm afraid that a part of me is Stryker. If I choose my father as the sperm donor, I lock out Stryker's genes, but how do I suppress his undesirable characteristics? Will I recognise them if they begin to manifest in me? And if they do, could I influence our children negatively?"

"Ok, you are less evolved emotionally in some ways than I thought. Can any person guarantee they won't develop undesirable habits in the future? I honestly believe you aspire to perfection that isn't human. Run the numbers. The risks are minimal. Share your fears with Chinta and Julia. Three watchful people are better than one. Be happy, Ilya. You deserve it."

Viking retreated, leaving Ilya wearing an idiotic grin. His alter-ego had forced him to face his fears. It was time to return to Chinta, who would be ecstatic to plan a family in the future if they wished. A weight lifted from Ilya's shoulders, and he ran back to the bunker.

Chinta was worried when she couldn't locate Ilya physically or telepathically. They were together constantly, and she felt his absence, so she sought out Julia. They both sensed his presence – he was home.

"Well, young man, did you have a healthy argument with yourself?" Julia raised an eyebrow at him inquiringly as Ilya burst out laughing. His mother knew him so well. In a child-like rush, he shared his fears and asked them to be vigilant as he aged.

"Oh, you silly sausage! EB my arse," said Julia. "Are you sure you want to reproduce with him, Chinta? You are a smart, attractive young woman who could have anyone," she teased.

"And just take a look at what a smarty-pants partners-mother you will be inheriting," smirked Ilya, poking his tongue out at Julia like the petulant child he had never been. Julia cuffed him gently around the ear and floated out, closing the door behind her so the youngsters could talk.

"Ilya, I'm so excited."

"I know. I can feel it. Children are a long way in the future, but we could practice?"

They locked themselves in Ilya's apartment and merged into one.

Tamara rolled her eyes and strengthened her walls because Ilya and Chinta's all-consuming love was exhausting. Her parents weren't much better. When I grow up, I will rely on myself to be happy - not someone else. And I am going to be a leader, have children, and protect the people I love most; she told her dolls before tucking them in bed. The childish play made her smile at herself, but she still enjoyed little girl activities.

"Xian, do you want to play chess? All of this love is making me nauseous."

The Unknown

The cryopods hissed open. It had been an uneventful journey from Earth. Before commencing the Return to Life protocol, the crew revived the migrants, bio-scrubbed and health-checked. Travellers spent fifteen days onboard the craft together. It allowed them to interact socially with their new planet peers, prepared them to assimilate to the environment, and provided an effective quarantine period. Space illness wasn't common, but occasionally unknown disease states of mind or body infected travellers.

The medical crew cleared all travellers to enter Caritas, the main settlement of Proxima Centauri. Architects modelled each domed colony on an area of planet Earth during the Miocene Epoch. Exploration of the universe gifted humankind another chance to create a healthy living environment. The people of Proxima Centauri were fortunate. The Council selected other stars, planets, and moons to exploit mineral wealth while building a biodiverse paradise - Caritas. The Council had chosen several alternative exile planets to occupy if Earth became uninhabitable.

Skyla unpacked her bag. Her cottage was simple but beautiful. She smiled as she made her new abode feel like home. This settlement was one of her projects. Complex technology drivers were involved in engineering environments similar to Earth, and Skyla was the leading authority universally. She was assigned to refine and duplicate Caritas. It was called the Genesis Project. Skyla would be authorised to participate as an 'Eve' on a new planet upon successful execution of the prototype plans. The opportunity thrilled her. She would be a mother, a birth mother, of a new civilisation. Humming to herself, she hung her work uniforms tidily in an old-fashioned closet, plumped the pillows on her bed, and picked some flowers from the garden. Satisfied with her unpacking and home-making, she removed her most treasured belongings from an earth-pressurised, padded valise.

Skyla cuddled a holocube to her breast with a sweet smile as memories flooded her mind. In the holocube were moving clips of her outings with the love of her life. She fervently hoped they would be reunited one day, and he would love her as much as she loved him. The fantasy made her happy, and Skyla believed destiny would allow them to find each other again. She was a loving woman now and could enjoy a mature and enduring relationship.

Skyla Montreaux lay down on her pillow with her eyes closed for a moment. The second item she removed was a tiny crystal cryotube containing the precious building block of life she had harvested. If she couldn't locate Viking Argos again, she could at least have his child.

There are many people to thank when you reach the end of writing and publishing a novel. This book is no exception. Not only do I need to thank my husband, Ieme de Wolf, for putting up with my endless rewriting and colourful language during challenging moments. This time, he also edited the book – on, I must say, very favourable payment terms. Reading a book several times, looking for plot holes, identifying unclear passages, and looking for spelling and grammar errors isn't everyone's idea of a good time.

Early readers are such an integral part of shaping the story. I received critique from Julian Bradbrook and Mariska van Galen, so thanks guys, for letting me know what you wanted as readers, which is valuable. Kerry Ngarimu-Ngatai, Paula Kearns, Taranga Kent, and Liz Steven also took the early manuscript for a test drive - awesome.

People who inspire me with their words and talent surround me – Teira Naahi, Wanda Thompson-Kiel, Katrina Reedy, Benita Kape, and Molly Pardoe, to name a few. I miss your encouragement and smile, Rodney Baker, but I still hear you asking, "how's your book coming along, R. de Wolf?"

In my last book, Poetry In a Pear Tree, I acknowledged my parents', siblings', and extended family's contribution to my literacy. My teachers also played an essential role in developing my love of the written word. Teachers who encourage, empower, and fire the imaginations and curiosity of children are hugely influential and, in my opinion, great teachers.

How lucky I was to be taught by many teachers who contributed to my writing - Rosanna Stevens (O'Brien), David Duncan, Cara Gilkison,

Chris Duckworth, Tweed Clark, Ann Volmuller, Charlie Lampitt, Bruce Fraser, Chris Day, Julie Farrell (we shared an obsession with Tolkein), and Leslie Minshall – thank you.

I will never forget my Ngarimu aunties, who were such natural teachers but especially Aunty Tusie - Tuhimoana Floyd, who taught me to play a mean game of scrabble and do a crossword. Not many people under the age of 10 years had a vocabulary like mine, and occasionally I had to explain the words I used to my teacher. Also, Aunty Peg - Ripeka Heeney was never my official teacher at school but taught me so much and lit the room with her singing. There were holidays with Aunty Bubby Maniapoto, learning stick games and songs, eating and mowing the lawn with my legally blind Aunty Saf Nepe and her quirky humour. I laughed with Godmother Aunty Mau Haua, ate mountains of delicious kai with Aunty Hindy Rangiuia, accompanied by her saucy commentary, and admired Aunty Sani taking charge of the entertainment at the Pa and received encouragement to be whatever I wanted to be from Aunty Kate Walker. Aunty Sal, Dad's 'little Mum' always welcomed us with a big hug and although I didn't know Aunty Whiu well, I have connected with a local artist and cousins - gosh, I miss you all.

I was a fortunate girl to grow up influenced by a bouquet of mana wahine - strong women. Ngati Porou women spoke on the marae and took charge of their lives, while later, Ngati Awa heroine, Wairaka, poised on a rock in the Whakatane harbour to save the day. How could I not grow up believing I could do anything?

The author acknowledges that she has referred to some actual people, places and publications in this novel. All information used is publicly available and sourced from the internet.

Although R. de Wolf refers to the Dunedin Study fictitiously, it is a very real, in-depth, piece of research.

'An internationally renowned **Dunedin Multidisciplinary Health and Development Study** (also known as the **Dunedin Study**) is a detailed study of human health, development and behaviour. Based at the University of Otago in New Zealand, the Dunedin Study has followed the lives of 1037 babies born between 1 April 1972 and 31 March 1973 at Dunedin's Queen Mary Maternity Hospital since their birth. Teams of national and international collaborators work on the Dunedin Study, including a team at Duke University, USA. The research is constantly evolving to encompass research made possible by new technology and seeks to answer questions about how our early years impact mental and physical health as we age.

The study is now in its fifth decade and has produced over 1300 publications and reports, many of which have influenced or helped inform policy makers in New Zealand and overseas; many of these can be found on the Dunedin Study -publications section of their website.' (Source Wikipedia 2022)

Animal Farm and Nineteen Eighty-four written by George Orwell are both referenced as reading material that Ilya remembers when he realises he is living in a controlled world.

'***Animal Farm*** is a satirical allegorical novella by George Orwell, first published in England on 17 August 1945 by Secker and Warburg, London, England.'

'***Nineteen Eighty-Four*** (also stylised as ***1984***) is a dystopian social science fiction novel and cautionary tale written by English writer George Orwell. It was published on 8 June 1949 by Secker & Warburg as Orwell's ninth and final book completed in his lifetime. Thematically, it centres on the consequences of totalitarianism, mass surveillance and repressive regimentation of people and behaviours within society.' (Source Wikipedia 2022)

R. de Wolf enjoys watching Heston Blumenthal's culinary adventures on his TV show. Blumenthal seems like a chef who would inspire Viking Argos, (caterer to the elite), when food in the 22nd Century is balanced and bland. The recipes and food concepts are figments of the author's imagination, stomach and tastebuds.

'**Heston Marc Blumenthal** OBE HonFRSC (/'bluːməntɔːl/; born 27 May 1966) is a British celebrity chef, TV personality and food writer. Blumenthal is regarded as a pioneer of multi-sensory cooking, food pairing and flavour encapsulation. He came to public attention with unusual recipes, such as bacon-and-egg ice cream and snail porridge. His recipes for triple-cooked chips and soft-centred Scotch eggs have been widely imitated. He has advocated a scientific approach to cooking, for which he has been awarded honorary degrees from Reading, Bristol and London universities and made an honorary Fellow of the Royal Society of Chemistry.' (Source Wikipedia 2022)

The Beehive is real and it is in New Zealand. All other references to The Beehive, its design and events are fictitious.

The **Beehive** is the common name for the **Executive Wing** of New Zealand Parliament Buildings, located at the corner of Molesworth Street and Lambton Quay, Wellington. It is so-called because its shape is reminiscent of that of a traditional woven form of beehive known as a "skep". It is registered as a Category I heritage building by Heritage New Zealand.

Construction began in 1969 and was completed in 1981. Since 1979, the building has housed the offices of government ministers. Thus, the name "Beehive" is closely linked with the New Zealand Government.[2] It is often used as a metonym for the New Zealand leadership at large, with "the 9th floor" specifically referring to the office of the prime minister, which is based on that floor.[3] Cabinet meets on the top floor. (Source Wikipedia 2022)

ABOUT THE AUTHOR

R. de Wolf, aka Regina Ngarimu - then Regina de Wolf-Ngarimu, was born on the East Coast of New Zealand and is of Maori descent. After leaving New Zealand to travel the world, she lived overseas for 29 years, returning to New Zealand in 2014. Currently, she resides in sunny Turanganui-a-Kiwa - Gisborne. The call to write came home with her.

In 2020 R. de Wolf published her debut fiction novel and hasn't looked back. In 2021 she established herself as an author and Indie Publisher, releasing a second novel and a poetry book. To kick off 2022, R. de Wolf is printing a poetry book for a local poet, tutoring a writing course with Katrina Reedy, editing the second edition of a local anthology with Gillian Moon and Chris McMasters and releasing two more books.

De Wolf writes about the issues she is passionate about – equality, women's rights, the balance of nature, and the spiritual connection to our ancestors and place. A self-confessed nerd and Sci-Fi fan, The Goodness Algorithm is R. de Wolf's first dystopian novel.

Other Work by R. de Wolf

Guardians of the Ancestors - Book One of the Spirit Voyager Series

Kaituhi Rawhiti - A Celebration of East Coast Writers featuring Crushed Violet a short story

The Future Weavers - Book Two of the Spirit Voyager Series

Poetry In a Pear Tree - An accessible book of poetry for anyone